LOVE AND HONOR

Knights Of Honor

Book Seven

Alexa Aston

Copyright © 2018 by Alexa Aston
Print Edition

Published by Dragonblade Publishing, an imprint of Kathryn Le Veque Novels, Inc

All rights reserved. No part of this book may be used or reproduced in any manner whatsoever without written permission, except in the case of brief quotations embodied in critical articles or reviews.

Books from Dragonblade Publishing

Knights of Honor Series by Alexa Aston
Word of Honor
Marked by Honor
Code of Honor
Journey to Honor
Heart of Honor
Bold in Honor
Love and Honor

Legends of Love Series by Avril Borthiry
The Wishing Well
Isolated Hearts
Sentinel

The Lost Lords Series by Chasity Bowlin
The Lost Lord of Castle Black
The Vanishing of Lord Vale
The Missing Marquess of Althorn

By Elizabeth Ellen Carter
Captive of the Corsairs, *Heart of the Corsairs Series*
Revenge of the Corsairs, *Heart of the Corsairs Series*
Dark Heart

Knight Everlasting Series by Cassidy Cayman
Endearing
Enchanted
Evermore

Midnight Meetings Series by Gina Conkle
Meet a Rogue at Midnight, book 4

Second Chance Series by Jessica Jefferson
Second Chance Marquess

Imperial Season Series by Mary Lancaster
Vienna Waltz
Vienna Woods
Vienna Dawn

Blackhaven Brides Series by Mary Lancaster
The Wicked Baron
The Wicked Lady
The Wicked Rebel
The Wicked Husband
The Wicked Marquis
The Wicked Governess

Highland Loves Series by Melissa Limoges
My Reckless Love
My Steadfast Love

Clash of the Tartans Series by Anna Markland
Kilty Secrets
Kilted at the Altar
Kilty Pleasures

Queen of Thieves Series by Andy Peloquin
Child of the Night Guild
Thief of the Night Guild
Queen of the Night Guild

Dark Gardens Series by Meara Platt
Garden of Shadows
Garden of Light
Garden of Dragons
Garden of Destiny

Rulers of the Sky Series by Paula Quinn
Scorched
Ember
White Hot

Highlands Forever Series by Violetta Rand
Unbreakable

Viking's Fury Series by Violetta Rand
Love's Fury
Desire's Fury
Passion's Fury

Also from Violetta Rand
Viking Hearts

The Sons of Scotland Series by Victoria Vane
Virtue
Valor

Dry Bayou Brides Series by Lynn Winchester
The Shepherd's Daughter
The Seamstress
The Widow

Table of Contents

Prologue 1
Chapter 1 9
Chapter 2 20
Chapter 3 31
Chapter 4 43
Chapter 5 51
Chapter 6 62
Chapter 7 72
Chapter 8 80
Chapter 9 89
Chapter 10 97
Chapter 11 105
Chapter 12 116
Chapter 13 125
Chapter 14 134
Chapter 15 143
Chapter 16 152
Chapter 17 160
Chapter 18 169
Chapter 19 181
Chapter 20 190
Chapter 21 199
Chapter 22 207
Chapter 23 214
Chapter 24 222
Chapter 25 229
Epilogue 235
About the Author 239

PROLOGUE

Shallowheart Castle—September 1365

BENEDICT BOWYAR RODE through the gates of Shallowheart as the sun dipped below the horizon, a calm descending over him. He was home—for good. Nothing would ever entice him to leave again. He had a job to do.

And a child to raise.

Every sight looked familiar to him as they trotted through the outer bailey and then crossed into the inner one. The blacksmith's hut. The kitchens with their fires lit. The steps leading up to the keep. He had spent the first seven years of his life here, returning each summer from fostering, his brother always by his side. But now Lawrence was dead.

And so was Lara.

Benedict pushed that painful thought aside and brought his horse to a halt. Shallowheart's longtime steward awaited him at the bottom of the stone steps. Benedict climbed from his horse and faced the slender man.

"Welcome home, my lord. I trust you had a safe journey from the west."

He was a true lord now. The Baron of Shallowheart. No longer a second son without a pence to his name, only possessing his armor and horse. The title and estate became his upon Lawrence's death two weeks ago. His brother had already been buried even as word was sent calling Benedict home to his inheritance.

Glancing at his wife, he saw Amicia didn't bother to hide a satisfied smile. He turned back to the steward.

"Greetings, Gershom. 'Twas a long way to Shallowheart. Lady Amicia is tired and needs to wash away the stains of the road. Have hot water brought to the solar at once. Something to eat, too, since we have missed the evening meal. You and I can speak tomorrow after we break our fast regarding matters of the estate."

"Very good, my lord."

Benedict helped Amicia from her horse and briefly spoke with the head of their escort party. The soldiers who had accompanied them east would return in the morning to his father-in-law's estate. He dismissed them and came back to where his wife stood proudly, her eyes taking in everything around her.

"Come," he told her. "We will go to our solar."

They entered the keep and found Gershom had lined up the entire staff of servants to greet the new baron and baroness. After moving down the row nodding when he saw a few familiar faces, Benedict led Amicia upstairs to the solar.

"Would you prefer to eat first or bathe?" he asked, not quite sure of her mood. Then again, he had never been comfortable around this wife of his and only spoke to her when absolutely necessary.

"Food can wait. I wish to remove the clothing I wear and burn it. I hate being on the road, especially for such a long time. 'Tis most inconvenient."

She gave him a pretty smile and Benedict knew to remain alert after their time together. Amicia could be pleasant one moment and lash out in rage the next, all without warning. His wife finally had what Benedict thought she wanted—to be known as the Baroness of Shallowheart.

Even if the wrong baron stood by her side.

"Mayhap we can go to town tomorrow and select new cloth. I would like to have many new cotehardies made up for me, in as many fabrics and colors that I can find. I want to look every bit the Baroness of Shallowheart." Amicia cocked her head and studied him a moment. "You, too, my lord. You must dress for the role fate has bestowed upon you. Coin will never again be a problem."

"Whatever you wish, my lady." Benedict was only too happy to give his wife whatever she asked for since her father had practically made them beg for the very morsels they ate from his table every day. To never worry again about how much food he put in his mouth, much less how much a horse might cost, still seemed foreign to him. Benedict realized it would take time to adjust to his new position. Despite how his heart remained heavy at the loss of his brother, he looked forward to being in control of his life as never before.

Servants arrived with the bath water and Benedict decided that he would also like to wash away the travel stains from the past week's journey. Once both he and Amicia were clean, they sat down at the table and partook of the cold chicken and round of sharp cheese that had been brought. Benedict poured wine for them and then refilled the silver goblets several times as they ate in silence. He still found it hard to believe that he was sitting at this table in the solar as the Baron of Shallowheart, just as his father had for many years, and as Lawrence had for a short time.

"We have had a long day," he told his wife. "My eyes grow weary. We should retire."

They went into the bedchamber and undressed and drew the bed curtains aside. Lying on the soft mattress and wrapped in the even softer bedclothes, he paused a moment before he relaxed. Lawrence had died in this very bed. His brother had taken his last breaths here, his head resting on these pillows. A dull ache filled him, knowing he would never see Lawrence again. Never hear his laugh or break bread with his brother.

Gradually, Amicia's breaths evened out and he knew she had fallen asleep. Despite his weariness, Benedict lay awake for a long time. Finally, he slipped from the bed, trying not to disturb her, and returned to the other room with his clothes in hand, carefully redressing.

But he wasn't fooling himself. He knew exactly what he wanted to do.

Go see Rosalyne.

Leaving the solar, Benedict moved silently down the hall to where he and Lawrence had slept all their lives, from the time they were babes until they both wed. As he suspected, Rosalyne had been placed in the same bedchamber. He entered the room and saw her in the arms of a wet nurse, who lifted the babe from her breast and placed Rosalyne against her shoulder as she burped the child. A loud belch erupted from the babe, bringing a grin to Benedict's face.

The nurse glanced up and noticed him. She rose.

"Lord Benedict. I did not expect to see you here so late."

"I wanted to see my brother's child."

Lara's child.

The servant turned the babe in her arms so that Benedict could see Rosalyne's face. The first look broke his heart. The babe had the Bowyar blond hair and deep blue eyes but her nose and mouth were all her mother's.

Benedict stepped toward the pair and brushed a finger against the babe's cheek. "She will be a beauty someday. She's already lovely to look at."

"Aye, my lord," the nurse readily agreed. "And she is a sunny child. Never seems to cry. I've never been around such a happy babe and I've cared for my fair share over the years."

"Do you stay with her every night?"

"I do, my lord. Lady Lara insisted. Especially . . . well . . . once she grew ill, that is. Before she and Lord Lawrence fell sick, Lady Rosalyne spent her nights with her parents. But Lady Lara feared the child would catch the fever that caused them both to waste away. As much as she loved Lady Rosalyne, she wouldn't allow the babe near the solar at the end."

Benedict realized how much it would have pained Lara—and Lawrence—to be away from their only child, but they had done the right thing. Their selfless actions had guaranteed that Rosalyne would live.

"May I?" He reached for the babe and brought her close to his chest. "I would like to spend a few minutes alone with her. You may return in half an hour."

"Of course, my lord." The nurse left and Benedict sat with his warm bundle, a pleasant glow radiating inside him. He studied her face, memorizing it, knowing Rosalyne was the best of both of her parents. She considered him, as well, her eyes gazing at him in curiosity. Her tiny hand reached toward him and Benedict gave her a finger. She grasped it and squeezed, surprisingly strong for one so young. Then she smiled at him and his heart nearly stopped—for 'twas Lara's smile.

Benedict had loved Lara Parry from the first time he saw her. They had never been officially betrothed but the understanding between their parents led him to believe that Lara and he were destined for one another. The same was true of Lawrence—and Amicia. From an early age, both couples knew they would one day become man and wife.

Until everything changed.

When it came time to wed, Lawrence admitted to Benedict that he only had eyes for Lara. Then Lara told Benedict how strong her feelings were for his brother. Neither of them wanted to hurt Benedict but they couldn't hide their love for one another anymore. Lawrence had gone to their father and explained the situation. As the older brother, their father had usually given in to every whim that Lawrence had, knowing he would one day succeed him as baron. Benedict could have fought for Lara—but why do so when she didn't want him? He refused to stand in the way of her happiness.

Even if it left him miserable.

By default, Amicia became his wife. The brothers married in a double ceremony that was the most difficult day of Benedict's life, seeing how Lara glowed every time she looked at her new husband. Lawrence became the baron less than a month after their nuptial mass, gaining the title and land and the woman Benedict loved, while Benedict and Amicia returned to her home. He became a knight in service to her father—and lived with his own private heartache—as well as Amicia's bitterness for having lost out on wealth and position.

Benedict pressed a kiss upon the brow of the babe, whose eyes began to droop. He sang to her softly as she fell asleep in his arms. Rosalyne touched a place inside him because of how special her parents had been to Benedict. He looked upon it as an honor to raise her in their stead. He would make sure he shared stories with her about her parents. Even though she would never see them, Rosalyne would know who they were and how much they'd loved her.

Standing, he placed the beautiful babe in the cradle and leaned over, watching her sleep for a few minutes. The door opened, a slight draft coming in, and he supposed the wet nurse returned to care for her charge. He turned and froze.

Amicia stood there, a dark scowl on her face.

"I might have guessed you would come here," she hissed. "To moon over that whore's babe."

Benedict's hands balled into fists but he calmly replied, "Lara was no whore. She was my brother's wife and Baroness of Shallowheart."

"She stole him from me!" Amicia cried.

"Quiet," he commanded. "You'll wake Rosalyne."

"I don't care if I wake her. I hate her." Rage glittered in his wife's eyes.

"How can you hate a small babe?" he asked. "She is an innocent. Rosalyne has done nothing to hurt you."

"I've had the last of hurt in my life, Benedict Bowyar," Amicia proclaimed. "I was embarrassed and humiliated when Lawrence rejected me. I could have had all of this and he took it from me because that woman crooked her finger and smiled beguilingly at him." Her eyes narrowed. "And you let it all happen. You could have stood up to him. Demanded that we keep to what our parents intended. Nay, like a coward, you backed down and gave in to your brother, all because you are weak."

"I acted honorably and did the only thing I could do," Benedict said solemnly, ignoring Amicia's insults. "Just as now the right thing will be to raise Rosalyne as ours, alongside our own children."

She burst out in laughter that sounded half-mad. "Nay. I will never do that. I want this babe gone from here." Amicia walked toward him and placed her hands on his shoulders, her nails sinking into his skin. "I can make your life miserable, Husband. You know I can. If you allow that child to remain at Shallowheart, you will never know a moment's peace until you are in your grave."

Fear struck Benedict's heart. "What do you mean?"

She shrugged. "Who knows? Babes die every day. Mayhap little Rosalyne simply stops breathing some night and we discover her dead in her cradle the next day."

"Are you saying you would *murder a child?*"

Amicia sniffed. "I am not saying anything." A smile played about her lips. "But you cannot watch her every moment, my lord. And if something happened? I supposed we would all be so very sad."

Benedict knew Amicia had it in her to carry through her threats. In the two years since they'd wed, he had found a cruel streak grew within her. She had done things to prove to him that she could not be trusted.

He couldn't risk anything happening to Rosalyne.

"What do you suggest?" he asked, keeping his voice neutral.

Amicia bit her lip and thought a moment. "Didn't Lara have a brother?"

"She did. Templeton. But I haven't a clue where he might be. By the Christ, he was a good dozen years older than Lara. All I know is he took off after their parents' deaths. She was left in the hands of a cousin until she married Lawrence."

"Find him," she ground out. "The quicker, the better. I want the brat gone from our estate. I refuse to allow her to share a nursery with my future children. She will not take away time nor love from them. She is to be banished from Shallowheart forevermore. Do you understand, my love?" Her nails dug deeper into his flesh.

Benedict certainly did. Amicia was a vindictive bitch and Rosalyne would never be safe under a roof shared by the two.

Wearily, he nodded. "I will set about tomorrow finding out Templeton Parry's whereabouts."

Amicia gave him a brilliant smile. "Good." She ran her hands down his chest. "You can accompany me back to our bed, my lord, and make love to me. Tonight might be the night you finally get me with child."

She whirled and left the room without a backward glance.

Benedict bent and rested his palm atop Rosalyne's head, then bent and kissed the sleeping babe's cheek.

"I love you enough to protect you the only way I know how, sweet Rosalyne." With that, he returned to the solar and the distasteful task of making love to his vengeful wife.

CHAPTER 1

Kinwick Castle—July 1385

PRIDE FILLED EDWARD de Montfort as he watched his brother, Hal, standing tall and alert before the altar of Kinwick's chapel. Hal had spent the previous evening alone in prayer and preparation for today's dubbing ceremony. Edward glanced to his right and saw his mother, Merryn, wipe away tears of happiness as she watched her son become a knight of the realm. She had also wept when her oldest son, Ancel, went through the same ceremony several years before.

Edward had been ten when Ancel had been dubbed a knight, the only time he had witnessed the Oath of Knighthood Ceremony. It made a lasting impression upon him and gave him a goal to strive toward as he completed his service as a page and continued on as a squire to Lord Hardwin at Winterbourne.

The newly-knighted Sir Ancel de Montfort left Kinwick soon afterward to serve in King Richard's royal guard, the young royal being crowned upon the death of his grandfather, Edward III. Edward, named after the old king by his parents, who enjoyed a friendship of many years with the Plantagenet monarch, wanted nothing more than to follow in his oldest brother's footsteps someday and serve in the king's guard.

Hal was keen to do the same and go to court, especially since Ancel had recently left the king's service to take over the management of Bexley. Ancel had become Earl of Mauntell and the owner of Bexley upon the death of his father-in-law four months ago, thanks to the petition granted by King Richard. Ancel and his wife, Margery, along with their young son, Cyrus, would remain at Bexley until Ancel became Earl of Kinwick upon their father's death. Hopefully, that would be many years from now. Edward couldn't imagine Kinwick without Geoffrey de Montfort's steady hand and larger than life presence.

He glanced toward his father as Geoffrey now rose to take part in the knighthood ceremony. At two score and ten, his father's dark hair had more streaks of gray in it than the dark black it had once been, but Edward thought it only made Geoffrey look more distinguished. His father's cousin and closest friend, Raynor Le Roux, along with his mother's brother, Hugh Mantel, joined Geoffrey as they solemnly walked toward the altar where Hal and Father Dannet stood waiting. Cousin Raynor and Uncle Hugh would act as sponsors for Hal's dubbing.

The sponsors handed over the sword and shield to Geoffrey as Hal took his oath of honor, pledging loyalty to his father and the de Montfort name and promising to fear God and maintain His Church, fight for the welfare of all, and at all times speak the truth.

For once, his brother wore a serious look on his face. Hal was known for being lighthearted and mischievous and had been a wild child, but even Edward saw that Hal realized the solemnity of this occasion. Hal knelt before his father as Geoffrey tapped his son on his shoulders with the flat side of the sword.

"I admonish you to conduct yourself at all times with courage, bravery, skill, and loyalty." His father paused and with a smile added, "I dub thee Sir Hal de Montfort, knight of England and loyal servant of King Richard the Second."

Hal remained on his knees while Raynor and Hugh placed a pair of spurs on his boots. He rose as they girded his sword on him before they stepped back. Then Father Dannet led everyone present in a closing prayer to complete the ceremony.

Those in attendance applauded as a grinning Hal embraced his father, then his uncle and cousin. Hal went to his mother and knelt for her blessing before kissing her cheek. Hal looked around and sought

Edward. He joined his brother and best friend, clasping Hal and pounding him on the back in congratulations.

"You did it," he told Hal. "I was impressed, for you looked quite grave up there. I wasn't sure you had it in you," Edward teased.

"I felt the weight of the moment," Hal confessed. "I don't think I've ever been so sober in my life." He smiled. "I tried to emulate you, Brother."

"You rose to the occasion," Edward complimented him, glad that Hal had given his dubbing ceremony the proper regard. The two brothers had been inseparable as children and remained the same while they fostered together and grew toward manhood, but Hal forever seemed cheerful and untroubled, while Edward served as the more sensible, earnest one.

Suddenly, all of his sisters surrounded them. Edward stepped aside so they could lavish praise upon Hal.

A weeping Alys said, "I never thought I would see you so restrained, Hal. To think I used to chase after you as you found trouble every minute of the day when you toddled about." She smiled. "I've never been more proud of you than when you took your oath of knighthood now."

Nan, younger than Edward by three years, added, "I rather like this new Hal. Mayhap he will take his oath seriously and look after the welfare of ladies." She gave Hal a pointed look. "That means you must put an end to your merciless teasing of me, of course." Her brows rose haughtily and then she laughed heartily.

The smallest de Montfort, nine-year-old Jessimond, wrapped her arms around Hal's waist. "I thought you looked lovely, Hal, all dressed in white and scarlet." She frowned. "I suppose you will leave Kinwick now to serve the king."

Hal picked her up and smacked her cheek noisily. "I may. I may not. I have yet to decide." He placed Jessimond back on the ground, as others came to congratulate him.

Edward moved further away, studying the scene as he was wont to do. Suddenly, he realized someone was at his shoulder.

His father said quietly, "We must talk before the feast. Come to the solar at once. Bring Hal, Ancel, and the men in the family. Hardie, as well. I need to have a word with them all. Recent events bear sharing."

"Aye, Father."

Edward signaled Ancel over. "Father wants to speak to all of our male relatives. We are to gather in the solar immediately. Help me round up everyone without alerting the women to what we are doing."

He and Ancel parted and worked their way around the chapel, giving a quick word to those his father wanted included in the meeting. Edward wondered what serious matter would be discussed. As the de Montforts and their relatives headed inside the keep, the women entered the great hall as the men made their way upstairs to the solar and seated themselves around the large oak table. A jug of wine made its way in a circle as cups were filled to the brim.

Edward knew he was in the company of some of the greatest knights in all of England. Besides his two older brothers and uncle, the group included Kit Emory, Alys' husband; Michael Devereux and Kenric Fairfax, husbands to Geoffrey's nieces; and his father's confidant, Raynor Le Roux. Geoffrey had also invited Lord Hardwin, Earl of Winterbourne and the man Edward and his brothers had fostered with, to the table.

"Thank you all for coming," Geoffrey said. "You know that Hal's dubbing ceremony had to be delayed because I was at court advising the king on the Scottish problem. I should say the French and Scottish problem," he amended.

"Not the Auld Alliance again," Ancel complained. "I have fought in skirmishes along the Scottish border several times over the last few years. If the rebels have support from France's treasury or even French soldiers, it will not be good for England."

"The Scots are still angry about the Duke of Lancaster's attack last year," Michael said. "He pushed north as far as Edinburgh."

"And only stopped after the burgesses bought him off," Kit added.

"Though he did destroy Haddington before the coin went into his pocket. Somehow, Lancaster always seems to earn a profit no matter what venture he undertakes." His look of disgust was shared by all.

"I don't see why the Scots would be gullible enough to trust the French again," Kenric noted. "The bastards reneged on their previous agreement with Scotland to send assistance two years ago."

"And don't forget that France entered into a temporary truce with England around the same time," Raynor said. "The fact that the Duke of Lancaster negotiated the truce would not be lost on the Scots."

"Nevertheless, we've received proof they have united again despite misgivings on both sides," Geoffrey said. "Our English spies recently learned that three weeks ago a force of twelve hundred French soldiers sailed to Scotland from Flanders, under the command of Admiral de Vienne. They landed in Leith with a gift of fifty thousand gold francs for the Scottish nobility and joined in a campaign with the Earl of Douglas and two of King Robert's sons to march on England. Although they've taken the castle at Wark in Northumberland, quarreling is rampant among the commanders on both sides." His father paused and Edward knew Geoffrey had come to the heart of their meeting. "Because of that, King Richard is now calling for a feudal levy in order to invade Scotland. As we speak, messengers are being sent throughout the country in order to bring an army to London and march upon the border in order to secure it."

Excitement filled Edward. Because of the halt in fighting against France, he had wondered if he would ever participate in battle as the older men in his family had in previous years. The king's levy guaranteed that he would see action.

As he looked around the table, though, grim faces stared back as those present pondered Geoffrey de Montfort's words. Edward realized that, except for Hal and himself, every man seated here had a wife and children. Going to war and leaving their loved ones behind would prove difficult.

And there was always the possibility that injury or death might come to pass. It occurred to him that the next time they gathered, it might be for a funeral mass for one or more of the men present. The thought weighed upon him heavily.

"We already have troops that will fight with our Portuguese allies soon regarding Castile and Lancaster's claims there, which is why the king has decided to use the levy to summon knights to fight the Scots," his father continued. "I wanted all of you to know so that you could make your decisions."

Lord Hardwin sighed wearily. "We could send others to fight in our places but I've never found that to be effective, Geoffrey. My men look to me as their leader. I will send soldiers to the king because he makes the request but I plan to accompany them and do my part as their liege lord. I would not ask of any man what I would not do myself."

Everyone nodded in agreement. Edward looked to his father, wondering if he also meant to fight.

"I support your decision, Hardie," Geoffrey said. "I, too, will send the required knights to our king and plan to ride with them for the very reason you mentioned."

"At your age, Father?" Hal asked. "Surely, you are of more value to King Richard as a military adviser than a soldier on the battlefield."

His father's eyes narrowed as he studied his second son. "I am in excellent health, Hal, and I will have my sword in hand in order to help the king deal once and for all with these miserable Scots. Not to mention the French bastards who are foolish enough to ally themselves with them."

Edward hid a smile. He might have known nothing would stop Geoffrey de Montfort from riding into battle. His father had always seemed immortal. Edward grew up hearing stories of his father's prowess as a warrior against the French.

As a group, the men rose, cups raised in their hands.

"To England—and the defeat of our enemies," Geoffrey declared.

Edward and his relatives echoed the words, each downing the remainder of his wine.

"Let us be off to the feast in Hal's honor, for he has earned our respect this day," Ancel declared. "We should wait and tell our wives of our upcoming absence after today's celebration. Especially Mother."

Geoffrey grimaced. "Believe me, I would rather face an army of French and Scottish soldiers than tell Merryn that I ride off again to war."

The assembled group filed from the solar. Edward held back so he could walk with his father to the great hall.

As they fell into step together, Geoffrey said, "I want you and Hal to stay near me the entire time we are gone from Kinwick. 'Tis important for you to accompany me to the meetings with the king and other advisers, for you will learn much by observing the proceedings. You two will stand in the background and be my eyes and ears. You may see something I or the king will need to be made aware of. Remain silent while there but we will speak after every strategy session with King Richard."

"As you wish, Father."

Being allowed to accompany his father to meetings with the king and gain battle experience?

Edward couldn't wait to ride from Kinwick to fight.

MERRYN ACCOMPANIED HER husband to the solar, the day's festivities finally over. While she'd enjoyed the gathering of their extended family, she knew something troubled Geoffrey and was determined to learn why now that they were alone.

He closed the door behind them and wrapped his arms around her. The feel and smell of him always brought her a deep sense of satisfaction. Merryn soaked in the moment and then pulled away, ready to address her concerns.

"Tell me why you are worried," she urged.

Geoffrey sighed. "I have never been able to hide anything from you."

"Nor should you," she retorted. She watched as he struggled and her gut told her only one reason would make this brave man so hesitant to speak to her.

War.

Merryn cursed aloud. "You're leaving. To fight."

Her husband nodded. "The king is calling for troops. We leave in the morning for London. From there, we will push toward Scotland."

Icy fear gripped Merryn's heart. She clutched his cotehardie. "Nay, Geoffrey. You cannot go." Even as she spoke the words, Merryn knew her pleas would fall upon deaf ears. "Let others go. You have answered the crown's call too many times to count. I don't want you riding into battle. Not at your age."

A deep frown creased his brow. "At my age?"

"Geoffrey, you are fifty years of age. War is a younger man's game."

He took her hand and flattened her palm against his hard chest. "Feel, Merryn. You, better than anyone, know my body. I train harder than any man in Kinwick's yard. I have the stamina of a knight half my age." He paused. "I also have the wisdom of age and experience in battle. You have nothing to worry about, love."

Merryn knew his strength of mind, body, and heart. Geoffrey de Montfort was the most confident man in England. If anyone could take on his enemies and survive, it would be this man she knew and loved so well.

Tears sprang to her eyes. "My mind understands your words but my heart refuses to let you go. It's not only you, Geoffrey. It's our sons I also worry about."

"Ancel has plenty of experience in battle."

"He does," she agreed, "but that doesn't mean my fears for his safety are not warranted. And what of Hal and Edward? They are just boys, Geoffrey, not hardened soldiers."

He framed her face in his hands. "I understand that you love us and will worry but remember, Merryn, Hal and Edward are no longer boys. They are men."

"They have never seen battle!" she cried, her vision blurring with the tears swimming and then falling down her cheeks.

Geoffrey kissed them away but Merryn was having none of it.

"I don't want you to placate me. I don't want you to go, Geoffrey," she said flatly. "I'm not sure if I can stand another separation from you. In all our years together, England's wars have lurked in the background, taking you from me time and again. I'm tired of it. I don't want to lose you. I can't lose you."

He pulled her to him, enfolding her in love. Her cheek nestled against the steady beat of his heart.

"You won't lose me, Merryn. This levy is only for a short time of service. I will come home to you as I always have. Our sons will be with me every step of the way. I assure you that I will watch over them and protect them. No harm will come to any of us."

She knew his duty was to the crown, even before family. Geoffrey would always be the most honorable man she knew, a knight whose honor made him the man he was. Much as she was loath to let him go, she must.

"Promise me you'll come back without a scratch. Hal and Edward, too," she said fiercely, holding him tight.

"I've always come back to you, my love. You are my home and my heart. I swear I will be back at Kinwick before you know it. Come to bed now."

Merryn gazed up into his warm, hazel eyes and saw the gleam in them. "I suppose we'll get little sleep tonight."

Geoffrey laughed and kissed her hand. "Sleep is the last thing on my mind, Wife."

"Go and warm the bed then. I'll be there shortly."

He smoothed her hair and kissed her. "Don't be long."

"I won't."

Merryn watched him enter the bedchamber and went to stand before the dying fire. She would accept her husband's choice to lead the troops from Kinwick—but she didn't have to like it. Though she worried about Geoffrey and all three of her sons, she was most concerned about Edward. Of her three boys, Edward had the most tender heart. She feared what seeing battle might do to him.

A light knock sounded at the solar's door. Before Merryn could answer it, Edward opened it a crack. Seeing her, he entered and came to her.

Taking her hands, he said, "I see Father has spoken to you. I knew you'd be upset."

Her throat was thick with emotion and she nodded. Her eyes roamed over her youngest son. At six feet, he was the shortest of the de Montfort men but he still possessed the same muscular frame. He had his father's eyes but her hair. Even now, the firelight brought out bits of auburn that ran through it. Edward was also her most sensitive child. It didn't surprise her that he'd come to comfort her.

"Mother, I want you to know that Hal and I will be fine."

"You've never seen war, Edward. It is far uglier than you can imagine. Taking a man's life stains your soul, even if he is your sworn enemy."

"I have been trained by the best knights in the land, Mother. No one will be better prepared than Hal and I as we march into battle."

She placed her palm against his cheek. Only yesterday she'd held him to her breast and nursed him. Now, he rode off to war.

"I know that. I'm not only uneasy about you and your brothers, though."

"You're worried about Father," Edward said. "About his age."

Merryn nodded. "He thinks he's a score and five, not double that."

Edward's hand covered hers. "Just as Father will look after me, I will watch over him. Hal and I both. We will constantly be at his side, whether it's when he meets with the king's military advisers or we take to the field. We will come home to you, Mother, I swear it. All of us. You and Father will live to a very old age. Together."

Merryn wrapped her arms around him. "When did you change from a boy into a man?" she asked softly.

Edward chuckled. "You've always told me I've been an old soul from the time I was born."

She kissed his cheek. "Get some rest."

"I will."

He took her hands and kissed them and then left. Warmth flooded her. She had been blessed with the most wonderful children. They had been raised well. She must trust in their training and judgment—though she would pray daily for their safe return.

Edward left and Merryn composed herself. Tonight would be her last with Geoffrey for some time.

She planned to make the most of it.

CHAPTER 2

Scotland

EDWARD BIT HIS tongue to keep from speaking out as he and Hal stood back from the table King Richard's council surrounded, viewing maps of the local area. He glanced at his brother. Hal rolled his eyes and looked away, disinterested in the proceedings before them. Hal was all about the fight and not the politics or strategy behind it.

He listened as his father made a suggestion, one of many Geoffrey had offered since the English army rode out from London in August. Again, Geoffrey de Montfort's idea was pushed aside, as other noblemen who had military experience discovered during this campaign. The king seemed only to have ears for what came from the lips of his favorite courtiers, many barely older than the king himself, and none with the background necessary to offer advice in this situation.

His father had told him he would learn much. All Edward had discovered was that sycophants surrounded the king, telling Richard only what he wanted to hear. Edward thought most of them were idiots. So far, the king's army of fourteen thousand men, a quarter provided by his uncle, the Duke of Lancaster, had done very little fighting, experiencing only a few encounters with pockets of Scottish troops. Spies and scouts had revealed that the French leaders could not settle their differences with their Scots' brothers and many had already left for the continent. With not enough men to match England in a fight, the Scots refused to be drawn into battle and kept retreating.

Time also was running out. The king's call to arms under the feudal levy only required soldiers and knights provided by medieval noblemen to fight for a limited period. His father had told Edward usually the time span amounted to forty days, though under certain circumstances it could be increased to ninety. Edward and Hal counted as men under his father's provision and Geoffrey had been required to provide trained men, including the soldiers' weapons and clothing. With the deadline fast approaching, the troops present would return to their liege lords' estates to ensure that the land would not suffer from neglect or attack.

The strategy session ended. Edward and Hal allowed the council members to withdraw from the tent before following them outside. Hal immediately took off, probably to throw dice or swap tales with fellow soldiers. Edward decided to eat something and made his way to a line of men who awaited stew and a bit of bread. Once he had his food, he settled on the ground and observed those around him.

"Mind if I join you?" his father asked, dropping to the ground with a bowl in hand.

They ate in companionable silence. When finished, Geoffrey asked, "So what do you make of the council and this campaign?"

Edward glanced around. Keeping his voice low, he said, "Saying I am bitterly disappointed in the advice the king accepts would be putting it mildly. In truth, I am horrified at how the king handles his council, much less the men who sit upon it. I know you have chosen not to be a permanent council member, Father, but you have military experience—which most of the others sorely lack. I cannot understand why the king seems to ignore what you have to say."

"Richard is not the man his grandfather, your namesake, was. I fear our young king let his success in the peasants' rebellion four years ago go to his head. Ever since then, Richard has become arrogant and insensitive."

"He acts as if he knows everything, when he is only eight and ten. That is a year younger than I am."

His father chuckled. "Ah, but you were born an old soul, Edward.

At least that is what your mother has always said about you." Geoffrey surveyed the army camp. "Richard will cut his losses here by week's end. He'll burn the border abbeys and depart with little gain."

"So what was the point of this campaign?" Edward asked.

Geoffrey sighed. "I wish I knew. Only that between the two of us, the king and I have spoken of making peace with France."

Shock ran through Edward. "What? The old king is probably turning in his grave at such blasphemy."

"I agree. But Richard isn't interested in war because his group of friends isn't." Geoffrey's expression grew grim. "I think this is the last time I will be advising our king, much less pursuing men in battle. I envision the next few years to be ones where our monarch completely believes everything those gathered around him say. He won't want an old man such as me around.

"And because of the change in the wind, Edward, I hope you will stay far from court. Hal, too. I plan to speak to your brother about this, as well. Richard's vanity only seems to grow. His hubris could bring a swift downfall and I wouldn't want you or Hal to be caught up in that. I am only grateful that Ancel has left the royal guard."

Edward hesitated and then asked, "You think rebellion might occur, Father?"

Geoffrey chose his words carefully. "Not outright rebellion, as when the peasants rose up. But I see the older nobles uniting, much as they did in King John's day, and confronting the king. 'Twould be best if the de Montforts avoid court—now and in the future."

Disappointment filled Edward but he would heed his father's warning. "You don't have to worry about me, Father. I am content to stay and serve you at Kinwick. Hal, on the other hand, has looked forward to the possibility of going to London. He longs to serve in the royal guard as Ancel did. He will be disappointed if you forbid him from doing so."

"Hal can learn to live with slight disappointment," his father said, his eyes bleak. "Better that than lose his head."

The sentiment shocked Edward. He didn't understand all the

machinations of the court, but if his father believed an uprising would take place, Hal should accept that advice. England had been stable for the fifty years the old king sat on the throne but cracks had appeared during these early years of his grandson's reign. The fact that Geoffrey de Montfort had decided to no longer go to court spoke loudly. Unfortunately, 'twas a warning the young king would more than likely neglect.

His father excused himself. Edward wandered the camp for an hour, walking off nervous energy. Tomorrow, if the Scots refused to be engaged again, the burnings would begin. He dreaded it would come to that. Already, in the few clashes between the two armies, Edward had hated running his sword through men wearing little to no armor and possessing few weapons. He had envisioned war to be glorious and grand. What little he'd seen during this campaign left him disillusioned and ready to return to a quiet life in the country. The dawn would tell if a decisive battle would occur or if the fight would be brought to the border towns themselves, with innocent people losing their homes—if not their lives. The king would burn everything in sight, including the abbeys, to send Scotland and its people a message before he returned to London.

Edward knew he would get no sleep tonight.

ANTICIPATION CRACKLED IN the early morning air as men readied themselves for battle, putting armor into place and gathering weapons and horses.

Edward finished assisting Hal don his armor and his brother returned the favor afterward since no squires had accompanied them from Kinwick. Geoffrey de Montfort did not like to bring children near battle, even if they saw no action. Though he had a reputation as a great warrior, Edward knew how much his father truly despised war. He glanced around and saw other soldiers who'd come from Kinwick also aiding one another as they prepared to make war on the Scots and French bastards today.

His father had shared with the members of his family that today's fight in the northwest of England would most likely be the last stand de Vienne and his French contingent would make in Scotland on behalf of the Auld Alliance in the foreseeable future. According to reliable spies, de Vienne would lead his men in an assault on Carlisle, a town directly on the Anglo-Scottish border. If the attack proved unsuccessful, as both sides expected, de Vienne would cut his losses and fall back into Scotland before making his way east with his men to his ships and returning the fleet to Flanders.

"Ready?" Hal asked, his expression solemn. Though his brother seemed forever lighthearted in life, Hal could always be counted upon to rise to an important occasion.

Edward nodded and retrieved his horse. He scratched Sirius between his ears and offered him an apple. Sirius quickly downed the fruit, spitting the core to the ground and looked to see if his master would offer him another treat.

"'Tis all you get from me now, boy," he told the horse. "I'll see what I can do for you once this day is done and the bloodshed is over."

He turned Sirius in the direction where his father now mounted his own war horse. Looking around, Edward saw the men of Kinwick settling into their saddles, alert and ready to follow their liege lord into battle. To their right, he spied Raynor and the soldiers he had brought with him from Ashcroft. On the left of the de Montfort group, Lord Humphrey Gardyner climbed into the saddle.

Gardyner had been designated to lead today's charge. Edward liked the gruff nobleman, who had little time for nonsense. Twice while observing tactical sessions, Edward had to stifle his laughter when Lord Humphrey barked at different royal advisers regarding fighting strategies. The man's shaggy eyebrows took on a life of their own as he dressed down courtiers half his age who sorely lacked military experience. Edward thought if Gardyner and Geoffrey de Montfort had been solely in charge of the king's army and its battle plans, the fight would already be done, with the Scots crawling back to their Lowlands and Highlands and the French sailing home with their tails between their legs.

That feeling of nervous energy soared through Edward again as it had each time he'd ridden toward the conflict over the last few weeks. He harnessed it and focused on the field ahead and the town of Carlisle to the north of it. Then the troops received the signal and he nudged Sirius into action. As the army galloped toward their enemies, Edward hoped this would be the final time the two sides would clash and that their enemies would have sense enough to lay down their arms and return home.

Riding closer, he unsheathed his sword, gripping the hilt as he swung and made contact with the first opponent in his path. He pushed away any pity he felt at the poorly-equipped man as his blade tore through the foot soldier. The Scot collapsed with what Edward knew would be a mortal wound. He never looked back as he rode on.

Minutes later, he'd made a dozen kills, mindless of whether they were Frenchmen or Scots that fell under his sword. He swung Sirius around for another charge in the opposite direction and saw Lord Humphrey's horse stumble when an arrow struck just below the crinet that protected the horse's neck and slightly above the peytral, which guarded the horse's massive chest. The arrow had found the tiny gap between the protective armor, a lucky shot that a bowman might never make again in his lifetime. The nobleman slipped from the saddle and yanked himself partly up into it again as the war horse veered and then collapsed, pinning Gardyner to the ground. Immediately, two Scots ran in the lord commander's direction, swinging their swords in glee as a war cry escaped their lips.

Edward dug in his heels and raced across the field. Reaching the first threat, he arced his sword with a fluid motion and beheaded the man in a single blow. The head went sailing as the legs propelled the body another few steps before it crumpled to the ground. Edward whipped Sirius around again as the second attacker, who'd watched his comrade fall, now moved to strike a death blow against Lord Humphrey, who flailed helplessly, trapped by his horse's great weight.

The Scot sensed Edward coming and wheeled. Edward feared the man would thrust his sword into Sirius, so he leapt from the horse's back as Sirius avoided injury by galloping away.

Now his enemy raised his sword against Edward and the two men began their fight to the death. The sounds of the battle surrounding them faded as only the clang of their two swords reverberated in Edward's ears. He blocked out the warm sunshine of the September day and the tinny smell of blood as he focused on his opponent and parried and sliced. Edward made contact twice, cutting into the man's shoulder and ripping through his thigh. As blood loss weakened the Scot, Edward delivered a final blow. The soldier fell to the ground, hitting it hard as blood bubbled from his mouth. His lips moved silently and then stilled.

Scanning the area, Edward saw the enemy retreating. He hurried to Lord Humphrey, who groaned softly under the immense weight of the now-dead horse.

Hal appeared, galloping toward them as he led Sirius by the reins. His brother dismounted. "What should we do?" he asked, assessing the situation.

"We need to get the horse off him quickly," Edward said. "Else he'll be crushed to death."

He explained to Hal what they needed to do and quickly rigged rope that he always carried around the fallen horse, knotting it tightly and attaching it to their own beasts.

"Come on, Sirius, pull!" shouted Edward, as he also yanked on the rope with all his strength.

Hal did the same, tugging from the other side. With the strength of the two men and their huge war horses, they dragged the dead animal from the suffering nobleman.

"Care for the horses," Edward instructed Hal. "I'll see to the lord commander."

He knelt next to Lord Humphrey and removed the man's helmet. The nobleman sweated profusely. Pain dulled his eyes as he inhaled in shallow breaths.

"I need to remove your armor, my lord, so we can tend to any wounds or broken bones you might have suffered."

"What about the damned Scots? And their French comrades-in-arms?"

"Both retreating as we speak. You led a successful charge, my lord commander."

Gardyner mumbled something Edward didn't understand and then his eyelids fluttered and closed. Edward removed the unconscious man's armor as gently as he could as men loyal to Lord Humphrey gathered around to assist him. Edward only wished his mother or Alys could be here. Both were renowned healers and would have known what to do to relieve the nobleman from his suffering and help set him on a swift road to recovery.

With so many hands, they made quick time stripping the nobleman down. Edward felt along the man's limbs, remembering this was something Alys used to do as she practiced the healing arts on her three brothers. Both arms and one leg seemed to be fine but the commander's left leg and hip had borne the brunt of the weight of the horse when it collapsed. Deep bruising already occurred. From its awkward angle, he surmised the leg must be broken, if not the hip itself. Edward's fingers continued their search, skirting the injured man's ribs. He moaned, leading Edward to believe several had been broken.

Suddenly, the soldiers around them parted and the king himself stood next to them.

Edward rose from where he knelt and bowed low.

"Rise," the king commanded. He studied Edward a moment. "You're one of de Montfort's sons. I have seen you as we have planned our war against the enemy."

"Aye, your majesty. I am Edward de Montfort, the youngest boy."

"Hmm." The king motioned and men flew into action. The monarch's personal healer directed Lord Humphrey's removal to a litter.

As a group of the king's guard lifted the nobleman from the ground, his eyes opened. He scanned the crowd gathered around him until his search proved fruitful.

"You," he said, pointing to Edward. "Come here."

Edward stepped to the litter. "Aye, my lord?"

"You are one of de Montfort's men?" asked Lord Humphrey.

"Aye, my lord. I am his son, Edward."

"And the other who freed me?"

"My brother, Hal."

"Bring him here."

Hal came to stand next to Edward as Lord Humphrey told the king, "Edward de Montfort saved my life, your highness. He struck down two Scots who would have murdered me as I lay trapped beneath my horse. Then he summoned his brother and they lifted the dead animal away before the beast could crush the life from me.

"If they are not knights, they should be."

"I underwent my knighthood ceremony before this campaign began," Hal said. "But Edward has yet to do so."

Lord Humphrey looked at Edward and said, "If a soldier fights with notable bravery, he can earn the right to knighthood on the battlefield. You deserve this honor for your actions today." He looked to the king. "I am afraid, your majesty, that I haven't the strength. Would you do the honors?"

King Richard smiled. "Of course." He pulled his sword from his side. "Kneel," he ordered.

Stunned, Edward did as told, his knees quaking.

The king placed the flat of the sword against first one shoulder, then the other. "For the bold courage and daring fearlessness you showed this day against the enemies of Mother England, I dub thee Sir Edward de Montfort. Rise!"

As if in a dream, Edward pushed himself to his feet. A sea of faces surrounded him but he picked out his father and Raynor among them. A beaming Ancel lifted his sword high above his head in recognition.

"For your outstanding actions this day, Sir Edward, I would like to invite you—and your brother, Sir Hal—to serve in my royal guard."

Edward turned back to the king, remembering his father's words and how the last place Geoffrey de Montfort wanted his sons was at court, much less in the king's guard. Yet, how could he refuse such an offer in the midst of so many?

He saw elation on Hal's face and his brother nodding encouragingly, telling him to accept the generous offer for them both.

Edward's gaze met that of the king's. "We would be honored to become your most obedient servants, your highness."

As a cheer went up from the soldiers encircling them, Edward spied his father looking on with dismay.

The crowd began to disperse and he saw his brother working his way toward him. Hal hurled himself at Edward, hugging him hard.

"We're members of the king's guard!" he exclaimed. "We'll be living at court, just as Ancel did."

By now, Geoffrey de Montfort had also reached them. "Come with me," he said and strode off.

Edward nudged Hal and they followed their father away from the army.

"He doesn't look pleased," Hal said. "Do you know what has him so upset?"

"Father doesn't want us in the royal guard," Edward said. "He spoke to me about his reasons why."

"I don't care what reasons he has. We're grown men and can make our own decisions. We're in the king's guard now," Hal said stubbornly. "He can't change that."

Geoffrey stopped and faced his sons. By the look of displeasure on his face, Edward guessed he'd heard what Hal said.

"I've already spoken to Edward about my concerns but you need to hear and take heed, Hal." He paused. "I know Edward had no way to graciously decline the king's offer, especially in front of so many men. I'm here to caution you both of what lies ahead."

"Aren't you proud of Edward, Father? Of us?" Hal demanded. "The king himself knighted Edward on the battlefield for his bravery. 'Tis an honor to serve as a royal guardsman. Ask Ancel."

"Be silent, Hal," Geoffrey warned sternly.

Edward knew that tone. He hadn't heard it often as a child but he'd cringed when he did. Beside him, his brother stilled, both realizing the severity of what Geoffrey de Montfort spoke.

"You must watch out for each other at all times," his father began. "The royal guard is full of Cheshire bowmen. You will be outsiders to them. The camaraderie you've experienced at Kinwick is not present at court. You will only have each other. Never forget that. Richard's court is full of false men and women who will not live up to the moral standards your mother and I have instilled in you."

A sick feeling washed over Edward.

"The king also plays favorites," Geoffrey continued. "Do whatever it takes to remain on his good side without compromising yourselves. Avoid court politics at all costs. You are present to protect the king, not gossip or take sides in petty disagreements that can blow up with major consequences."

Geoffrey drew in a long breath and expelled it. "I warned Edward of this but you must also understand this above all else, Hal. The king's vanity has grown, thanks to the band of men about him that tell him whatever he wants to hear. Discontent is growing throughout England and will continue to spread. I'm not saying it will lead to insurrection but you must be aware of your surroundings at all times. Is that understood?"

Both he and Hal nodded, sobered by their father's words.

Geoffrey placed a hand on each of their shoulders. "Promise me if the opportunity arises and you can leave the guard that you will."

Hal reluctantly agreed but Edward said, "I understand your concerns for us, Father. Hal and I will be united as one. If it's possible to leave court without alienating the king, we will."

Edward wondered what his future now held.

CHAPTER 3

Canterbury—May 1386

ROSALYNE PARRY DRESSED for the day before heading outside to the small, enclosed yard behind their cottage in order to feed the chickens. The hens—or rather, their eggs—helped provide a livelihood for her and her uncle. She scattered the grain along the ground and watched to see that none of them got into any fights over it. One young rooster was beginning to strut about, wishing to exert his rights within the group. She would need to keep an eye on him in order to see that peace was maintained within the flock, which definitely had a pecking order that must be adhered to.

Under her watchful eye, the chickens feasted. Rosalyne enjoyed watching them. Over the years, she had learned how entertaining and personable they could be. Uncle Temp had even trained a few of them to retrieve small objects.

"I will be back to collect your eggs after mass," she told the group and returned inside the cottage, brushing her hands up and down her arms to ward off the chill she felt. At this time of year, the hens usually laid their eggs in the early hours after the sun had risen. On Sundays, it gave her time to attend mass and break her fast before she gathered the eggs. Some would be sold but the largest of them would be used in creating her uncle's tempera paints.

Rosalyne pushed open the door to her uncle's bedchamber and heard his heavy snores. Chuckling at the noise he made, she shook his shoulder gently.

"Arise, Uncle. 'Tis time for you to ready yourself for mass."

Templeton Parry cleared his throat loudly and rubbed sleepy eyes. "Good morning, Rosalyne. Thank you for waking me."

"If I didn't, you would probably sleep until noon," she teased.

Her uncle often sat up late into the night, thinking about his current work and ways to improve his painting. He'd spent his early years training to be a knight but when his parents died and left him a small sum as he reached manhood, he'd followed his dream and gone to Italy to study art instead of taking his knightly oath. The secrets he'd learned from his two years abroad had been put to good use, for he always seemed to be gainfully employed, either producing portraits for various nobleman or working on panels for churches throughout southern England.

"Go ahead," he told her. "I know you will want to visit with Metylda before mass begins. I will see you afterward."

"Thank you, Uncle Temp."

Rosalyne slipped on her cloak and tied the cords together. It was one thing to step out and feed the chickens in the yard but quite another to walk the two miles to Canterbury Cathedral against a brisk wind. May afternoons in England were mostly pleasant, but early mornings usually had a chill hanging over them. She longed for the arrival of the warm days of summer, her favorite time of year.

"Rosalyne!"

She waved as she saw her closest friend, Metylda Hann, closing the door to her family's home.

"Good morning, Metylda. How are you today?"

Her friend linked arms with Rosalyne as they continued down the street.

"I am well, though Father suffers from a most dreadful cough. He was up all night and, this morning, his nose is bright red and raw."

"I am sorry to hear that, but better coughing than snoring," Rosalyne said. "Uncle Temp's snoring could wake the dead. Sometimes, I fear our roof will cave in after shaking so much. Many a night, I have buried myself beneath the bedclothes and held my pillow to my ears in order to try and block out the noise he makes."

"I like your uncle. I will defend him since he is not here to do so himself," proclaimed Metylda.

"Oh, I love Uncle dearly. He's all the family I have or could ever want."

Rosalyne knew very little about her parents, only that they had died when she was not even a year old. She never quite understood why she hadn't remained with her father's brother, Lord Benedict, at the family home once he inherited the title, as custom allowed. Uncle Temp told her that the situation was complicated but he had been happy to take her in as his own daughter.

She laughed to herself. His last name was Parry and so she'd assumed for many years that hers was, as well. When she was nine and introduced herself to someone as Rosalyne Parry within his hearing, Uncle Temp sputtered until she had to clap him hard on the back several minutes. By the time he could speak, the acquaintance had left.

That was when he told her that her true name was Rosalyne Bowyar. How foreign it sounded to her ears, especially when paired with her first name. She told him that she'd always felt like a Parry and would continue to remain one. He had laughed and said she sounded exactly like Lara, his sister and Rosalyne's mother.

"Lara always knew her own mind, even from a young age. 'Twas how she found herself married to Lawrence."

His laughter died down after that cryptic statement, piquing her curiosity. But Uncle Temp changed the subject and rarely mentioned her parents after that comment. Rosalyne knew there was some story behind what he did not share with her but she had never pressed him to divulge it. Whatever it involved seemed to make him unhappy and she would never do anything to trouble him. Templeton Parry had been both father and mother to her and taught her everything she knew, from reading and writing to cooking and painting.

More than anything, Rosalyne wanted to be a painter as Uncle Temp was.

Yet, she could not think of a single person who might hire her, no matter how much talent she possessed. Women did not paint or draw, much less get paid to do so. They did not act on stage as mummers. They were not called upon to be troubadours.

Despite the slim possibility that she would ever earn a commission as a painter, Rosalyne practiced her art every day in hopes that the time would come when she would be able to show the world what she could accomplish if given a chance.

They arrived at Canterbury Cathedral, a massive structure and one of the oldest churches in England. It held a tender place in Rosalyne's heart, for her uncle had painted some of the panels inside. She thrilled to pass them each week when she came to mass, knowing his work would stand on display for many years to come. Mayhap one day, her children—nay, her grandchildren or even *their* children—would enter the sacred building for worship and smile when they passed by the work of their blood relative.

Glancing around, she saw the usual group of strangers in attendance. These pilgrims had streamed to the cathedral ever since the murder of Thomas Becket, the cathedral's archbishop, over two hundred years ago. Thanks to the thousands who made their pilgrimage in order to visit Becket's shrine, revenue was raised from the sale of pilgrim badges made from lead alloy. The badges depicted the archbishop and his martyrdom or even the shrine itself. Her uncle often supplied these badges to the current archbishop to be sold and Uncle Temp had even begun to let Rosalyne create these for him so that he could focus more on his paintings. He told her it must be their secret and she certainly understood why.

Mass ended and she and Metylda exited the cathedral. Once outside, she saw her uncle in conversation with the archbishop himself, who had conducted this morning's service. William Courtenay always intimidated her. He was an imposing man, a great-grandson of Edward I and once King Richard's Lord Chancellor of England, before being named Archbishop of Canterbury.

"I wonder what they are discussing," Metylda said quietly as they stopped and observed the two men. "Your uncle looks very serious." She paused. "I think I will go. You need to see to your uncle." Metylda scurried off like a mouse being chased by a cat. The archbishop must frighten Metylda, too.

Rosalyne decided to put on a brave face and join the two men. Her uncle saw her coming in their direction and held out a welcoming hand.

"Ah, my niece. You remember Lady Rosalyne, Your Excellency?"

The archbishop nodded at her regally. "I do. Greetings, Lady Rosalyne." He extended his hand toward her and she knelt on her left knee and kissed the massive ring that was a sign of his exalted office.

Uncle Temp helped her rise and said to the priest, "Rosalyne is of great assistance to me in my work." He looked pointedly at her and said, "The archbishop would like me to complete one more panel. It will be placed inside Trinity Chapel."

Her eyes grew large. The chapel contained the shrine of Thomas Becket and was where each pilgrim visited.

"Many people will see your work there, Uncle," she said, swallowing as she realized the importance of him being asked to complete such a task.

"Aye, and I told the archbishop I would take it on if you could assist me."

Rosalyne maintained her composure though her insides quaked. "I would be honored to help in any way you see fit, Uncle."

The archbishop laughed. "You respond like a seasoned courtier, my lady. Politics aside, will you do it, Parry? And how long will it take you?"

"I am delighted to accept this commission, Excellency. I will take time to consider it and share my proposal with you. Once you have approved of the drawings, the actual painting will not take long. I think in a month's time or so, the panel will be resting inside Trinity Chapel."

"So be it. Go contemplate what you will produce. I hope to meet with you by early next week if not sooner, so you can share your sketches with me." He glanced her way. "You may even allow Lady Rosalyne to accompany you to our meeting if you wish."

The archbishop gave them a dismissive nod and sauntered away, his robes flowing in the slight breeze. Rosalyne waited until the priest entered the cathedral before throwing her arms about her uncle and squealing in delight.

"'Tis a big task we will undertake," he proclaimed after swinging her around and placing her back on the ground.

"But we are up to it. After all, we are Parrys," Rosalyne said. "And Parrys meet every challenge head on."

EDWARD AWOKE, DRENCHED in sweat. Images of Saint Giles Cathedral and Edinburgh's Town Hall in flames slowly receded from his mind as the nightmare dissipated. He'd often dreamt of the burnings that occurred in Holyrood and Edinburgh after that last skirmish outside Carlisle—though never of the fighting itself. He supposed his mind justified battle and the deaths that occurred on the field between armed opponents.

What troubled him still after all these months was the deliberate destruction of government buildings and places of worship, with innocent bystanders being caught in the crossfires. As he'd laid torches at Richard's command, Edward's heart told him his king wronged the Scottish people. The monarch's anger at not gaining a decisive victory on the battlefield resulted in the deliberate destruction the royal guardsmen and other knights and soldiers partook in.

Not only did he resent following orders he believed to be detrimental but Edward hated serving the king as a member of his select guard, mostly because he felt like an outsider. In years past when other Plantagenets sat on the throne—or even in the very early years of Richard's reign when Ancel served the king—royal guardsmen were drawn from the best knights in the kingdom.

That had all changed in recent years.

The royal guard's majority belonged to the bowmen of Cheshire, known as the best archers in the land. Some of their number had been recruited by the old king to serve him, wearing the green and white livery issued to them by Chester Castle's chamberlain. The Black Prince had even used Cheshire bowmen at both Crecy and Poitiers, resounding English victories in which the bowmen played a crucial role. Now, though, King Richard used the Cheshiremen to fill the ranks of his bodyguards. The bowmen guarded the king's bedchamber all night, rarely allowing any other knight of the royal guard on this duty. To Edward's disgust, King Richard had unofficially sent members of the bowmen on a mission of intimidation recently. A group of handpicked bowmen surrounded the Westminster Hall during the trial of one of Richard's enemies to ensure the correct verdict would be reached.

The bowmen's conceit often got in the way since they'd been given full reign within whichever palace the king resided. Edward heard rumors of cases even involving murder, where various bowmen had been granted pardons for their crimes as the king turned a blind eye to their illegal activities.

His short time at court had disillusioned him, much as it had his cousin, Avelyn. She had served Queen Philippa for a year as a lady-in-waiting and begged to come home to escape the petty politics at the royal court.

Edward was ready to do the same, though as a grown man, he didn't know how to go about solving his dilemma. That's why he eagerly waited to speak to his father today. Geoffrey de Montfort, much to the surprise of those at court, had been called to Windsor Castle by the king two weeks ago to help negotiate a new treaty between England and Portugal. Edward had only seen his father in passing but Geoffrey told him yesterday that he would ask for his sons to be present at the signing of the treaty this morning.

Because of that, Edward nudged a sleeping Hal, who lay next to him, and said, "We are to report to the king's chambers once we break our fast."

Hal grumbled good-naturedly as he threw back the bedclothes. His brother seemed to be enjoying their time at court far more than Edward had. Often, Hal was assigned to Queen Anne and watched over her and her numerous ladies-in-waiting. Very few, if any, of the Cheshire bowmen pulled that duty. Mayhap Edward should request that he spend more time in the queen's wing of rooms. He might feel more useful than he did now.

The brothers headed to the large room designated for the royal guardsmen's meals when they weren't attending the king or queen. As they ate, Edward revealed to Hal what would happen today since Hal had arrived after Edward fell asleep last night.

"Father said that everything has been agreed to with Portugal and signing the documents today is a mere formality."

"You spoke to him?" Hal asked, tearing off a piece of bread and chewing on it.

"Only briefly. The negotiations have gone 'round the clock and only were settled late last evening. Father said he would ask the king for permission to allow our presence at the signing of the treaty. 'Tis why we need to report to the king's rooms as soon as possible."

They finished their meals, washing the last of them down with cold ale, and made their way toward the area where the king's rooms were located. Edward liked Windsor more than any of the other Plantagenet palaces, especially the park land surrounding it. Richard's grandfather, King Edward III, had been born at Windsor and spent much of his time here, using ransom money from prisoners taken at successful battles in France to build additions and improvements to this royal residence.

When they reached the hallway that led to the king's rooms, a double line of Cheshire bowmen greeted them. Before Edward consulted one of them to gain admittance, his father arrived.

"My sons are here to accompany me," Geoffrey de Montfort said coolly, and the way parted for the three men to enter the king's chambers.

The monarch, already dressed, sat eating. The three de Montforts greeted him and bowed.

Richard looked them over. "I can tell you, Lord Geoffrey, that Sir Hal has proven to be quite popular with the queen and her attendants.

She often asks for him by name."

His father's lips twitched in amusement. "Hal has always proven to be good company and I am sure he takes his duties seriously."

"Quite so." The king dabbed his mouth with a cloth and pushed away his empty cup. "Sir Edward, on the other hand, is most solemn and steadfast. He earnestly takes on any task that I ask of him, much as his oldest brother did. How do Sir Ancel and Lady Margery fare?"

The king looked in his direction, so Edward responded, "They are well, sire. Ancel has enjoyed making various improvements at Bexley. Cyrus turned three last month and talks constantly. Lady Margery is with child again and she will deliver come October."

"I am happy to hear this." The king paused. "I know that my grandfather is your namesake, Sir Edward."

Edward glowed with pride as he recounted, "Aye, your majesty. King Edward and Queen Philippa came to Kinwick several times on summer progress over the years. Mother was a great favorite of them both. She honored me by giving me his name. I only hope I live up to the ideals the old king represented."

"Hmm." Richard grew thoughtful. "Sir Ancel served as my eyes and ears on many occasions away from court, being places I could not go and informing me of things I needed to know. Would you be interested in doing the same for me, Sir Edward?"

Excitement burst within him. "I would be honored to go wherever your majesty wishes and report on whatever you need me to investigate."

"Good. Then I wish you to leave for Canterbury today in order to view the progress being made there on the city walls. Grandfather worried how they'd fallen into disrepair and began rebuilding the old Roman defenses in fresh stone, integrating them with the older walls that still remained. He worried about the French raiding the city since it lies on the coast."

The king stood and began pacing the room as he spoke. "I have continued this task, though progress is slow. The royal treasury is almost exhausted, thanks to the costly wars against the French and

Scots, so I have used murage to fund the repairs instead."

Edward had never heard the term before. "What is murage, sire? If I am to go, I wish to understand the situation before I arrive in Canterbury."

"'Tis a toll that is used to build or repair town walls throughout both England and Wales. I called for murage again last year because some of the recently completed construction suffered tremendous damage after the earthquake that occurred there three years ago. We even felt the earth rumble here in London, so you can imagine what damage it did in Canterbury. The funds from murage are helping continue work on shoring up the walls, as well as repairing the bell tower of Canterbury's cathedral and the cloister walls that were damaged."

"So what is the mission, your majesty? What am I took look for?"

"Observe the work at hand. See what has been accomplished at this point and how much is yet to be done. Speak to the men in charge of this project and gauge both their leadership and the work ethic of the laborers."

"How long do you wish for me to be gone?"

The king shrugged. "As long as it takes. Use your judgment in the matter."

"Then I foresee a few weeks, your highness, if not a month or more. They will know I am your emissary and might put on a show if I am there but a handful of days." Edward thought a moment. "In fact, I may choose to become a common laborer at these walls and see for myself how the work progresses and how the hands are treated. It might extend my time there but I would gain invaluable knowledge this way, with no one knowing who I truly am or that I represent your interests."

"Excellent idea, Sir Edward," the king proclaimed. "I knew I could count on you."

A servant appeared at the door and cleared his throat. "Your majesty, the Duke of Lancaster has arrived and wishes to speak with you."

"Send him in." Richard returned to his chair.

John of Gaunt swept into the rooms, a tall and impressive nobleman. Despite constant rumors that the duke wished for the crown of England to rest atop his own head, Lancaster continually supported Richard and had never gone against the king, nor tried to usurp him in any way.

He greeted his nephew and then turned to Geoffrey. "I hear I have you to thank, de Montfort, for the smooth negotiations with Portugal."

"I am at the king's service," his father replied. "You will be satisfied with the terms, your grace. The diplomatic alliance signed between England and Portugal today will be one of lasting friendship between our nations."

"And my daughter?" Lancaster prompted.

"The treaty will be sealed by the marriage of Philippa of Lancaster to King John of Portugal. The battle at Aljubarrota assured Portuguese independence from Castile, firmly establishing the House of Aviz, with John the Good as the first king of Portugal. King John is most grateful for English intervention on his behalf and wishes to unite our countries through marriage."

"So the treaty will be one of mutual support, held together by my daughter's marriage to King John?"

"Aye," Geoffrey confirmed. "Your daughter will be Portugal's first queen and mother to its next king."

"I hope you are pleased, Uncle," the king said.

Lancaster's eyes gleamed with approval. "More than pleased, sire."

Richard rose. "Then we should go meet the Portuguese ambassador so I can sign this treaty and make Lord Geoffrey's work officially completed." He looked at Geoffrey. "What will we call this document?"

"The Treaty of Windsor, your majesty," Geoffrey replied. "And may it last many years."

The king exited the chamber, his uncle close behind him.

Geoffrey turned to his sons. "Come, and you can witness an historic day for England."

Hal strode from the room but his father touched Edward's arm to hold him behind a moment.

"The king does you a great service by favoring you so, Edward."

"I will not disappoint him, Father. And I am most eager to leave court."

His father gave him a sympathetic look. "I feared as much. Do this task well, Edward, and mayhap it will create enough good will to free you to come home to Kinwick."

Edward sighed. "I would like nothing more than for that to happen, Father."

CHAPTER 4

WORRY FILLED ROSALYNE as she stood watching her uncle struggle to bring his sketch to fruition. His drawing hand trembled noticeably. He would place his left hand over it and it would still for a moment but when he lifted the stabilizing hand, the right one would begin to shake again.

How could he finish the sketches for the chapel's new panel—much less paint it?

She slipped away and went to sit outside in the sun with her chickens for company. Rosalyne had noticed a slight tremor in Uncle Temp's hands when he ate. His wooden cup wiggled slightly and she had stopped filling it to the brim so that none of the contents would spill from it. Raising a bowl to his lips, she also saw the slight movement in the right hand.

It began back in the autumn, before cold weather set in. When he rejected a few portrait commissions months ago, it surprised her. He usually enjoyed painting people in the colder months. He had told her he merely put off the offers and planned to reschedule them for a later time. Uncle Temp had said his joints were starting to ache in winter and he preferred to paint when the weather turned mild and his fingers didn't pain him so. Now, she wasn't certain that he would be able to complete the commitment to paint those portraits—or any future work.

And that included the triptych the archbishop had asked for.

Picking up Mary, one her favorite hens, Rosalyne placed the bird in her lap and gently stroked the silky feathers as the other chickens waddled around the yard, clucking away.

She bent and brushed her lips against the back of Mary's neck and whispered, "Oh, Mary, what will we do if Uncle Temp can no longer paint? Though I sell the extra eggs that we do not use to create paints, that is not nearly enough to clothe and feed us."

At least their large cottage belonged to them and they paid no landlord to reside within it. But how would they survive? Uncle Temp had been a soldier—almost a knight—in his youth. But those days were long past. He had reached two score and ten three years ago. 'Twas old, indeed, and he could never go back to being a soldier at that advanced age, much less with the shaking in his hand. Besides, he had no armor and had even sold his sword many years ago, saying he no longer needed it.

True, she kept all of the monies from his commissions and proved frugal in running their small household. They had one servant who came in a few times a week to help with some cleaning and washing of clothes but Rosalyne performed the rest of the household tasks herself. Mayhap, they would need to let Martha go. That would save a few coins each month.

"Rosalyne?"

She started from her reverie, releasing Mary. The chicken flew a few feet to the ground and began picking up feed, a rooster giving the bird an appreciative glance.

"Aye, Uncle Temp? You have need of me?"

"I do. Let us walk."

Templeton Parry did his best thinking as he walked the streets of Canterbury. Often, Rosalyne joined him and they would walk for miles around the city. They might not speak the entire time but sometimes he discussed with her ideas he had regarding his art.

He offered her his arm and she took it, glad that she felt no tremors within it. She glanced at his hand. It, too, seemed to be fine. Mayhap, she had been imagining things earlier.

But her heart told her otherwise.

Usually, her uncle set a rapid pace but this time he moved more slowly. After they had strolled past many of their neighbors' cottages and beyond a local blacksmith's shop, he cleared his throat. Rosalyne knew that was Uncle Temp's cue to speak about serious matters. She braced herself for what he would reveal to her.

"Over the years, I have tried to teach you everything I know about art," her uncle said. "I have shared with you what I learned during my sojourn in Italy. Taught you how to view a subject and capture it. Explained which colors to use and how to layer paint to show dimension and shadows. You have been an excellent student, Rosalyne, and listened well to my lessons. You draw better than I ever have and your painting of people has started to rival mine."

She grew warm from his praise but wondered where this conversation might be headed.

"Something is wrong with me," he continued. "I know it—and I know you have noticed, as well."

"I have seen your drawing hand shake some," Rosalyne admitted. "But nothing beyond that."

Uncle Temp shook his head. "'Tis far worse, I'm afraid. I am starting to move more slowly. My legs feel as if I walk underwater and am dragging them through it. My face and neck have become stiff and harder to move. I awoke last night and found myself shaking the bed, the tremors were so great."

"Oh, Uncle!" she cried. Rosalyne stopped and studied him. "I wish you would have told me."

"I did not want to worry you, my dear," he said. "But now it's time you knew in order for me to carry out my latest commission from the archbishop. I have prepared you for this day all along. You have aided me by preparing the woods that I work on and creating the paints I use. 'Tis why I have allowed you to do some of the actual painting when no one else is present."

He placed his hands on her shoulders. "You will be the artist who creates the sketches for the archbishop to see and approve. And you, my dearest Rosalyne, will be the artist who paints the panel for Trinity Chapel."

Rosalyne rolled the set of sketches up, fighting the nerves that danced inside her. They would leave soon for their meeting with Archbishop Courtenay and she thought she might lose her noon meal before going. Sitting in a chair, she tried to calm herself as she wrung her hands absently. The anxiety mounted as her mind whirled.

Would the archbishop endorse the drawings that she had created? Would Uncle Temp continue to grow worse? Would they be able to pull off the deception and allow her to paint the panels? How could she earn a living to support them both if they failed in this matter?

Exhaling a long breath, Rosalyne had a partial answer to only one of those questions.

When her uncle came to Canterbury, he'd used the last of his coin to purchase their cottage. Both had their own bedchamber and a third also existed which had originally been designated as the place for his work. Unfortunately, the room proved too dark, so Uncle Temp had added on to the rear of the abode, creating a space to work in and store all of his art supplies. He had purchased large panes of expensive glass and included two huge windows in the room, needing as much natural light as possible. On mild days he would throw open the windows to work, allowing the paint fumes to escape while the light shone in. Even in cooler weather, he would allow the windows to remain open while he worked, not closing them until it proved absolutely necessary.

That meant they had a free bedchamber and Rosalyne intended to rent this out for the income it would bring in. It wouldn't solve all of their problems but it would be a start. She hoped a widow with a little one might choose to move in with them, for she would love to hear the sound of a child's laughter. Though she longed for a family and children of her own, Rosalyne doubted that would ever come to pass because of her odd position in the community. Thanks to the lineage from her father's side, she could claim the title of lady. But the only nobility she even encountered involved those she met when she and Uncle Temp traveled to paint some nobleman's portrait. She was invisible to whoever had hired them, merely someone who mixed the master's paints and cleaned his brushes while he labored over the portrait. Rosalyne doubted any nobleman would wish for his son to marry a painter's assistant—even if she was of the same class.

For the most part, she and her uncle kept to themselves. When they did mingle in society, it was with others who were in trade—carpentry, brick makers, and the like. They all knew her as Lady Rosalyne and, though she never put on airs, it was obvious others held her at a distance because of her background. Only her friend, Metylda, who possessed a carefree spirit, treated Rosalyne as she wished others would.

A shadow crossed her vision and Rosalyne looked up to see Uncle Temp standing in the doorway.

"'Tis time to leave for the cathedral."

Gathering up the rolled sketches, she accompanied him outside. They walked to Canterbury Cathedral in silence as her distress grew.

"You're trembling," he said as the church came into view. "What has you so upset?"

"What if Archbishop Courtenay doesn't like my sketches?"

Uncle Temp smiled gently. "You mean the ones you have labored over till they are perfection themselves?" He chuckled. "The archbishop won't know they are yours. At least, not now. That will change later."

His plan involved gaining the archbishop's approval and having Rosalyne complete the triptych for the chapel at home before having it carried to the church. Once installed, Uncle Temp would meet privately with the priest and reveal to him the identity of the true artist. She feared the man of the cloth would reject the panel outright—and refuse to compensate them for the hard work that would go into the process. Though Rosalyne had not expressed these fears aloud, they had kept her from sleeping well the past week while she and her uncle discussed what the panel should look like and even after she'd finished her drawings.

"We're here," she said, tamping down her fear.

Instead of entering the church, they went around the massive structure in order to visit with the archbishop in his private quarters. A servant admitted them and led them to a small room, promising to return soon with the archbishop in hand. They seated themselves and, after some minutes, William Courtenay made his appearance. They kissed his holy ring before he greeted them warmly and sat on the bench next to a large table.

"I am eager to see what you have to show me, Master Parry."

"I discussed the panel at length with my niece, your grace. Together, we have come up with several drawings to show you. Hopefully, one will meet with your approval."

The first of the seeds had been planted, with Uncle Temp making sure to divulge her part in the sketches that Courtenay would view.

Rosalyne handed the rolled designs to her uncle and he unfurled the parchments. Handing the first one to Courtenay, he let the priest study it without conversation. After some moments, the archbishop set the drawing aside and reached for the next one. He continued to do so for four sketches and paused.

Frowning, he said, "I wonder . . . mayhap if you could somehow combine the ideas in the first and third drawings, it would be more pleasing to the eye."

"Then you will appreciate this one." Uncle Temp passed a fifth drawing to the archbishop.

Rosalyne watched the man's face alight. "This is more what I had in mind," he said eagerly.

"Then you have Rosalyne to thank," Uncle Temp said. "'Twas her idea to merge the two together."

"Mmm." The priest reached for the final sketch and looked at it before resting it on the table. He spread all of them out so he could see each design as he looked from one to the next. Finally, he said, "The last one is obviously the best, though all are thoughtful pieces. It calls to mind everything I desire in the panel, even if it looks to be the most complicated of the lot."

"I agree," Uncle Temp stated. "It will take a talented artist to complete this task."

Courtenay laughed. "And I suppose you are up to this challenge, Parry?"

"I am—along with help from Rosalyne."

The archbishop turned in her direction. She stiffened her knees to keep herself upright under his scrutiny.

"So, you discussed with your uncle what my panel should include?"

"Aye, your grace. And I will help prepare the wood that the panel will be drawn upon, as well as mix the paints for Uncle."

"Because you have chosen the most complicated of all the designs, your grace, it will take some weeks to complete," Uncle Temp said. "Longer than I had first anticipated."

She knew he tried to give her as much time as possible. Rosalyne didn't know if she would be skilled enough to complete the panel on her first attempt. Or the tenth, for that matter.

"Shall we say a month from now?" suggested Courtenay. "Surely, that is enough time for an artist of your ability." His tone did not allow for compromise.

Nodding slightly at her uncle, Templeton assured the priest, "The panel will rest inside Trinity Chapel in a month's time, your grace."

"Good." The archbishop rose. "I look forward to seeing your creation, Master Parry. I suppose you are somewhat like the Almighty in that you are able to create something from nothing." His face grew stern. "But always remember that every talent, including yours, is God-given and should be used for His glory."

Both she and her uncle bowed their heads as the archbishop exited the room. Once gone, Uncle Temp hugged her tightly.

"I told you that was the best of all of your drawings. He was delighted."

Rosalyne shrugged. "I don't know if Archbishop Courtenay is every truly delighted. He always looks so stern. Being in the same room with him terrifies me."

"Come. I want to go to Trinity Chapel now and show you exactly where the panel will reside. It may inspire you to see its final resting place."

She rolled up all of the sketches and thrust them under her arm. They returned to the front of the cathedral and entered, heading east to where the chapel lay. Not only did Trinity Chapel hold the remains of Thomas Becket but also Edward Plantagenet, the Black Prince, who had been interred within the chapel. It was near where the Black Prince's remains lay that her uncle stopped.

"The panel will be placed here," Uncle Temp said.

Rosalyne deliberated over the size of wood she would use for her triptych, ignoring the numerous pilgrims that moved about the chapel. Now that she had seen the space in which the panel would rest, she knew exactly what she wanted.

Turning to her uncle, she said, "I am eager to return home and go through the wood we have. I believe I can use some we already possess."

Uncle Temp kissed her cheek. "I think I will remain behind for a while and pray over this task you will undertake."

"Oh, mayhap I should do the same," she said, feeling guilty that she had not thought to stop and pray for heavenly guidance.

"Go," he urged. "You will have plenty of time later to make your bargains with God."

"Bargains?" she asked, unsure of what he meant.

He shrugged. "I think all artists think to barter with God as they work on a piece." He placed his hands on her shoulders. "There will be times of doubt as you work, Rosalyne. Times you fear to continue. Times you are afraid to stop and consider alternatives. But the Living Christ will guide you in this endeavor." He smoothed his hand against her hair. "I will see you at home."

"All right."

Rosalyne left the cathedral and ventured out into the busy thoroughfare. She was keen to reach home and begin the most important task of her life.

CHAPTER 5

EDWARD APPROACHED THE city of Canterbury after traveling for two days. Before his arrival, he needed to change his clothing, so he turned Sirius off the road and veered into the forest that paralleled the road. It seemed odd not to wear his armor while traveling but he would have nowhere to keep it once he arrived at his destination. He had decided not to wear his usual clothes, for it would distinguish his class and not allow him to pass for the common laborer that he would pretend to be.

Because the king requested that Edward leave immediately, there hadn't been time to find anyone to make peasant clothing for him, so he'd ridden through the streets of London before his departure and looked at what laundry hung outside drying. It took a while to locate something to accommodate his large height and broad chest but Edward thought his search was worth the effort. What he now donned would look well-worn, as if he'd possessed it for a long time. He needed to look the part for the role he would play.

Fortunately, the Black Death had caused increased movement in England. Before plague struck, decimating the population, workers stayed on the estates where they'd been born for their entire lives. The only people who left were soldiers headed to war or the nobility who either followed the king on his summer progress or returned to their estates upon leaving London. With a reduced working class, laborers found they could leave their birthplace instead of staying in one spot and find work at a wage they wanted. It led to growing cities and even other towns springing up. It would not seem odd for him to turn up in

Canterbury because of this.

Edward slipped on the frayed gypon and pants. He was lucky to have convinced the woman he bought the used clothing from to give him an extra set. Of course, he had rewarded her with ample coin in order to claim two changes of clothes. Folding the clothes he had just discarded, he would leave them in the bag attached to Sirius' saddle. His horse's fine lines would be another thing that could give him away, so he would stable Sirius outside the city. Only when he had worked the wall for a couple of weeks and observed the behavior of both laborers and the men leading the construction would he return for his horse and change from commoner's clothes to that of a knight and meet with the men in charge.

He brushed his fingers against his soft hunter green gypon before slipping it into the bag. It had been made for him by his mother. Not only was Merryn de Montfort a healer of some repute but she still enjoyed sewing clothing for her children and grandchildren. Securing his things with the leather strap, he gave Sirius a firm pat.

More than anything, he missed wearing his own boots, which he had left in London with Hal. Once again, Edward would have had nowhere to leave them and their outstanding workmanship and spurs that he'd received after being awarded his knighthood on the battlefield were more dead giveaways as to his identity. He smiled, thinking of the thoughtful Humphrey Gardyner, who had made it a point to find Edward at court after the lord commander recovered from his battle injuries. Lord Humphrey himself placed the spurs on Edward's boots. He appreciated the nobleman's kindness. Few men would have found time to make such a generous gesture.

Edward wished more men at the royal court could be like Lord Humphrey but men such as Gardyner and Geoffrey de Montfort seemed in scarce supply in King Richard's London. Most courtiers thought only of how they could station themselves to become wealthier and more powerful, with little regard to others. He supposed his Father's words had proven truthful—that his day at court had passed. The old guard of Edward III's no longer was welcomed in a court that grew convincingly self-centered by the day.

Mounting Sirius again, Edward rode a short distance before he could see Canterbury on the horizon. He spotted a blacksmith's shed and saw a young boy of about six playing alongside a fence next to the road. The boy climbed up and then jumped down. As Edward rode up, the lad froze, his eyes wide as he stared in Edward's direction.

"Greetings," he called out. "Is your father nearby? I wish to speak with him."

"'Tis a fine horse you have there, my lord," the lad said.

"Oh, I'm no lord," Edward said humbly, "but I would like to see your father."

The boy turned away from the fence. "I'll fetch him." He ran into the shed.

Moments later, a burly man with muscled arms and a thick chest appeared, a hammer swinging in his hand. His son followed closely behind.

"My boy says you wish to talk, my lord."

Edward dismounted. "As I told the lad, I am no lord."

The smithy appraised him. "You may say so but your horse tells a different story. So does your bearing and your speech, despite the mean clothing you wear."

He winced. It never occurred to him that his speech might give him away. He would need to add to the story he'd invented as he traveled to Canterbury and remedy that.

"The horse was a gift. My father was steward to an earl and he wanted a better life for me. Told me to pay attention and imitate everything about our liege lord that I could, from the way he spoke to the way he walked." Edward smiled shyly. "I have a gift for mimicry. It pleases me that you thought me highborn."

The smithy gave him a toothless grin. "'Twas that or to think you had stolen the horse. You didn't look the thieving type to me."

Edward laughed heartily. "Nay, I am honest to a fault. At least, that is what my mother always told me. But I have a favor to ask."

The man grew wary. "What would a stranger wish from me?"

"I will be in Canterbury for a few weeks and would rather keep a horse with these bloodlines out of the city. You yourself noted his fine lines. I would rather Sirius be somewhere away and safe, where he could be cared for. He is rather spoiled for an animal. My fault, I'm afraid, and that of my liege lord before he passed on and the horse came to me for services I'd rendered to him. I have ample coin to pay you. Would you be interested in stabling my mount until I return?"

He glanced to where the boy peered around from behind his father and tried to sweeten his offer. "Your son could help. Sirius loves children."

"Could we keep him, Father? Just for a little while?" the boy begged.

The blacksmith considered the proposition as he rubbed his bushy beard. "You say you have coin to pay?"

"Aye. Enough to feed and house him." Edward winked at the boy. "And, hopefully, for someone to brush Sirius and talk to him every day so he won't feel so lonely without me."

The man came to a decision. "Aye. We will care for your horse, my son and I." He extended his hand. "I am John. This is Will."

"Short for William," the boy said. "Mother named me. But she lives with the angels now."

"I am sorry to hear that," Edward said. "You must miss her very much. But I'll wager she looks down upon you from Heaven and watches over you every day."

"That's what Father says," the boy proclaimed.

"Then your father is a wise man."

The blacksmith said, "We were about to stop and eat our noon meal. Would you care to join us?"

"That would be most kind of you, John. And I am Edward. Edward Munn. Most pleased to meet you both."

He'd already decided he could not use the de Montfort name, with it being one of the oldest, most noble in England.

"Bring Sirius into the shed. You can rub him down and give him some oats. I'll prepare something for us to eat."

"Can I stay with Edward, Father?" Will begged. "He can show me how to brush Sirius."

His father ruffled Will's hair. "You may. But do everything Edward says."

"I will!"

Will led him and Sirius behind the shed to an enclosed structure.

"This is where Father shoes horses. Sirius can stay here."

Edward removed the horse's saddle and the small bag that contained his own clothing and the extra set he'd purchased from the London fish wife. He decided he would take the satchel with him instead of leaving it behind. Though John seemed a good man, it wouldn't do for him to become curious and go through Edward's things.

"Let me tell you about everything Sirius wears and why he does so."

He passed a pleasant half-hour with the boy, discussing the horse's equipment and how to care for both it and the animal. Edward demonstrated how to brush Sirius and gave Will a chance to try his hand at it.

"Talk to him the entire time you brush him," Edward suggested. "He likes that."

Will looked puzzled. "What do I say to him?"

"Just speak to him as if he were your friend, for that's what a horse can be. And be sure to scratch here, between his ears. Sirius likes that most of all."

After they finished, Will brought him inside a one-room cottage. John gestured for them to be seated and they ate a simple meal together. Edward thought of the rich foods eaten at court and how these two would be happy with a few morsels of court leftovers.

As they ate, Edward asked John about construction on the wall.

"Been going on for some time. It creates steady work for those men who come to Canterbury, which is a good thing."

"Who leads the construction?" Edward asked, though he already knew. He wished to draw out what he could from the smithy. Local gossip would be something to consider during his time in Canterbury.

"The Crown appointed Lord Botulf to be in charge." John shrugged. "From what I hear, he only goes to the site on occasion. The actual work itself is in the hands of Perceval Rawlin. He is head of all the crews spread throughout the wall and decides who does what."

"What do you think of him?"

John grew thoughtful. "I have not met the man in person but I know others who have. Even some who have worked under his direction."

"And?" Edward thought John was being evasive.

"He's a bloody bastard," the blacksmith said. "Deceitful. Corrupt. Why do you ask?"

"I was curious. I've heard of the work on the Canterbury walls and thought it had been going on for far too long. Mayhap they need someone else in charge."

"That won't happen anytime soon. Not with Rawlin lining his own pockets, not to mention Lord Botulf's. The great lord seems to look the other way. Most venture to guess that Rawlin gives at least half of his profit to Lord Botulf, which guarantees no questions are asked." John paused. "But who am I to say? I'm but a humble smithy."

They finished eating and Edward told John he would be happy if the blacksmith chose to exercise Sirius each day.

"For such a large horse, he's gentle as a lamb. You would have no trouble riding him if you wish to do so."

"I may." John stroked his beard. "I haven't ridden in some time but I would love to be on the back of a magnificent beast such as Sirius."

"Then feel free to do so. Take young Will with you." Edward winked at the boy. "I think he might like that."

He gave John several coins for the horse's care and promised more upon his return. Saying his goodbyes, Edward slung the bag over his shoulder as he stepped out into the road and turned toward Canterbury. It felt good to stretch his legs after a couple of long days in the saddle.

A short time later, Edward entered through the city's gates and decided to walk the streets for a bit. He wanted to familiarize himself with Canterbury and would need to find a place to sleep. He wondered if someone in his position would stay at an inn or even eat there, or if that would be too much coin for a day laborer. He would ponder that as he walked the city.

The main thoroughfare teemed with people that afternoon, much as London did. Edward passed cottages, stalls, and street vendors selling their wares. Though he'd already eaten, the meal hadn't filled his belly and the smell of meat pies enticed him enough to purchase one and down it in a few, swift bites.

Edward ventured down side streets and then wound back around to the main road that cut through the city. More than anything, he was eager to see the cathedral, which was said to rival any structure in London. As he drew closer, the church did not disappoint. Its majestic beauty nearly took his breath away. He entered and wandered about the main church, soaking up its grandeur. He knelt and said a quick prayer, hoping all in his family were well and that he would accomplish his mission in Canterbury to the best of his ability.

After that, he headed toward Trinity Chapel, where he wished to pay his respects to the Black Prince. Edward had grown up hearing tales about Edward of Woodstock from his father and Raynor. Both men had fought under the Plantagenet prince during the wars in France. Geoffrey de Montfort had stressed to his three sons that not only was the Black Prince a brilliant military strategist and commander but he was one of the best men that ever walked the earth. The Black Prince was known for his generosity as much as his leadership and Geoffrey had emphasized to his sons that both were equally important in life.

Multitudes of pilgrims milled about the chapel, most making their way toward the front. Edward assumed that was where Thomas Becket's shrine lay. He looked around and spotted what had to be the place where the Black Prince was interred. As he approached, he saw a man close to his father's age standing nearby.

But it was the woman next to him that drew Edward's interest.

The candlelight of the chapel bathed her golden hair in warm, rich tones. He longed to reach out and run his fingers through her tresses.

That gave him pause. He hadn't a romantic bone in his body, unlike Hal, who could wax poetic without thought. Yet everything about this woman made him long to speak to her. She was petite in height, with small, round breasts and an even smaller waist. Her fair skin glowed in the candlelight. He studied her profile a moment and liked the pert, upturned nose. He only wished he could see her eyes as she looked at the wall in concentration.

Edward glanced away, not meaning to stare. He heard the two speaking to one another in hushed tones as he looked upon the final resting place of the Black Prince. This was a knight for all knights to admire. He wondered what kind of king the Black Prince would have made if his life hadn't been cut short by illness and then felt guilty for the thought. 'Twas the man's son who now sat on the throne and Edward had sworn allegiance to Richard.

Lost in his reverie, he didn't notice when the woman left. Edward stepped back and saw she was now missing. The companion she'd stood by offered him a friendly smile.

"Not a pilgrim come to see Becket, but one wishing to pay homage to our famous Black Prince?"

"I have heard many stories of him," Edward said, reminding himself to remain in his role of Edward Munn, a simple worker and not a knight who aspired to be like the Black Prince.

"This is the man who should have been England's king," the older man said firmly. "His son makes a mockery of his grandfather's ways."

The stranger's words shocked Edward to his core. If spoken in London, 'twould be considered treason. Edward felt tainted merely standing next to someone who had voiced such a blasphemous opinion. He tried to mask his surprise but he obviously failed.

"I have disturbed you, my friend. If so, I am sorry," the man apologized.

"Excuse me." Edward turned away and left the chapel, not wanting to be lured into a conversation with the outspoken fellow. He would return another time to see the rest of the chapel and study the architecture of the church in more detail.

What he wanted to do now was find the mystery woman.

He hurried outside and scanned the crowded street in front of him, looking in both directions. Luck was with him. He caught sight of her moss green gown and hair, made more golden by the sunshine that fell upon it. Striding her way, he quickly closed the gap between them, thanks to his long legs and her much shorter ones.

As he drew close, he grew curious at the scrolls she carried under one arm. Edward had never seen a woman serve as a messenger and wondered if she delivered missives for a living. Something about her intrigued him like no woman ever before.

He came within a few feet of her, ready to reach out and touch her shoulder—but something held him back.

'Twas his knightly code.

Guilt rose in him. A knight was sworn to tell the truth at all times. How could he speak to this lovely creature and introduce himself by giving her a false name? That was no way to approach a woman, especially one who interested him so. Edward backed off, slowing his pace to allow distance to be created again between them.

But what of when his task had been finished? He would like to meet her then. Leaving matters in Fate's hands wasn't good enough. Canterbury was a huge city and he might never lay eyes upon her again.

Edward once more closed the gap between them. He would merely see where she went and that she arrived at her destination safely. If she went into a cottage and stayed, he might assume she resided within and he would know where to go when his time in Canterbury came to an end. But what good would that do him? To meet an intriguing woman and then leave the next day, never to see her again?

What foolishness had overcome him?

Still, he continued to follow her and decided he would make sure she got to where she headed without a problem. He thought it odd that she was unaccompanied and used that as an excuse to shadow her.

Suddenly, he heard something rumbling in the distance, above the din of the street noises. Then a scream. Then more. His eyes looked ahead and saw a team of horses running wild, with no driver to slow them.

And they ran straight for the woman.

With a burst of speed, Edward reached her seconds before the uncontrolled horses did. He flung himself through the air, knocking her out of the way in the nick of time.

They both landed hard on the ground, Edward falling on top of her and then scrambling off so as not to crush her. He quickly came to his feet and latched on to her elbows, drawing her up.

The deepest blue eyes he'd ever seen met his. Her mouth fell open. Nothing came out.

"Are you all right?" he asked.

"I . . . I think so." She looked around. "What happened?"

"Someone must have lost control of their team of horses. They stormed toward you."

"I could have been killed," she whispered. Her eyes grew larger and she licked her full, bottom lip, causing something to stir within him.

"I am Edward. Edward Munn."

The woman bestowed a radiant smile upon him. "And I am Rosalyne Parry."

"'Tis a good name for you, for roses seem to bloom in your cheeks." Edward winced after the poetic words left his lips. He never said anything that wasn't practical. To blurt out something whimsical like that to a woman he had just met was unthinkable.

"I thank you for the compliment, Edward Munn." She smiled a moment longer and then it dissipated. "Oh, no!" she cried. "My sketches!"

Edward looked and saw the wind had carried them away. Rosalyne broke away from him and began chasing the parchments as they blew down the street.

Though he did not know the significance of the drawings, he knew they meant a great deal to her. He would save them—and learn something about this woman who intrigued him so.

Edward raced past Rosalyne. He planned to retrieve every bit of parchment.

And gain a few answers along the way.

CHAPTER 6

ROSALYNE SCRAMBLED AFTER her drawings. She had spent far too long on them only to lose them because of an unexpected accident. If she could save the single one the archbishop approved of, all would be well.

The trouble was, she didn't know which one that was—and didn't have time to inspect a page when she retrieved it.

The man who'd saved her from what most likely could have been death raced by her. His long legs covered twice the ground that she could in half the time. He grabbed one of the parchments and kept running. She tried to keep up with him as he dodged between people and carts and behind stalls. Finally, Rosalyne gave up, out of breath. She moved from the middle of the road and watched as he collected every one of her sketches.

Without breaking stride, he hurried back to her, hitching the bag he carried back up on his shoulder. As he approached, she admired his tall, muscular frame and handsome looks. His hair seemed dark at first but glints of burnished auburn shone through in the bright sunlight. A strong jaw and sensual lips drew her in. She had been mesmerized by his hazel eyes, seeing both greens and browns within them in the short time they had spoken together.

"I think I have them all," he said as he reached her. "Were there five total?"

"Aye." Rosalyne watched as he placed one atop another, resting them on his knee so they didn't touch the ground. He rolled them up as a group and handed them over to her.

"Much thanks, Edward Munn," she said gratefully and winced as she reached out to collect the drawings from him. Her left wrist throbbed painfully. It hadn't bothered her during all of the excitement but now that she had her artwork in hand, she realized she must have injured it in the fall when Edward pushed her from the path of danger.

He shrugged. "They seemed important to you. And 'twas partly my fault that you lost them." He paused. "May I ask what they are for?"

"Why don't you come home with me and I'll tell you? I feel I owe you something. At least a cup of ale." She slipped the parchments under her left arm and tried to keep the wrist of that hand still.

Edward grinned. "I have never been a man to turn down a cup of ale, least of all if offered to me by a charming woman." He offered her his arm and she slipped her good right hand into the crook.

"Why don't I carry them for you?" he asked. When she didn't speak, he added, "I promise nothing will happen to them. If any more wild horses come our way, I'll run like the wind with your drawings—even if I must leave you behind to fend for yourself against the runaway beasts."

She chuckled. "All right."

Taking the group of parchments, he secured them under his arm. "Which way?"

Rosalyne led him down the street, enjoying the nearness of him. His arm seemed hewn from rock where she gripped it. He smelled wonderful, a mix of something masculine that gave her a heady feeling. Never had she reacted to a man in such a way. She seemed almost lightheaded as her heart pounded fiercely in her chest. A swirl of something ran inside her, something she couldn't put a name to.

But it felt splendid, all the same.

They strolled at a leisurely pace as Rosalyne asked, "What do you do in Canterbury, Edward?"

"Nothing, so far. I only arrived in the city a few minutes ago. I hope to join the workers who toil on the wall."

"You should have no problem in being hired. You are young and strong. They are always looking for new men."

"'Tis good to hear this. I am only a score and I have the strength of two men or more."

"And you are so modest," she teased.

Edward laughed. "Should I hide what few talents I possess? I have a hardy back and can lift whatever stones need to be moved. I could easily lift you, Rosalyne, and move you wherever you needed to go."

She sensed the blush spilling across her cheeks. "My own two feet will get us back to my home, Edward. No need for you to carry me anywhere."

He gave her a lazy smile, making her heart skip a beat.

"Do you live far?"

"Nay, our cottage is up ahead on the left." She pointed it out. "The large one on the end, with the enclosed yard."

They reached the front door and entered. Edward had to duck his head since he was taller than the door's frame. He placed the rolled drawings on the table. Reluctantly, Rosalyne released his arm.

"This is a large abode," he noted. "Do you live here with your husband? Your children?"

"Nay, I have no husband. 'Tis my uncle's place. I have lived with him since I was a babe. My parents both died of fever and Uncle Temp took me in and has cared for me ever since."

"Was he the man you stood with in Trinity Chapel?" Edward asked.

"You were there?"

"Aye. Visiting the great cathedral was the first thing I did when I arrived in Canterbury. I saw you in the chapel but you stared at the blank wall and saw nothing around you."

"I was there with Uncle Temp. He is a painter and I assist him in his work."

"A painter? Why would someone paint the stone walls of a chapel?'

Rosalyne laughed. "Nay, he paints people and panels. Noblemen hire him to paint their portraits. It is becoming a practice within the nobility, to capture your likeness in a picture to pass on to your descendants. Uncle Temp paints several portraits each year. I accompany him to the great houses and prepare the surface of the wood and mix his paints."

"You do?" He gave her an appreciative glance. "That is most unusual. I would enjoy hearing you tell me about this process." He thought a moment. "But the sketches I saw were not for portraits, were they?"

"Nay. Archbishop Courtenay commissioned Uncle to create a new panel for Trinity Chapel. He and I had come from a meeting where the archbishop approved the final sketch to use in the project. Uncle Temp showed me where the panel would rest inside the chapel today. I wanted to see the space so I could envision where the triptych would be displayed."

"And your uncle needs to view his sketch while he paints this panel?"

"Of course. Some artists refer constantly to the sketch they've made while they paint. Others actually duplicate the sketch faintly on the wood itself and then use it as a guide while their brush strokes over it."

"Hmm. Which does your uncle do?"

"Actually, he has used both methods in the past."

But Rosalyne preferred drawing what she would paint directly onto the wood. That was why having the exact sketch she had labored on for hours proved critical. She wanted to use it to include every detail before she ever picked up her brushes. It would aid her immensely as she painted since tempera paint dried at a fast rate. An artist had to commit quickly and be assertive with the brush when working with this paint.

"Please, have a seat, Edward," she told him. "I have been remiss. I promised to offer you ale. I will return shortly."

Rosalyne went to their kitchen and tried to pour the ale but her wrist had now begun to swell. She found it difficult to do anything with one hand and groaned in frustration.

"Do you need help?" Edward stood in the doorway, his large frame filling it.

She frowned. "I seem to have injured my wrist when I fell. It is troubling me some."

But what really troubled her was that she needed both hands to begin work on the panel. Rosalyne drew and painted with her right hand but she needed both of them to attach the wood planks together and sand them down, as well as glue the linen atop the wood and apply multiple layers of gesso. She feared the injured wrist would stall the process and knew her uncle's unsteady hand could not replace hers. She had yet to begin the panel and she was already far behind.

Tears welled in her eyes as frustration built within her.

"You are distressed. In pain," Edward said. "Let me help you."

Rosalyne angrily brushed a falling tear away with her good hand. "What can you do?"

He smiled. "More than you think. My sister, Alys, is a healer and she practiced on my two brothers and me while we were growing up. Mother would give us different complaints to act out and it was up to Alys to determine what ailment we had and work to bring us back to good health."

"There were four of you?" she asked wistfully. "I always longed for a brother or sister."

"Not four but six of us. I also have two younger sisters."

"Where are all of them now?"

She watched him frown a moment and wondered why he was reluctant to share information about his siblings.

Finally, he spoke. "Alys married and has children of her own. Her twin, Ancel, works the land with his wife, Margery. My brother, Hal, has gone to London to try and earn his fortune. Nan and Jessimond are still at home with our parents."

"And you left to come to Canterbury, to do the same as Hal?"

"Aye. I did not want to farm. I would rather use my hands. Canterbury seemed to be a place of opportunity. But enough talk about my family. Let me examine your wrist and see if I can bring you some relief."

Rosalyne offered it to him. It amazed her that a man with hands so large could be so gentle as he ran his fingers around her wrist and probed it. A sensation of butterflies flapping their wings erupted in her belly and she swallowed, trying to tamp down the giddy feeling.

As Edward manipulated her wrist, he said, "I actually learned quite a bit from Alys. For instance, I know to rub the slime of a live snail against a burn. If you do, 'twill heal quickly."

Rosalyne shuddered. "Then I am glad I don't suffer from a burn. I cannot imagine allowing a wriggling snail to rub against my skin." Her nose wrinkled in disgust.

"The good news is that it is not broken, only sprained. Tell me how your wrist feels now," Edward said. "I can see it's slightly swollen when compared to your other wrist."

"It is somewhat tender. I feel mild pain but nothing severe."

"Even better. I wouldn't begin to guess what type of poultice you should put on it. It may bruise some but you haven't injured it greatly. It should be good as new in two to three days but that means you must rest it until then. I know Alys would wrap it tightly and have you keep it elevated." He thought a moment. "I can also make you a sling. That way 'twill be cradled against you and you won't be tempted to use it. Do you have some cloth that I can use to fashion one?"

"Aye. I will retrieve it for you." Rosalyne went to her bedchamber and found a long length of material that would work. She paused and took a deep breath before re-entering the room. The effect this stranger had on her confused to her no end.

But his company proved fascinating.

"Will this work?" she asked.

Edward nodded and took the cloth from her, using his teeth to split it before he yanked hard to tear it apart. He wrapped the smaller piece around her wrist several times, binding it firmly and tucking in the end carefully to keep it in place. Then he stepped behind her and reached around, placing her wrist against the material. His chest brushed against her back, causing frissons of electricity to skirt through her. He brought the ends up and tied them behind her head, his fingers brushing against her neck. The blood pounded in Rosalyne's ears.

Edward turned her around by her shoulders so that she faced him. They stood so close that she feared he would see her cotehardie jump from her heart bumping fiercely against it. Rosalyne stared into Edward's dreamy, hazel eyes, bewitched by them. She fought going up on tiptoe to place her lips against his. Never had she kissed a man before—and never had she longed to do so.

Until now.

"That should hold it in place," Edward said, his voice like a silken caress.

They stood gazing into one another's eyes until the sound of the front door creaking open startled her. Rosalyne stepped back guiltily, feeling her face flame.

Uncle Temp entered the room and stopped in his tracks, a puzzled look pinching his brows together. "What's this?" he asked. "Why, 'tis the stranger from Trinity Chapel. What are you doing here?"

She quickly said, "This is Edward Munn, Uncle. Edward, my uncle, Templeton Parry. This man saved my life today and the sketches you drew for the archbishop."

Her uncle closed the door behind him and faced them. "How so?" Then he studied her more closely. "What has happened to you, Rosalyne? Why is your arm in a sling?"

"I am fine, Uncle, but I promised Edward a generous cup of ale for coming to my rescue. I'm also famished. Would you help me bring in food and drink and we shall tell you the story?" She looked at their guest. "Please, have a seat, Edward. We will return shortly."

Uncle Temp followed her into the kitchen. He never questioned her as he helped retrieve a small round of cheese, a few apples, and the ale. Rosalyne knew she would not have been able to manage with a single hand but she hadn't wanted to leave everything to her uncle with his shaking hand. Glancing at him, though, the tremors seemed to be absent at the moment.

"Are you able to carry the tray in?" she asked.

"For now. The quivering comes and goes. Right now, I have no shaking, nor do I sense any coming on."

He scooped up the tray and they returned to where their guest patiently waited. Rosalyne distributed the cups of ale with her right hand, feeling odd to only use it. Edward pulled out his dirk and sliced cheese for them while Uncle Temp made sure each of them had an apple.

"So, how did you rescue my niece?" he asked, curiosity written on his face.

Edward explained to him about the runaway team of horses that crashed down the street and that he had made sure Rosalyne hadn't been struck by them.

"You are far too modest in telling this tale, Edward," she chided. "The wild horses came perilously close to trampling me. If not for this man's swift actions, I might have been crushed under their hooves and the cart's wheels. At best, I would be battered and have numerous broken bones. At worst, I would not be sitting here talking with you, for I would have been killed."

Uncle Temp's eyes glistened with tears. "Thank you, Edward. My niece means the world to me." He squeezed Edward's shoulder briefly and then turned his attention to his ale.

Rosalyne saw he struggled to get his feelings under control and wanted to take the focus from him. "In the commotion, I let go of the sketches. The wind picked them up and scattered them along the thoroughfare. Though I gave chase, Edward was the one who gathered all of them up and returned them to me."

Uncle Temp had regained his composure. "Then we are in your debt, Edward. The drawings are the result of many conversations Rosalyne and I shared. Archbishop Courtenay gave his approval today after viewing them. One, in particular, will be used to create a new panel to hang inside Trinity Chapel. In fact, 'twill be right where you and I stood today when we spoke."

"You've met?" Rosalyne asked, looking from one to the other.

"Only briefly," Edward murmured.

"I am afraid I scared young Edward off," her uncle admitted.

"What did you say?" Rosalyne knew Uncle Temp could be free with his opinion at times.

He shrugged. "'Tis neither here nor there." He brightened. "But I am glad to make your acquaintance, Edward Munn."

"And I am pleased to meet you. And your niece," Edward added. He bit into the apple and then drank some of his ale.

Uncle Temp asked Edward what he did for a living and where he lived in Canterbury.

"I have only arrived this very day and will seek work tomorrow. I plan to speak to the men who are in charge of rebuilding Canterbury's walls. Hopefully, they have need of another laborer."

"Have you a place to stay?" Rosalyne asked. She thought about her plan of how they could add to their coin and saw this as a golden opportunity—in more than one way.

"Nay. I suppose I will look for an inn to stay the night and then seek something more permanent in nature tomorrow. If I am hired, that is."

Though she had not discussed her idea with her uncle, Rosalyne said, "Uncle Temp and I have a spare bedchamber. It has sat empty for far too long, so I have thought recently that we might rent it out." She glanced at her uncle to gauge his reaction. He didn't seem to object, so she pushed on. "Mayhap you would be interested in staying here with us. We are not far from where a bulk of the current construction takes place. It would be convenient for you and you would not have to look elsewhere."

Hope fluttered inside her as she saw him consider the option.

Then Edward beamed at her. "I would be happy to reside here during my time in Canterbury," he declared. "I will pay you a fair price for use of your bedchamber and extra coin if you will provide me with two meals a day, one before I begin my day's work and one at the end."

She named a price and he agreed to it without hesitation. She raised her cup and said, "Then here's to our new resident—and new friend."

Rosalyne drew a long drink from cup as she considered how she could manage to steal a kiss from the handsome man seated across from her.

CHAPTER 7

ROSALYNE ROSE AFTER a night of fitful tossing and turning. Normally, the moment her head hit the pillow, she fell fast asleep and did not wake until morning.

Not last night.

Images of the very handsome Edward Munn constantly invaded her thoughts. His ready smile and hazel eyes. The sensuous lips that she wished would touch hers. The dark hair that shone with auburn highlights in the bright sunlight. She had laid first on one side, then the other, trying to urge sleep to come. She shifted to her back and then her belly, only to return to her side again, yet sleep had eluded her. Somehow, she must have drifted off at some point but her eyes now felt grainy and dry.

She dressed in light blue, which Metylda pointed out made Rosalyne's eyes seem an even deeper shade of blue. Though she had never dressed for a man before, Rosalyne wanted to draw Edward's attention. Why it was important to her to do so puzzled her. She had met many men in her one and twenty years but none of them had drawn a second glance or a lasting thought. A few had flirted with her, including two different noblemen's sons. Uncle Temp had painted the portrait of one of them for the man's grandfather. The other had come and watched his own father's image being captured, constantly asking Rosalyne questions and then following her about like an eager puppy.

But neither man interested—much less fascinated—her the way Edward did.

She couldn't say why he stood out from others of her acquaintance, only that she couldn't wait to see him again. Talk with him. Laugh with him. Share something about herself and learn more about him and his large family.

Rosalyne went to his bedchamber's door and knocked softly upon it with her good hand. Her wrist still proved tender, so she would ask if he could help her put their morning meal together. He had offered to pay for it and another one when he returned from work each night. Mayhap she would tell him to save his coin until she could prepare the food and drink on her own.

After waiting a few moments, Rosalyne knocked again, this time more loudly. Edward might be a heavy sleeper. When he still did not respond, she decided to be brave and push the door open in order to call out to him. If he snored as Uncle Temp did, he might not have heard her summoning him. Since he was eager to find work today, she did not want him to oversleep.

She scanned the darkened chamber and saw with the light streaming from behind her that the bed did not look slept in. The bedclothes remained in place and Edward was nowhere to be found. Rosalyne blinked back unexpected tears that sprang to her eyes.

Why had he agreed to stay with them, only to sneak out after she and Uncle Temp had gone to bed last night?

Disappointment flooded her. She had started the day eager to see Edward—and now she probably never would again.

Had he regretted his hasty decision to stay with her and Uncle Temp? Or did he already grow homesick and leave Canterbury to return to his country home?

Rosalyne chided herself for trusting a stranger. She had admitted him to their home, hoping for his coin and company. Now she would have neither. A wave of sadness overcame her, thickening her throat with unshed tears.

As she started to close the door, she glanced down and saw Edward's satchel sitting on the ground next to the door. Hope sprang within her. If his things were still here, surely he was, too. She didn't know where he might be at the moment but she believed he would return.

She had to. For if she didn't, she would have to admit how empty her life seemed before he entered it.

True, that seemed a foolish thought. Rosalyne had an uncle who loved her and was lucky enough to live in a roomy cottage. She helped her uncle with interesting work and traveled with him whenever he went to paint portraits. She had a steadfast friend in Metylda and cared for her chickens.

But beyond that? Nothing.

Edward's appearance had sparked something within Rosalyne. It made her think that there might be more to the life she was living—if he were in it.

"I am being irrational," she said aloud.

She had only spent a few hours in the man's company and knew very little about him. Why, all of a sudden, did she have such wild ideas and unexplained longings where Edward Munn was concerned?

Rosalyne closed the door and went to awaken Uncle Temp. As usual, his loud snores rattled the bed. Bending over to touch his shoulder, she paused.

His hands, crossed over his chest, shook. Both of them. Not just his drawing hand but the other, as well. And in his sleep. She pushed aside the panic that loomed within her. For now, she would ignore it. She needed to focus on the panel for Trinity Chapel and making it her best possible work.

Then she would confront her fears regarding the future.

"Uncle Temp? Time to rise."

He started. "Oh, 'tis you, Rosalyne." Pushing himself upright, he coughed. The coughing continued until she tapped him on the back. It sounded as if it came from deep within his chest and that worried her.

"Dress yourself and come to break your fast," she said gently before leaving the room.

In the kitchen, she struggled to place bread she'd baked onto a tray. She would have to get her uncle to slice it. The same with the chicken she'd roasted yesterday. Trying to cut it without being able to steady it with her left hand proved impossible, so she set it on the tray with the bread. She retrieved a pitcher of ale and took it into the other room, where she placed it on the table.

"Where is Edward?" Uncle Temp asked.

"I know not, Uncle. I went to be sure he was awake and ready to eat but he was not in his chamber."

"He left without filling his belly? I know he is young and eager to find work but 'tis foolish to try and put in a hard day of labor on an empty stomach."

She shrugged, not sure how to answer him. Before she could return to the kitchen and figure out how to get the tray from there to here, Edward suddenly appeared in the doorway.

Rosalyne sucked in a quick breath. "You startled me!" she proclaimed.

He blushed as he walked in and took a seat at the table. "Mother always called me her ghost. She said of all six of her children, I was the one who came and went silently. I am sorry if I surprised you."

"I did not think you were here," she said.

"I wasn't. I went to mass."

"Oh! We thought you might have gone to the wall."

"Nay. I always start my day at mass as my parents taught me to do. I was pleased when I stumbled across a chapel about half a mile from here. Though I long to hear mass said in the cathedral by the archbishop, this nearby chapel will be much more convenient on a daily basis."

It impressed her that he was so devout. She and her uncle attended mass each Sunday and on holy days but they did not make an effort to go every day.

"Would you help bring in our morning meal?" she asked. "My wrist is still a bit tender."

Edward rose. "You shouldn't lift anything for a couple of days. It needs time to heal. Please sit, Rosalyne. I will get everything."

She took her seat at the table and waited. He brought out what she had placed on the tray and had added a small round of cheese to it.

"Let me slice everything," he said. He did so and distributed the food among the three of them.

As he finished, Uncle Temp began coughing again. He quickly downed the ale Edward had poured but still continued hacking. Edward pounded him steadily on the back. Finally, the coughing ceased.

"You do not sound well at all, Master Parry."

"Call me Temp, Edward. Everyone does." Her uncle wiped his watering eyes on his sleeve.

"Once you break your fast, you should go back to bed and rest," Edward advised. "I know you feel you must work on your panel but Rosalyne told me she is the one who prepares the wood and the tempera paints for you. With her wrist ailing her, she won't be able to do so. That means you cannot work until she does, so getting extra rest would be good for you."

"Mayhap you are right," Uncle Temp said.

Rosalyne couldn't believe he had given in to Edward's advice so quickly. That alarmed her even more than the shaking in both hands had.

They finished their meal before Edward accompanied her uncle back to bed. He had continued to cough off and on while they ate. She cleared the table, bracing the tray against her waist and holding it there firmly with her good hand, returning to make additional trips to bring their cups and the jug of ale back to the kitchen.

"Rosalyne, can we speak frankly?"

She looked up and saw Edward standing in doorway to the kitchen. He seemed larger than life, full of vitality and energy but she saw the concern on his face.

"Is this about Uncle Temp?" she asked.

He nodded. "The cough is a deep one, buried within his chest. He did not have it yesterday. For it to come on so quickly is distressing, especially for one his age."

"I know. He is never sick, much less so fast."

"What about the tremors in his hands?"

So Edward had noticed those. She hesitated.

"Has he had them long?"

Rosalyne saw nothing but kindness and sympathy in Edward's eyes and decided to speak freely.

"It started a few months ago. 'Tis the right hand which he draws and paints with that has been affected. Until now."

"So whatever is wrong will affect his livelihood. And you."

"Aye." Her vision blurred as tears filled her eyes.

Then she found herself wrapped in Edward's strong arms, her face pressed against his worn gypon. Rosalyne gave in to the tears, crying against the soft wool, her fingers clutching the gypon as desperation filled her. His large hands stroked her back as he murmured comforting words. A sense of peace filled her. Despite all the worries about what the future would bring, this moment gave her a sense of relief as Edward consoled her. She gave in to it, savoring the feel of his embrace.

As her tears subsided, a new sensation rippled through her. This time, instead of comfort, Rosalyne's heart began to beat furiously as butterflies danced in her belly. She became aware of Edward as a man. His height and broad shoulders. The hardened chest her cheek rested against. The hands splayed against her back. Her breath quickened as she drew her head back and stared up at him.

She saw he was also conscious of the change between them. His brow furrowed as the brown in his hazel eyes receded and more of the green and gray came out. The mischief that usually shone in them changed now to that of desire. He was as aware of her being a woman as she was of him being a man. A very handsome, physical man.

And one that she burned to kiss. Now.

Rosalyne didn't know which of them moved first toward the other or if it occurred at the same time but suddenly his mouth was on hers, warm and inviting. She leaned into him, her fingers tightening on his gypon as he brushed his lips against hers. A mellow feeling poured through her, making her bones turn to liquid.

Then his tongue outlined her lips with a sensual slowness that drove her to the point of madness before it glided along the seam of her mouth. She opened to him, not knowing what to expect.

And found paradise.

His tongue teased, playfully dueling with hers. She joined in the battle wholeheartedly, her body heating up as he drew her closer. When his tongue grazed the roof of her mouth, she shivered. They continued a game of cat and mouse as his kisses became deeper and more demanding. The soft gentleness turned into a flaming passion as his kisses became harder. Faster. More possessive. Her good hand moved up and clutched his shoulder, holding on for dear life as she seemed to rocket skyward, though her feet remained on the ground. Never had such sensations occurred within her.

Rosalyne heard a low moan and realized it came from her. A throbbing at the apex where her legs joined began as Edward's hands dropped lower and cupped her buttocks. The feel of his long, lean fingers gripping her caused the throbbing to pound harder. She desperately wanted *something*—but she had no idea what that something entailed.

His hands went to her waist and encircled it, then he broke their kiss and eased her away from him, holding her in place as he gazed down at her. Her body felt as if a fever had struck her from out of nowhere. She blinked, dazed as she looked at him, confused by what had just occurred.

"Rosalyne?" His voice was husky and she realized that came from need—need for her.

"Aye?" It surprised her that she could find her voice.

"I am going to release you. Do you think you can stand on your own?" he asked softly.

"I . . . I am not sure," she admitted.

"Let me try."

She locked her knees, bracing for the moment his hands left her waist. He loosened his grasp on her, allowing his hands to hover next to her, in case she wavered. She swallowed and took a huge breath.

"I think I am fine," she told him, hoping that was the case.

"All right."

Edward stepped away from her. She missed the immense heat that had come from him. Her own body started to cool.

Rosalyne found she wanted to be back in his arms. She moved toward him but he held up a hand to stop her forward progress.

"Nay. I should not have kissed you as I did."

"Why not?" she asked.

He remained silent.

Rosalyne didn't know if he knew the answer or not.

CHAPTER 8

WHY HAD HE *kissed her?* Edward never acted on impulse. He always weighed his decisions and came to the proper answer.

And yet, he had kissed Rosalyne with abandon. Not a simple kiss, a light brushing of his lips against hers. Nay, it had been multiple kisses, growing in fervor and passion as their tongues waged war. He had wanted to possess her. Learn everything about her. Brand her—as his.

The depth of his feelings frightened him beyond measure.

Marriage was something far off in his mind and his future wife would need to be kind and intelligent for, to spend a lifetime with someone, he did not want to be bored. Especially by some court-bred beauty with an empty head and no thoughts to call her own. He wanted a friend, a true companion, someone he could share every thought with. A woman who was lively and interesting.

A woman . . . like Rosalyne Parry.

Both his mother and father had told him that when he met the woman destined to be his bride, he would know without a doubt. 'Twould be a feeling deep inside, both in his gut and heart. Geoffrey de Montfort and Merryn Mantel had been a rare love match and they insisted their own children should follow their hearts. It was the reason why none of the de Montfort children had been betrothed at a young age. His parents did not care for wealth or power, the two reasons families united through their children and planned marriages far in advance. Position meant little to Geoffrey and Merryn. What mattered most was family—and the happiness of their children.

Was he meant to love Rosalyne? Spend a lifetime with her?

Edward had only known her since yesterday, yet he'd been drawn to her in inexplicable ways. Her beauty was obvious, with her oval face and midnight blue eyes and thick, blond hair that he longed to unbraid and run his fingers through. But he saw past that to her soaring spirit and sweet disposition. Add that to the fact that she aided her uncle in his painting and Rosalyne Parry proved to be the most fascinating woman of his acquaintance.

It made him long to know even more about her.

"I cannot explain why I kissed you," he shared. "I am not a spontaneous man. I think through each decision, carefully pondering both sides of an argument before I act. I am meticulous to a fault. I have never acted rashly in my entire life. Until now."

Edward struggled to find the words to say to her. "I did not know I was going to kiss you," he admitted. "It happened before I realized what I was doing."

Rosalyne worried her bottom lip, driving him to distraction. He fought the urge to capture her and kiss her again.

And lost.

Once more, he moved toward her, enveloping her in his arms before she could protest or question him further. One hand went to the small of her back. The other wrapped around the nape of her long, slender neck. His fingers touched its silky smoothness and held her in place as he lowered his lips to hers again.

This time, Edward found himself more in control. The fervent, passionate kisses that had spun out of control the first time their mouths collided gave way to a different kind of kiss, one more leisurely, but no less ardent. He brushed his lips against hers slowly, not rushing the sensations that began to build. She opened to him all the same and he began a languid exploration of her mouth and tongue, drawing on the essence of the sweetness he tasted within.

He became aware of more than her mouth, which had dominated the previous kisses. As Edward took his time, he not only tasted her but inhaled the scent of roses that rose from her heated skin and hair.

He smiled against her mouth, thinking it appropriate that given her name, she smelled of the same flower. His callused fingers rubbed against her neck, the skin like fine silk against them. Though her injured arm hung in the sling between them, he pressed close enough to her to feel her breasts swelling against his chest.

Time stood still as his kisses remained unhurried, though they were no less passionate than the ones which came before. He let the heat build, savoring her scent and taste and feel, holding her prisoner within his arms. His mouth eased from hers, feathering soft kisses along her cheek and jaw, trailing to her ear. His teeth tugged lightly on her lobe and he felt her tremble as a small moan escaped her lips. He kissed her eyelids, her temple, and then brought his lips to her brow. He pressed them tenderly against it, wishing he could stay this way forever.

Edward lifted his head but kept Rosalyne tightly against him. Her skin was flushed with heat, her lips swollen from their love play. Slowly, she opened her eyes and met his. He saw a mixture of confusion and desire in them.

"I still cannot reveal why I kissed you," he said. "Only that something compelled me to do so." He gave her a tender smile.

She returned it. "I am glad you did, for I have never been kissed before. I did not know I could feel such a way."

Part of him swelled with pride, knowing his kisses had been her first. An even stronger part of him wanted to be the last man she would ever kiss. But Rosalyne did not even know his true name. She had no idea that he was a knight of the realm, in service to the king as a member of his royal guard.

And from the little that he knew of her, she would not take kindly to having been lied to.

His thumb caressed her cheek, reluctant to release her. He wished he could show her that kissing was only a small part of what a man and woman could share between them. He longed to take her to bed and remove each layer of clothing she wore and touch every part of this woman.

But he wouldn't. He couldn't.

Edward dropped his hands and stared at her for a long moment.

Rosalyne said in a shaking voice, "I am glad to have shared these kisses with you, Edward, but I fear you must make haste. I know you are eager to get to the wall and find work."

That was the last thing he wanted to do, despite the fact that being at the wall and observing what went on there was his sole mission while in Canterbury.

Instead, he countered with, "The wall will wait. They have worked on it for years. Another couple of days without me there won't make a difference. Besides, I have saved up enough coin. I am not desperate for work just yet."

"What are you saying?" she asked, frowning at him.

"I am the one who caused you to injure yourself. You cannot help your uncle because of it. I plan to devote a few days to helping the two of you. You can instruct me what to do and I will act as your hands in readying the wood and paints."

She hesitated, mulling over his offer. Edward thought to sweeten the pot and nudged her by saying, "I am sure the archbishop expects the panel to be finished by a certain time. Men in his position have little patience. You would not want to disappoint him, Rosalyne, and affect the reputation of your uncle by delaying the panel's completion."

She sighed. "Archbishop Courtenay is the second most powerful man in all of England, next to the king. He has given Uncle Temp the date he wishes the panel to be placed inside the chapel. I would not want Uncle to let him down." Rosalyne paused. "All right. You may assist me so everything will be ready when the time comes."

"And I believe that I can help your Uncle with his cough," Edward volunteered. "But first, I shall have to go to the market."

"Why? How will you help him?" she asked.

He laughed. "Remember, I explained to you that my sister practiced the healing arts on me while we were growing up. A severe cough was one of the complaints I acted out on several occasions. I coughed better than Hal or Ancel, making it sound both deep and nasty."

Edward demonstrated as Rosalyne laughed. "You sound worse than Uncle Temp!"

He loved hearing her laugh, so carefree and unpracticed, unlike the women at court.

"I might have missed my calling as an actor," he offered. "Still, when Alys ministered to me, Mother always had Alys speak aloud what was wrong with her patient and how she would remedy the illness. I actually learned quite a bit over the years and would like to treat your uncle's cough if you will allow me to do so."

"What would it involve?"

He thought a moment. "I will need to mix horehound with diapenidion."

Rosalyne cocked her head. "I have little knowledge of those things. What are they?"

"Horehound is an herb. A plant that is a member of the mint family, which makes it ideal to treat coughs."

"And dia . . . diapenidion?"

"That is a confection made up of barley water, sugar, and the whites of eggs. I will draw it out into slender threads, like strands of fine hair and have your uncle eat it. The sweetness of the sugar, along with the mint, gives it a pleasant taste." He chuckled. "I never complained when Alys made me ingest it."

"I can boil the barley water for you and I can also collect the eggs from our hens for you to use."

"Then all I need to purchase is the horehound and sugar. I can leave now and head to the market. It shouldn't take me long. I will return shortly. I hope that the concoction will calm Temp's cough. If it does, it may also help the tremors to subside and he will be able to return to his painting sooner rather than later."

This time, Edward refrained from kissing Rosalyne, though he wanted to very badly. He opened the door to the cottage and gave her a friendly wave.

As he stepped into the May morning, he tried to push the memory of their kisses from his mind and remember why he'd been sent to Canterbury in the first place.

ROSALYNE CHECKED ON Uncle Temp and found him resting comfortably, though he coughed in his sleep as both hands trembled slightly. She closed his chamber door and went outside since it was her usual time to gather the eggs from her hens. Placing the basket over her arm which was in the sling didn't work, so she rested it on the ground and collected the eggs with her good hand and placed them in the basket. Once she had gathered all the hens had laid, she scattered feed across the yard and then leaned against the fence as they ate.

Her best thinking occurred as she watched her feathered friends eat. But today, all her thoughts seemed more scrambled than any egg ever had been.

It was all because of Edward's kisses.

She gave in to the sweet memories, closing her eyes and reliving different moments. The first kisses startled her. Rosalyne hadn't known she was supposed to open her mouth to him. She had only seen a few married couples peck each other on the cheek or briefly on the lips. What she and Edward had done went far beyond that.

Only now, away from his presence, did she feel her body finally cool from the fiery heat that had possessed her from the inside and spread outward to flush her skin and make her flustered. She brought her fingertips to her lips and touched them, knowing Edward's lips had been against hers a short while ago.

It felt as if he consumed her whole during that first round of kisses. They couldn't get enough of each other. A fervor raged inside her as they seemed to go up in flames. She longed to crawl inside his gypon and run her hands across his bare flesh, half-believing her fingers would be scorched by the contact between them.

When he kissed her a second time, the desire still remained—banked, smoldering, until his slow examination of her mouth brought intense waves of need within her.

Rosalyne had enjoyed both kinds of kisses. She desperately wanted Edward to do it again.

And even more.

It was the *more* that troubled her. She had no idea what that might entail. She knew what she felt like doing—stripping her clothing off and tossing it aside so she could press her flesh against his. Rosalyne wanted to remove the layers between them. Curl up in his lap. Kiss him. Not just his lips, but *him*. She wanted to run her mouth along his muscled arms and chest and have him do the same to her.

Just the thought of his mouth on her bare flesh made her tremble. A wicked, wicked thought came to her.

What if Edward kissed her breasts?

As they'd pressed against him, she felt them growing in size. Her nipples ached as she rubbed them against him. Suddenly, Rosalyne pictured his large hand on her breast, stroking it. His lips teasing her nipple. His tongue licking it. She began to burn with need.

And shame.

Only an evil woman would have such terrible thoughts, ones that made her breasts tingle and her nether regions start to pound. Rosalyne wanted to touch herself down there and fought the urge to do so.

What had Edward done to her?

She pushed off the fence and returned to the kitchen with her basket of eggs. She would put the barley water on to boil. That would keep her busy. But as Rosalyne waited for the water to boil and then cool, her thoughts returned to the image of the man who kept pushing himself inside her head, invading every thought she had. Breathing now even seemed different, thanks to her experience in Edward's arms. He'd stolen the very breath from her with his constant kisses yet somehow she had survived.

And Rosalyne wanted more of it. And him. Much, much more.

She heard the door to the cottage open and tamped down the excitement that flooded her, knowing he had returned.

"I found what we needed," Edward said, looming large in the doorway.

Rosalyne glanced up at him and looked away. Already in his presence again, her heart slammed against her ribs. It seemed harder to breathe. A fluttering in her belly and chest made her want to scream. She wanted to hurl herself at him and devour him.

He came and stood next to her. "Let me." He took the pot in which she'd boiled the barley water and dropped some of the herb he'd brought back into it.

"It needs to rest there for a few minutes."

Edward busied himself, adding a small amount of sugar a bit at a time and, soon, his created concoction was ready for her uncle to sample. Rosalyne went and woke Uncle Temp, who looked better than he had when he first rose this morning. She led him to the table, where Edward explained what he had made and why he did so.

"I believe this will calm your cough if not rid you of it outright. That way, you can return to working on the panel for the chapel. In the meantime, while you and Rosalyne both heal, she will instruct me on how to ready the wood and paints for you so that no time will be wasted."

Uncle Temp smiled at their guest. "You are an interesting man, Edward Munn. Who knew when we took you in that you had healing powers?"

"I only hope this will help you," Edward said modestly. "If so, 'tis because of what I learned from my mother and sister. They are both remarkable women, strong in their convictions and two of the most intelligent people I have known."

"I feel the same about Rosalyne," Uncle Temp said, giving her a smile. "She is talented in many ways."

She felt a blush heat her cheeks as her uncle digested Edward's blend.

"This is most delightful. Even if it does not cure me, I will still enjoy drinking it."

"This mixture of sugar and mint flavor is pleasant," Edward pointed out. "Not all of Alys' brews were so tasty. My sister often had me drink horrible potions, all in the name of perfecting her craft."

Uncle Temp finished and said, "I think I will go back to my bed. Already, the tickling in my throat has subsided."

"That is good news, Uncle." She led him back and settled him in bed, plumping his pillows.

"I am glad you suggested that Edward stay with us," he said. "The coin he provides will be helpful but his company is even better."

Rosalyne tossed the bedclothes over him. "His offer to help with the wood and paints will make sure that we are back on schedule. I should be able to produce the panel in the timeframe the archbishop requires."

His eyes began to droop. She excused herself and left the room, already hearing his soft snores start up as she shut the door.

Edward was nowhere to be found when she returned to the kitchen. He wasn't seated at the table. Then she heard a noise and went to her uncle's studio. She found him there, sifting through various lengths of wood.

He looked up, giving her a smile that warmed her in a way nothing had before.

"So, where do we begin?"

CHAPTER 9

EDWARD WATCHED ROSALYNE sort through various stacks of wood using the arm not in a sling, enjoying the view of her rounded bottom against the soft wool of her gown as she bent over and tossed planks here and there.

"Tell me about what you are looking for and what your uncle's panel will involve," he suggested. "Remember, I am to be your hands for the next couple of days until your wrist mends and you can return to your normal activities."

She moved a few pieces of wood to the side. "Painted panels can be one piece or involve multiple pieces. Uncle has created some altarpiece art in the past, which hangs over the altar in a church or chapel. He has done diptych and triptych, which are two- and three-panel works. Polyptych panels are truly complicated, for they involve multiple panels and many hinged joints."

"Which one did Temp promise the archbishop he will produce?"

Rosalyne shifted and dropped to her knees as she examined a large plank, running her hand against the grain of the wood. "This commission is for a triptych, so it will have a large painted panel in the center and two related but smaller panels, on each side."

"Is there a certain type wood needed?" Edward asked, moving closer to her. "I see many different kinds here in his workshop."

She leaned back on her heels. "Uncle studied art—painting, in particular—for two years in Florence. The Italians prefer to paint panels and portraits on white poplar but most European artists tend to use oak."

"Oak is plentiful here in England. I see many fine pieces of it present."

"True. And uncle uses many other woods in his work. Walnut. Beech. Even spruce. But I know he'll wish to use the poplar for this commission. It is one of the most important—if not the most important—that he has ever accepted." She touched her right hand to a piece next to her. "It looks like this. If you can help me remove all the planks of this type, we can lay them out and see what we have and then consider the dimensions of the space which the panel will occupy."

He helped her sort through the various woods. Soon, they had a hefty stack of white poplar, which he separated by size and placed every piece in a row.

Rosalyne's brow crinkled in thought as she studied what was available. She had him move pieces around, eliminating some and keeping others, till she chose what she wanted.

She pointed to the planks on the left. "These are the ones that we will use. They must all be sanded smooth and flat."

"What should I do?"

"You must saw through some of the wood so that every piece is the size of this one." She indicated the one that would be the model for him to use. "Once they are of equal length, I will select the ones that will need to be reduced again for the two side panels, which will be smaller in size. After that, you can use my plane to smooth and scrape the wood. No bumps can remain because they could affect the integrity of the work."

Edward busied himself, sawing through the longer planks and lining each bit of wood beside the next until every bit of the approved poplar proved equal in size. Rosalyne studied the wood and told him which to leave in the center and what pieces should be moved to the left and right. Once he completed that task, Edward sawed through them in order to reduce the size for the remaining wood.

Rosalyne gave him shave-grass and he rubbed the herb into the wood and smoothed and scraped it with the plane till no flaws remained. He began to sweat and wished he could remove his gypon, as he did when he trained with his sword and other weapons. Instead, he mopped his brow with a sleeve and opened the door that led from the workshop to outside, hoping to catch a breeze from the sultry May day.

Next, she instructed him on how to mix the glue and had Edward join the edges of different boards together, pressing them tightly so that the glue would hold the wood in place.

"You can rest for a while," she said once he completed the lengthy task. "Let me get you some ale to drink. The day has grown quite warm."

Edward followed her to the small kitchen and insisted he pour ale for both of them since he saw it was still awkward for her to work with only one good hand.

"Shall we sit for a bit?" he asked and took their cups to the table.

"Let me check on Uncle first."

After a few moments, she returned and said, "He is peacefully asleep. No coughing at all. Your potion has done wonders, Edward. I wish I had known to give it to him before."

"I am happy to help him. Temp is an interesting man. What was it like being raised by him?"

A dreamy smile crossed Rosalyne's face. Edward wanted to reach out and run his thumb over her full, bottom lip. He kept his hands in his lap, exercising control he did not know he possessed.

"I have never heard a cross word come from Uncle Temp's lips. He loves everyone he meets and relishes each day." She chuckled. "At least after he rises. It is hard to get him to leave his bed in the mornings. He claims it goes back to his days in Florence, where he would paint far into the night and then not arise until long after the sun came up. But my childhood was one of happiness. Uncle taught me how to look at an object and see it, really *see* it, and how to draw and then paint it."

"So, you have been an artist yourself from an early age?"

She nodded. "I cannot remember a time when I didn't have a

brush in my hands. Art is what Uncle Temp knows through and through and he passed his love of it along to me."

"You said he also paints portraits sometimes."

"Aye, it has become a large part of how he earns his living. I suppose noblemen fancy letting future generations see how they looked, for Uncle has been kept busy painting their likenesses the last several years."

"You mentioned before that you accompany him."

"I do. My friend, Metylda, feeds the chickens we leave behind but we take some with us so that we have their eggs to use in creating the tempera paints."

"Describe how you create the paints," he urged. "This is all so new to me."

Rosalyne smiled. "Uncle Temp prefers a pure egg tempera, which is egg yolk mixed with a pigment. 'Tis what the Florentines that he studied under always used. Before tempera painting, Byzantine panels only contained darker colors. With tempera paints, an artist can give an impression that daylight is falling across a scene. The colors created with tempera are also incredibly vivid and bright and last for an incredibly long time."

She sipped her ale and continued, her eyes bright and eager as she said, "The Latin word *temperare* means 'to mix in proportion'. But Uncle says that the verb *temper* means 'to bring to a desired consistency'. So from the two words, we get tempera. An artist must take dry pigments and temper them with a binding agent, such as egg yolk. Only then can the paints be used to bring people and objects to life."

Edward's curiosity about the process grew. "But what do you mix with the yolk? What pigments give color to the paint itself?"

Her rich laugh drew him in. "I am sorry I didn't make myself clear. Working with pigments so often, I forget that others are not as familiar with them. They come from nature—plants, animals, and even minerals within the soil itself. Shades of siennas, ochres, and umbers can be dug from the earth, often from iron, clay, or silica. Those pigments are the most inexpensive to use and so the most common colors in a painting draw from these earth tones."

"I see. You dig them up and then what? Grind them?"

"Aye, to a very fine powder." She shrugged and indicated her arm in its sling. "That is why I was upset about losing the use of my arm and hand with this injured wrist. You already see how much physical labor goes into preparing the wood."

"You usually do all of what I have done today by yourself?"

Rosalyne's dark blue eyes sparkled. "Of course. I watched Uncle do it for years and he now allows me to do all of the preparation. I saw and sand and glue and grind."

His respect for her talents grew.

"Other pigments can be bought," she continued, "but at a much higher cost. You rarely see blue in a painting and if you do? 'Tis reserved for the most special person who is the focus of the work because lapis lazuli and azurite are outrageously expensive."

"Ah, that is why the Madonna is always pictured wearing blue."

"You are quick to understand, Edward." She gave him an admiring smile. "Also, the precious metal of gold is used in small amounts within paintings. Uncle melts the gold and applies it directly to the wood, shaping it quickly. After it dries he possesses tools, including a soft brush, which can remove the excess."

"Which will then be put to use in a different painting or portrait, I gather."

She beamed at him. "You have the mind of an artist, Edward. I wonder if you possess the skill to actually paint something."

He laughed. "I doubt it. I have never picked up a brush in my life and have no intention of doing so."

Rosalyne studied him. "Mayhap I will give you a lesson or two and you can see for yourself if you possess any talent." She paused. "But for now, we have more work ahead of us."

They returned to her uncle's workshop. Rosalyne inspected the wood to see if the glue held and gave him an approving nod.

"Our next step will be to cover the panel with a thin linen cloth. I am afraid it will be up to you to glue this cloth to the front of the wood. I can help hold it in place with my good hand but the majority of the work will be left up to you."

"May I ask why we do this?" Edward asked. "The wood has already been smoothed. Surely, your uncle can paint on the surface now."

"The cloth helps to conceal where you joined the various planks together."

He frowned. "I don't see how that will hide it."

She grinned. "Because you will cover this linen with many, many layers of gesso and then rub it smooth between each coat. By the end, the surface will be flat and stable and incredibly easy to paint upon."

"And how many layers of this gesso must I apply?"

"Usually ten and five," she replied. "And they must dry between each layer being swept across the linen. But the layers are thin and dry quickly. By the end, the surface is a brilliant white."

He sighed in mock exasperation. "Who knew wood preparation would prove to be so complicated?"

"Come, Edward. I will instruct you on mixing the gesso. It's a simple formula of combining chalk and glue."

"But in just the right amounts," he added, his lips twitching in amusement.

"You learn quickly," she complimented him, though a wisp of a smile played about the corners of her mouth and he thought she might be teasing him.

They spent a few hours cutting the cloth and gluing it to the surface of the wood. Rosalyne used her right hand to hold it tightly in place as Edward smoothed the linen against the planks. Gradually, the seam between the planks started to disappear. She assured him once the numerous layers of gesso were applied, the many planks of poplar would seem as a single piece.

"That is enough for one day," Rosalyne proclaimed. "I like for the linen to dry overnight before beginning the next step."

"Who knew I could build such an appetite with simple wood preparation?" he remarked. "I think I could eat an entire roasted chicken by myself."

"I am afraid I haven't got that," she apologized. "We have been so caught up in work for Uncle Temp that I neglected to prepare anything for our evening meal. 'Twill be stale bread and cheese for us."

"Nay, I will go out and purchase some meat pies," Edward said. "I had one yesterday when I arrived in Canterbury. It was absolutely delicious and I promised myself I would eat many of them in the coming weeks."

"Oh, I cannot let you do that. You are our guest."

"Nay, I am your paying tenant."

"But I promised to provide meals for you. Already, I am neglecting my duty." She sighed. "We have never had someone rent out our spare bedchamber. I fear I have much to learn about managing my time now that you are in our household."

"Why don't you prepare a little of the mixture I gave Temp this morning? While you do that, I will see to purchasing those meat pies."

"I will repay you, Edward," Rosalyne promised.

He winked at her and exited the cottage, heading in the direction of the cathedral since all of the stalls and vendors seem to lie that way.

The day had proven to be interesting and educational. Edward already had much more respect for the painted panels he'd viewed in various churches. Knowing what he did now about how much work went into them, he could appreciate the time and effort spent to produce one.

It felt good to be out and about, stretching his limbs, though he had enjoyed the labor put in today. Edward realized how quickly the day had passed in Rosalyne's company. It surprised him at how physical this portion was and how strong she had to be to organize and complete the steps leading up to her uncle working with the wood. Though a woman, she must be very sturdy to do everything he had done today.

Edward imagined her strong, callused hands taking his. No court beauty could have done a tenth of the kind of work Rosalyne did for her uncle every day. They never lifted a comb to their own hair, much less bathed or dressed themselves. And their conversations revolved around only what they saw and heard at court. He had tired of the gossip and empty chatter almost immediately after his arrival to serve in the royal guard.

He thought of the women he had coupled with during his time in London and Windsor and all of the other palaces the king frequented. Suddenly, each of them paled against the liveliness and intelligence of Rosalyne Parry.

In that moment, Edward knew he had to find a way to gracefully leave the king's guard because he wanted a life apart from all the shallowness that had surrounded him for the past year. He wanted a life away from serving the king.

One with Rosalyne.

CHAPTER 10

As Rosalyne gathered eggs from her hens, she looked forward to another day in Edward's presence. Though part of her felt guilty that he would remain again to help her in her uncle's workshop, she enjoyed his company too much to insist he leave her on her own. Besides, after today, her wrist would be sufficiently healed so that he could seek work in the city. She only needed both hands when readying the wood and all of those stages would be completed today. Her right hand did all the work when it came to sketching and painting.

And this would be the most important piece she had ever worked on.

She fed the chickens once her basket was filled and entered the house, surprised to hear voices. She realized both Edward and her uncle had risen. Coming into the main room, she saw them seated at the table with food in front of them.

"Good morning, Rosalyne," Uncle Temp called out cheerfully. "Come join us and break your fast."

She took a seat and marveled, "When did you ever wake up in such jovial spirits?"

He gave her a sheepish smile. "Mayhap Edward's concoction has something to do with it."

"Good morning," Edward said to her. "I have already mixed some of the herbs to suppress your uncle's cough and he partook of it."

"I feel like a new man," Uncle Temp proclaimed. "Younger certainly, though my sides and chest still ache from coughing so much."

"Alas, I have no cure for that," Edward lamented. "Still, under Rosalyne's supervision, your panel will be ready for your brush to touch it later today."

"You had Edward's help?" Uncle Temp asked her.

"Aye. He served as my hands and did quite well. I will have him apply the layers of gesso today, so by early afternoon the panel will be ready for you to start." Rosalyne gave him a pointed look and saw that he understood what to say next.

"Then I will try my best today to sketch out on it what I will paint later."

"Only if you feel up to it," Edward said.

They ate in companionable silence and then her uncle said, "I have missed the sunshine while lying abed."

Rosalyne told Edward, "Uncle Temp enjoys walking the streets of Canterbury as much as he does painting."

"Instead of walking, how about sitting in the sunshine?" Edward suggested. "The fresh air might do you some good and you can enjoy it and still conserve your strength for your drawing. I could place a chair outside the door for you."

"I would appreciate that, Edward. Thank you."

"I'll do it now." He rose and picked up a chair to carry outside.

The moment he stepped through the door, Rosalyne said, "Remember, Edward has helped me prepare the panel and knows I always do that for you."

"But we must keep the secret that you will be the one who produces the final work for the chapel," Uncle Temp added. "Once it is in place and has the archbishop's approval, I will let Courtenay know you were responsible. Only then can Edward—and the rest of the world— know what you are capable of."

Edward rejoined them. "Would you like me to assist you, Temp? I have found the perfect spot where you can soak up the sunshine and speak to passing neighbors."

"That is very thoughtful of you, Edward." He allowed Edward to help him to his feet.

"I will clear the table," Edward said to her. "Your wrist still needs a last day of rest in its sling with no straining."

Rosalyne nodded in agreement and sat until he returned and took everything into the kitchen for her. She heard him rinsing the cups and putting away things. He was a kind, thoughtful man, handsome and well-spoken.

And his kisses stirred something unnamed within her.

She wondered if he would ever kiss her again and thought not. She would not encourage him to do so. He seemed too polite to try again without her permission. Rosalyne supposed their brief encounter had been one of curiosity on his part. He had not attempted to touch her since. His tone had been light and friendly. She hoped they would become—and remain—friends.

Though a hidden part of her desired much more.

"I am ready for mixing the gesso," he said. "And proud that I remembered such an unusual name."

She had been lost in thought and had not realized he stood beside her. Rosalyne rose and accompanied him to her uncle's workshop, where the panel awaited them. Checking to see that the linen had dried completely, she found it to her satisfaction.

"Time to create our gesso," she said, showing him where the chalk and glue were located.

Edward ground the chalk to a fine powder. "Is this also how you would grind pigment for the tempera paints?"

"Aye."

It took him time to perfect the gesso mixture but once he did, the process went quickly. Edward would apply a thin layer across the linen-covered poplar and then they would talk for a few minutes before he stroked another coat onto the wood.

Several hours passed until Rosalyne decided he could stop.

Edward studied it a few minutes. "This was a laborious process but I see now how hard and smooth the surface truly is. The layers of gesso have turned it opaque and a brilliant white."

"Aye. The treated surface will actually help reflect the light of the paints."

He gave her a smile. "This has been most interesting, Rosalyne. I know I will never enter a church and view a painted panel in the same way."

She laughed. "And this was the easy part."

"So what will Temp do now?"

"Uncle will use the sketches Archbishop Courtenay approved as his guide and replicate them in charcoal directly onto the panel before he ever applies the paint. The most difficult aspect is to take his smaller drawings and transfer them to a much larger scale."

"I can see how that might be complicated," Edward said. "Has he ever had to start over? Add more layers of gesso to cover a mistake?"

Rosalyne shrugged. "Not that I know of. Mayhap in his early days but Uncle Temp is skilled and has much experience. He says besides getting the sketch to his liking, the most difficult aspect is mixing the paints correctly."

"And you also do that for him?"

"He has given me that task for the last four years. In my youth, I would watch him as he tinkered with amounts of pigment and yolk. Later, he supervised me in mixing them, much as I have done with you these past two days."

"Will you be able to grind the pigments? Has your wrist healed enough to do so?"

She saw the concern in his eyes. "I think by tomorrow I will be fine, Edward."

"May I examine it?"

Her gaze met his. Rosalyne swallowed at the intensity in it. She didn't trust herself to speak and simply nodded.

Edward moved toward her. His unique masculine scent invaded the space between them, causing her to grow lightheaded. She stiffened her knees, willing them not to buckle beneath her.

Leaning into her, he reached behind her neck and untied the sling, bringing the ends over her shoulders and drawing them away. Rosalyne kept from throwing her arms about his neck and pulling his mouth down to hers.

Barely.

He tossed one end of the cloth over his shoulder and lifted her arm by the elbow. Bracing her arm, he placed it against his own forearm to steady it and then used his free hand to touch her wrist. The callused fingertips glided against her skin, gently prodding it, encircling it. Rosalyne couldn't breathe. Couldn't think. Couldn't speak.

Then Edward released it and guided her arm down to her side. He stepped behind her and reached around, using the material to recreate the makeshift sling once more. As he tied the two ends together, she could feel his warm breath on the nape of her neck. Her belly flip-flopped wildly. She began to turn toward him, only to realize he moved away.

"That should hold. You aren't feeling any more pain, are you?"

"Nay." It surprised Rosalyne that she was able to get the word out.

"I think by tomorrow, you will be as good as new. If not, I can remain and grind your pigments for you." He thought a moment. "In fact, could I do so this afternoon? That way, you would only have to mix in the egg yolk and stir. You could do that with your right hand."

"All right." She swallowed hard, willing herself to regain the power of speech. "I will show you what can be ground. Mixing paints can sometimes be a slow process. Or Uncle will use one color in part of the painting and then I add more pigment if he needs a deeper shade for shadowing or another section of the painting." She sighed, trying to regain control of her emotions. "But having the pigment already ground will definitely save me time."

They spent another hour together, Edward grinding various pigments as she enjoyed watching the muscles in his forearms and his long, lean fingers at work. Finally, she decided he could stop, knowing she had more than enough pigment at this point to mix and paint large sections of the triptych.

"I don't mind fetching the eggs for you and mixing the paints," he said.

"Uncle Temp needs to be here for that. We won't need to begin that process until he has transferred the ideas from his sketches onto the wood."

Edward propped one elbow on the table and asked, "So why tempera paints? What is so special about them?"

"Egg tempera is incredible durable. Generally, it is unaffected by either temperature or humidity and it is long-lasting. When a painting is completed with egg tempera paints, nothing can match the satin sheen of its finish or how vivid the colors are."

"It sounds almost too good to be true. Are there any drawbacks to using it?"

Rosalyne laughed. "Tempera is thin when applied."

"Like the gesso?"

"Even thinner, which means is dries rapidly. An artist must truly commit when using it and use quick, deliberate brushstrokes in a crosshatching pattern. That helps add depth to the composition of the piece. When finished, the surface is a smooth matte."

He frowned. "That sounds complicated."

"Artists have used egg tempera paints for over a thousand years."

"Then 'twill probably be used for a thousand more." He gave her a crooked smile. "Unless you or your uncle can invent something new."

Being in Edward's presence had caused all thoughts of her uncle to flee. "Oh, I should go check on Uncle. I wonder if he is still sitting outside after so long a time."

Rosalyne found the chair moved back inside and Uncle Temp snoring softly in his bed. She returned and told Edward, "He is resting now but I know he enjoyed being in the sunlight."

"I used the last of the horehound this morning when I mixed the tonic for him. If we are through for the day, I would like to return to the market and purchase a bit more to have on hand in case his cough returns. Could I bring back anything for you?"

She thought a moment. "Since today is Friday, the fish market is open. Let me get a few coins for you, for I would like to make fish for our meal tonight."

He waved her away. "I have enough to spare. Do you favor a

certain kind of fish? Or does Temp?"

"Choose your favorite and I will cook it however you like," Rosalyne said. "It will also allow me to save the bones and burn them. Once ground, they are what will become the black in Uncle's painting."

Edward looked at her as if she might have gone mad and shook his head. "If you don't mind, I may be gone for a while and wander about Canterbury some, even take a look at the work going on at the wall."

"Then I will see you later." He gave her a quick nod and left the cottage.

Rosalyne retrieved the sketches so she could study them and decide what colors would be needed. She laid out the ones she wanted to use for the panel and deliberated on the colors she would use for each part. It was important that she see the entire painting in her mind before she committed to drawing anything on the wood.

Satisfied with her final vision for the triptych, Rosalyne retrieved her charcoal. Bowing her head, she offered a quick prayer to the Living Christ, begging Him to guide her hands as she worked to glorify Him through this panel. Selfishly, she added her wish for Archbishop Courtenay's resounding approval and acceptance of her as the artist of this work. If she had the holy man's approval and it was made known that she had produced the triptych, mayhap she would begin to receive her own commissions. That would allow Uncle Temp to stop working and she could be the one who provided for their needs.

Yet deep within, she knew this would never occur. A woman, as an artist, would never be accepted in society.

With a deep breath, Rosalyne began to outline various people and objects on the glistening surface. It had done her good to go through the preparation process with Edward. Since she had done it so many times before, she went into it sometimes without being mindful of her actions. But this piece was much too important for her to grow careless. She had enjoyed sharing each step along the way with Edward, seeing his wonder as the bare wood became something different and important.

Now, she needed every bit of her talent to produce a work of art worthy to reside in Canterbury Cathedral. Thousands of pilgrims would see this each year when they visited Trinity Chapel to pay homage to the martyred Thomas Becket and the Black Prince. Knowing how many people would view her panel should have made her nervous but Rosalyne instead felt uplifted, believing she could accomplish anything.

The charcoal glided effortlessly over the poplar and she lost herself in the drawing as it slowly sprang to life. Excitement grew within her. She couldn't wait to mix her paints and apply them. This would be her best effort. Already, she knew Uncle Temp would be so proud of her.

Finally, she lifted the charcoal away and stepped back to study what she had done. Rosalyne cocked her head one way and then another, happy with what she had accomplished. Her fingers itched to pick up her sable brush and paint over these outlines, then fill them in with color.

"Rosalyne?"

She froze. Edward's voice came from behind her. She had lost all track of time and should have been aware of her surroundings. Rosalyne gripped the charcoal in her fist to hide it from him. She plastered a huge smile on her face and turned to greet him, hiding her drawing hand with its charcoal slightly behind her in the folds of her gown.

"Uncle has done a wondrous job!" she proclaimed. "I cannot wait to see the paint added to these figures."

Rosalyne saw the question in his eyes turn to anger.

Edward marched toward her and grasped her shoulders, towering over her. "Your uncle did not draw this, Rosalyne. You did."

CHAPTER 11

Edward clutched Rosalyne's shoulders in his fingers. He did not understand why anger pulsed through him.

But it did.

He looked beyond her to the wood he had labored over the past two days and thought how it transformed from mere poplar to what he now beheld. The small sketches on parchment had come to life in bold lines. Lines that Rosalyne had drawn.

His gaze returned to her. "You did the drawings, as well. I am certain of it."

She shrugged away from him, crossing her arms protectively. "And what if I did? But, why do you think so?" Defiant eyes stared back at him.

"Because I just spoke to Temp. He was seated in his chair in front of the cottage when I returned. His eyes still looked sleepy from his long nap and he mentioned he had only risen a few minutes ago and decided to take in more fresh air before we ate. He could not have completed what I see, much less neglect to tell to me that he had worked so diligently on the panel."

Her teeth caught her bottom lip. Defiance melted away into worry. She dropped something from her hand and then rushed toward him. The fingers of her right hand bunched the material of his gypon, grasping it in desperation.

"Please, please—do not tell Uncle Temp what you know," she begged. "He means for me to do all the work on this triptych in secret and I do not want him to worry."

"I won't tell him," Edward promised.

Relief flooded her face, flushing it a rosy hue. "Thank you." She released his gypon and let out a long sigh.

A fierce need to protect this woman swept over him. Edward took her hand and found it cold, despite the warmth of the late May afternoon.

"Why must you keep your talent a secret, Rosalyne? If I could do what you can, I would shout it to the world."

Tears welled in her eyes. "Uncle Temp has taught me everything he knows. From the time I was small, he's guided me. He believes I have already surpassed his skills and that my talent is rare." Her mouth trembled. "I'm afraid nothing will ever come of it."

"Why do you say that?"

She snorted. "Who would hire a woman as a painter? Not the Church. Uncle has the foolish idea that once Archbishop Courtenay sees the finished panel and gives it his resounding approval, we will step forward and reveal who the true artist is. I have humored Uncle Temp in this scheme but I cannot allow him to make the facts known. The Church does not allow women to hold any kind of role. Having a triptych placed in the most holy chapel in all of England, where it would be seen by thousands of pilgrims each year, would be considered blasphemy if the truth came out and others learned a woman created it."

Rosalyne pulled away from him and brushed the falling tears from her cheeks. "We will earn a goodly sum from the archbishop for this painted panel, more than ever before. I will continue to accompany Uncle to any portrait commissions he receives. It is his habit to never paint a subject in person. He only sketches them from different angles and then uses the sketches to paint in private. I will be in the same room with him and do my own drawings. No one ever notices me. I am always in the background. That will allow me to produce the paintings for as long as Uncle's health remains and the tremors in his hands are not obvious.

"After that? We will have to live frugally. We own this cottage, so there will always be a roof over our heads. I can continue to sell eggs at the market. We can take in renters such as you once you leave. If Uncle Temp's health grows worse, I might even sleep on the floor in his chamber to care for him better. That would allow me to rent out my room, as well."

Edward saw how fiercely independent Rosalyne was. He also understood the argument for keeping her role in the triptych silent. But he would never allow her to live in penury, especially after Temp was gone. He planned to take care of her. Even marry her.

He just couldn't reveal his plans to her—yet.

Rosalyne had no idea who he was. If she knew he came from one of the oldest, most noble families in England, she would withdraw from him. Edward needed to gain her trust and accomplish his mission in Canterbury before he shared his identity and offered for her.

He took her chin in his hand, drawing it up till their eyes met.

"Temp will not learn from me that I know you are the true artist," he pledged. "Nor will anyone else." His thumb stroked her smooth cheek, lighting a fire deep within him. He wanted to bank it yet assure her.

Assurance won out.

Edward lowered his mouth and pressed it softly against hers. He felt the shudder that ran through her at his touch, knowing she had the same effect upon him. He kept the kiss gentle so that it wouldn't rage out of control as it had yesterday. Lifting his head, he brushed his lips against her forehead, hoping to comfort her.

"I will tell you that I find what you've already done to be extraordinary. I look forward to seeing your actual painting."

"Thank you," she said, sincerity shining in her eyes. "I need to begin preparing our meal." She stepped back and he dropped his hand from her chin.

"Since tomorrow is Saturday and a half-day, work will cease by early afternoon. Because of that, I will wait until Monday before I speak to those in charge," he said. "Would you care to join me as I explore Canterbury? I would enjoy seeing more of it and definitely want to return to the cathedral."

Rosalyne gave him a brilliant smile. "I would enjoy spending Saturday with you. And that would allow Uncle Temp to pretend that he completed the charcoal on the panels while we are gone. I will make sure he understands."

Edward returned her smile. "I brought back haddock from the market. Let me help you with the evening meal and we can talk about what we will see tomorrow."

ROSALYNE KISSED THE top of her uncle's head. "Finish your bread and ale. You know you need your strength to begin working on the panel today."

She caught the quick wink he gave her before she stepped away to return the pitcher and her cup to the kitchen. She rinsed the cup and dried it as Edward joined her. He washed his own cup and took the cloth from her hands so he could dry it before setting it on the wooden shelf.

"Are you ready to show me Canterbury?" he asked, looking as eager as a small boy who'd just been given a sweet.

Rosalyne was more than ready to spend an entire day in this man's company and not think about the triptych. Now that she'd outlined what she would paint, a sense of calm had descended upon her. Mixing the colors always proved challenging but she had vast experience in doing so and already knew what shades would go where on each of the three designs. When Edward left on Monday to seek work, she would get a good portion of the panel completed. Once he returned, Uncle Temp could take credit for the work, just as he would when they came home this afternoon from exploring the city.

"The weather is most pleasant today. There was a slight chill in the air when I went to mass earlier but it already had begun to burn off when I returned," Edward volunteered. "I doubt you will need to bring a cloak to warm you."

"Then we can be off."

They bid her uncle a good day and left the cottage.

"Where to first?" Edward asked.

"I think that we should walk toward the heart of town," Rosalyne replied.

She thought that he was reaching for her hand to place on his arm, much as a knight or nobleman would do when escorting a lady, but then the moment passed.

Did he know she was a lady? she wondered.

Rosalyne couldn't remember encountering anyone she knew calling out to her by name when he had escorted her home several days ago from the cathedral. No one had stopped by the cottage while he was there. Their neighbors knew how she and her uncle often worked on his paintings during the day while the light was good and so they never bothered to visit.

Then it hit her that Edward had offered her his arm when he had accompanied her to the cottage upon their first meeting. It seemed so natural at the time that she hadn't thought to question it. Mayhap he had done so to steady her after her encounter with the runaway team of horses. She had been shaken by the incident and almost losing her sketches.

Still, it struck her as odd.

As they strolled side by side, Rosalyne decided to put the thought aside and enjoy the day. She asked, "Do you know anything about the city you have come to?"

"Other than it has a cathedral?" Edward gave her a teasing smile, his hazel eyes full of mischief. "Aye, I know when William invaded England in 1066, he gained Canterbury without a fight. Why the citizens chose to surrender and not lift a sword to their enemy is a mystery to me."

Rosalyne looked up at him, noting the auburn highlights in his dark hair gleaming in the morning sun. "So you could fancy yourself as the fighting type? I suppose I could see that. If not for your humble birth, you have the size to be a formidable knight."

His jaw hardened. She wondered if she'd mentioned something he was sensitive about. She knew very little about where Edward came from, only that he had a large, loving family that he spoke fondly of and probably missed very much.

Trying to smooth over the silence, Rosalyne said, "The city was once called *Durouernon*, which means 'stronghold by the alder grove', though the Romans who built their settlement here named it *Durovernum Cantiacorum*. When the Jutes came after Rome fell, they christened it *Cantwareburh*, meaning 'Kentish Stronghold'. That is how the present name came about."

"That still does not tell me why an entire city would surrender without a fight," he said without pity.

Rosalyne defended Canterbury's ancestors. "Ah, but I can answer that. Danish raids occurred here several times over the years. They pillaged and plundered and even burned the former cathedral to the ground, even murdering its archbishop. When William the Conqueror invaded England, the destruction the Danes caused was still fresh in the minds of Canterbury's residents."

Edward grew thoughtful. "So that could be the reason the people did not resist."

"I believe that to be true. William ordered a wooden motte-and-bailey castle to be built at once by the old Roman city wall to reassure Canterbury that its people would always have his protection. Years later, the Normans rebuilt the castle with stone. They also reconstructed the cathedral twice—once to replace the burned one and a second time when that one burned, too. The structure you see today is what remains of that Norman effort."

"And three hundred years later, many English people have Norman blood running through their veins," Edward said. "At least in the nobility."

Rosalyne decided it was time to tell him about her background. She didn't want him being taken by surprise upon hearing it and she also hoped he might open up to her more about his past if she did the same.

"More than likely, I have Norman blood in my ancestry," she began.

"What?" Surprise knit his brows together. "You are—"

"I am Lady Rosalyne. Actually, Lady Rosalyne Bowyar, though for the sake of convenience, I go by Rosalyne Parry."

"Is Temp a knight?" Edward asked.

"Nay, though he came close to becoming one. He fostered with a nobleman for many years as the man's page and squire. When it came close to the time for his knighthood ceremony, he did not undergo it." She paused, wanting to protect her uncle's privacy. "You might ask him about why he decided to forego it if you wish."

"Temp certainly has the size to be a soldier," he said, "though he seems a most peaceable fellow. I suppose art won out over war." Edward grinned. "And the world is a better place for that."

"Uncle would take that as a compliment."

"But how did he come to raise you?"

Rosalyne frowned. "I know only a little of my story. I fear there is much more to it, probably parts that are too ugly to discuss, which is why he has kept the entire truth from me. I do know my father was named Lawrence Bowyar and my mother was his wife, Lara, who was Temp's younger sister. They were the Baron and Baroness of Shallowheart, though I could not tell you where the property sits. My parents died of a fever ravaging the land and Father's younger brother, Benedict Bowyar, became the new baron."

Her pace slowed as she shared her story with Edward. "I am not sure if Uncle Benedict did not want to care for a small babe or even if he had children of his own but he sent for Uncle Temp soon after my parents' death."

"And Temp answered the call. He took you away and raised you as his own," Edward concluded.

She nodded. "I always knew him as Templeton Parry and assumed I was Rosalyne Parry. When I discovered I wasn't, Bowyar sounded odd when coupled with my first name. I chose to remain being known as Rosalyne Parry in order to honor Uncle Temp since I have always looked upon him as my father."

Edward stopped and faced her. "So I should address you as Lady Rosalyne, I suppose," he reflected.

"Oh, no. 'Tis not necessary. I would not want things to change between us."

As he studied her, Rosalyne sensed the warmth staining her cheeks, remembering the kisses they had shared and hoping what she had revealed would not prevent Edward from kissing her again in the future. In truth, as a common laborer, he should not even touch someone of her rank—much less steal kisses from her.

And yet, that very thing was all she could think about every time she looked at his sensual lips.

"What I mean is that I hope things will remain friendly between us and that you will not think less of me because of my sire," she added.

"Think less of you?" Edward chuckled. "Only you would believe being a member of the nobility would be something to hide or be ashamed of." He placed a hand on her shoulder. "Nay, Rosalyne, I will think the same of you today as I did yesterday." He paused. "But tomorrow and the days after might change my mind."

His touch caused the unusual flutters she'd experienced before to begin in her belly. "Why would tomorrow be different?" she asked, her mouth growing dry.

Edward squeezed her shoulder gently. "Because once I see the panel take shape and come to completion, I am sure you will only grow in my esteem. I have a feeling I will think even more highly of you and your talents once the triptych stands finished and rests in Trinity Chapel."

Rosalyne felt her blush heating up with his complimentary words—and because of the heat that she saw in his eyes. She turned away from him and set out again, determined to regain control of her emotions.

Pointing to her left, she said, "That is the Hospital of Saint Nicholas. Both it and the Hospital of Saint Katherine, which we will see shortly, were built for the poor."

In a few strides, Edward caught up with her. "I seemed to remember passing a hospital located near the cathedral. Is that Saint Katherine's?"

"Nay. What you saw most likely was Eastbridge Hospital. Eastbridge was built as a shelter for poor pilgrims."

"Do many pilgrims come to Canterbury?" he asked. "Trinity Chapel and the cathedral itself teemed with people when I was there a few days ago."

"They come from all over England and even Europe in order to see the place where Thomas Becket was martyred by the four knights who responded to the king's call. The needs of these pilgrims must be met."

"I assume there are many places for these pilgrims to seek shelter near the cathedral."

"Along with many merchants selling goods and vendors peddling food to all the visitors that flock here. Even Uncle and I are part of that trade. We create badges for pilgrims to purchase at the cathedral. Several local artists contribute to this effort. The monies raised help fund the cathedral's upkeep and additions."

"What do these badges depict?" Edward asked.

"The archbishop prefers that they show Becket, his martyrdom, or the shrine to him. We can make the same badge repeatedly since Courtenay does not require them to look different from one another. 'Tis another source of income for us when Uncle is not working on painting portraits."

They drew closer to the center of the city and Edward said, "I am recognizing places now from being here yesterday to buy more horehound. Is the cathedral nearby?"

"Aye. It is in the heart of the city," Rosalyne told him. "The River Stour, which inhabitants sometimes call the Great Stour, has one branch that flows through the city in the south and east. I doubt you have been that far south yet."

"Nay, but I can smell it," he said.

"Another branch of the Stour runs around the city, near the walls. If you find work there, the scent of fish will remain in your nose during your work day and beyond."

He inhaled deeply. "Besides the river, I definitely smell leather."

Rosalyne laughed. "You do have a good nose. Besides supplying the needs of those on pilgrimage, our main industries are wool and leather. If you pay close attention, you will see many of the stalls sell shoes, gloves, and even saddles that are made in town."

"Even I have heard of the saddles that come from Canterbury. They are said to rival those made in London."

She sniffed playfully. "I think they are better than those fashioned in London."

"Have you ever been to the great city?" Edward asked.

"Nay, but I long to see it one day." Rosalyne decided to press him a little about his family and see if he would reveal anything new to her. "You mentioned that your brother has traveled to London and is seeking his fortune."

"Aye, Hal, who is two years older than I am. And if any man can meet with success, 'twill be Hal."

"Why do you say that? What is he like?"

"Hal is the most charming man you will ever meet. He is comfortable in the company of men or women. Everything has always come to him easily. He is friendly and kind and may not possess a serious bone in his body. We are nothing alike. I am but a mere shadow of Hal."

Rosalyne stopped in her tracks, surprised by his words. "But Edward . . . *you* are friendly and kind. And you are constantly smiling and teasing with me."

His jaw dropped. "I . . . am?" Doubt flickered in his eyes.

"And you are brave, of course," she added. "For you saved me from that runaway team of horses. Thoughtful, too, because you realized what the parchment that blew away meant to me and ran yourself ragged till you retrieved it." Rosalyne gave him a warm smile. "I think you are every bit as wonderful as your brother Hal. Mayhap you are even better, Edward."

She saw the astonishment on his face turn to pleasure. "No one has ever spoken of me in such glowing terms, Rosalyne. I have always been the plodding, serious, younger brother."

Rosalyne gripped his arm. "Then you have no idea how others truly see you, Edward. Mayhap separating from your brother and family and coming to Canterbury will do you some good. You just might learn more about who you truly are."

"Indeed," he said, a mysterious look crossing his face.

CHAPTER 12

EDWARD FOUND IT hard to believe what Rosalyne thought of him. As the youngest de Montfort son, he had always idolized Ancel, the eldest, while he had fostered with Hal, whom he followed blindly from the time he could walk. Ancel had been the leader. Hal had been the charmer.

Edward had been the invisible one, never seeking attention, serious about life and his duty from the time he was a young boy. He stayed in the shadows while his older brothers shone brightly.

His parents loved him, as did his siblings. That had never been the problem. But others tended to overlook him. He had never been ambitious, rather valuing being steadfast and loyal. It was only a stroke of luck that he found recognition for carrying through with his responsibilities on the battlefield and killing the Scottish soldiers before they could murder the pinned-down Lord Commander. Lord Humphrey seemed to think him especially brave but Edward knew any man would have come to Lord Humphrey's aid.

The act had earned him his knighthood—and a position in the king's guard—something he'd grown to hate.

The past few days in Canterbury, away from the royal court, had by far been his favorite in the past year. Not only did Edward enjoy being away from London but he had savored his time in Rosalyne's company. Being around her was like breathing in fresh country air after being trapped in the fetid, stale atmosphere that hovered over the streets of London.

Mayhap she was right. He didn't seem so solemn here. He was

more relaxed and smiled readily. He liked conversing with Temp Parry, who had a wealth of interesting stories.

And he had cherished the kisses he'd shared with Rosalyne.

She brought out something within him that Edward hadn't known he possessed. His spirits seemed lighter when he was around her. He enjoyed her quick wit and admired her artistic talent. Rosalyne Parry might be of the nobility but she was living life on her own terms.

Edward wanted this woman in his life. Now—and forever.

He wished he had followed his instincts and the good manners which had been drilled into him and placed her hand on his arm when they set out. Just the feel of her fingers would have brought him comfort and, at the same time, filled him with an urgency. If they were not in the midst of the busiest street in Canterbury, he definitely would capture her in his arms and never let her go.

Instead, he tried to emulate Hal and gave her what he hoped was his most charming smile. His hand took hers and tucked it into the crook of his arm.

"Now that I know I escort a lady, I must do so in proper fashion," he told her.

Edward enjoyed the becoming blush that tinged her cheeks. He longed to sink his teeth into her tempting bottom lip.

All in good time.

"Thank you, good sir," she replied playfully.

If only she knew he was a knight. Would she treat him differently? Act in a more formal manner? It didn't matter. For now, he would take what grew between them and enjoy it for what it was. Once he finished his work for the king in Canterbury, decisions must be made, ones that would affect his future—and hers.

They continued along the street while she pointed out various sites, such as the leper hostel dedicated to Saint Nicholas.

"I thought Saint Nicholas already had a hospital named after him," Edward pointed out.

Rosalyne smiled up at him. "Then I suppose Nicholas was a very saintly saint in order to have two important buildings in Canterbury named in his honor." Her head turned away abruptly and he saw she inhaled deeply.

He did the same and asked, "What is that divine smell?"

She sighed. "Eel pie. At that cookshop." She pointed to their right. "Uncle Temp and I sometimes spoil ourselves and buy one there."

Edward began pulling her in that direction.

"Oh, no," she cried. "We don't need to stop."

"I want eel pie," he declared. "I have never had this particular delicacy. I insist we try it."

They entered the cookshop, which had a narrow frontage to the street. He saw the place was small, with a long corridor running behind it. He supposed it led to the kitchens and quarters where the owner lived.

"Two eel pies," he said, handing over the coin the man asked for.

Soon, he and Rosalyne had their food in hand. They returned to the cloudless day and leaned against the wall of the cookshop as they ate.

"Mmm," she murmured, the noise low in her throat.

Edward only wished she could make that sound while he pleasured her.

He bit into his pie and moaned in a similar fashion. The golden crust melted in his mouth. The stewed eels, swimming in a delicious green sauce, were tender and slightly salty.

"I told you," she said, her deep blue eyes sparkling. "Eat slowly and savor it. Most men gobble down a meal without properly enjoying it."

"As you wish, my lady," he said.

Her brows shot up when he addressed her in that manner but she remained silent and took another bite.

They took their time, eating in silence. Edward enjoyed every morsel. "I may need to purchase another one."

"Not now," she chided. "We have more to see, including the cathedral. That will take a good deal of time."

"Do you know much about its background?"

"I have lived here all of my life, Edward. Of course, I can share with you what I have learned over the years."

He placed her hand on his sleeve again and led her back into the throng of people in the main thoroughfare as she described the history of the church and the murder of Archbishop Becket over two hundred years before. Edward was familiar with the story of the martyr's death, so his mind wandered as he reveled in the scent of roses that came from her skin and hair and the feel of her body's heat so near him.

"Are you listening to me, Edward?" she demanded.

Glancing down at her, he said, "I was distracted."

"By what?"

He looked up and saw they had arrived at the cathedral. The church rose in magnificence before them. Vendors hawked their wares, including the badges that Rosalyne had described to him. Another stall drew his eye, so he pointed to it.

"What does that man sell?" he asked.

She looked in the direction he indicated. Her lips narrowed in displeasure. "He is one of many who take advantage of the pilgrims who visit here."

Out of curiosity, Edward led her closer and frowned. "What is in those vials?"

"After Becket's murder, some of the citizens managed to acquire pieces of cloth soaked in the archbishop's blood. Rumors abounded that a person could be cured of disease by merely touching the cloth. I think that must have started many on their pilgrimage to Canterbury. Those with leprosy or blindness made their way to the cathedral and the monks began to sell small, glass bottles that they claimed contained Becket's blood."

Astonishment filled him. "People truly believed that?" He glanced at the small vials, all filled with a dark brown substance. "And they think the archbishop's blood has survived for over two centuries?"

Rosalyne nodded. "Though the monks no longer trade in this, others took up the idea. Many a pilgrim has purchased it, hoping to be cured of their ailments thanks to the martyr's blood."

Disgust rose in Edward. "I now better understand the story of the

Christ entering the temple in Jerusalem and expelling the merchants and money changers in anger, accusing them of turning that holy place into a den of thieves. These merchants do the same and take advantage of those on pilgrimage."

She pulled on Edward to lead him away but it still bothered him that many people, including those who had little coin to spare, found themselves deceived by these vendors who surrounded the church.

They entered the cathedral. It took a moment for his eyes to adjust from the bright sunlight to the dim interior as he dipped his finger into the holy water and made the Sign of the Cross. As on his first visit, the building bustled with people, including many workers using hammers and chisels. Scaffolding filled a section of the nave.

Edward motioned at all the activity. "What are these men constructing?"

"The fire that occurred after Becket's death did not touch the nave but it has fallen into disrepair. If you look closely, you can see some of the decay. About half a score ago, Archbishop Sudbury ordered that a new nave be constructed. One of the old king's master masons, Henry Yevele, is in charge of the work. 'Tis said it will take beyond the turn of the century before its completion."

Edward scanned the large area. The laborers were limited by the length and width of the nave but he saw they had compensated for that in height. From his estimate, the nave might one day be seventy to eighty feet high. He swore that he would return someday when the work had been finished and admire the mastery of the place.

They strolled through the south transept and along the quire and he marveled at the stained glass windows of Adam and Methuselah. She brought him to the presbytery and he looked back across the length of the building, taking in the grand scale of the church.

Rosalyne said, "Archbishop Sudbury lost his life in the Peasants' Revolt a few years ago."

Edward remembered that the holy man was one of several government and church leaders who had lost their heads in the uprising. Ancel had been in London during that chaotic time and shared with him and Hal how frightening those days had been.

"The people of Canterbury thought a great deal of Archbishop Sudbury. He even used his own funds to rebuild the West Gate and planned to do more for the city had he lived. We remember him each year during the Christmas season. The mayor of Canterbury leads a procession to Sudbury's tomb here at the cathedral."

She took him to see the deceased archbishop's tomb. Eventually, they made their way to the far end of the cathedral and entered Trinity Chapel, even more crowded than it was on his last visit. They joined the other pilgrims and shuffled along till they arrived at Becket's shrine and gave it their attention for a few moments. Then the swell behind them jostled them away.

Edward wanted to see the Black Prince's final resting spot again, so he steered Rosalyne south of Becket's shrine. A gilded copper effigy of Edward Plantagenet in armor marked the prince's tomb. It reminded him of the old king, Edward III's effigy in Westminster Abbey, but this one seemed even grander with its marble tomb chest surrounded by a dozen coats of arms. He thought it a fitting tribute to England's greatest soldier and, once more, remembered how Geoffrey de Montfort emphasized his admiration for the Black Prince's compassionate nature as much as his soldiering skills.

Rosalyne had drawn away from him and stood a few feet from where her triptych would soon rest. He studied her profile—the elegant nose and sweeping, blond hair that caught the highlights from the hundreds of lit candles burning in the chapel. She turned her head slightly as she perused the area, lost in thought.

He moved toward her and bent to whisper in her ear. "Can you picture your panel here?"

A satisfied smile danced on her lips. "Aye. I can."

After giving her adequate time to view the spot, Edward escorted her from the chapel. They crossed the north transept and aisle in a circular sweep of the building and worked their way past the busy construction until they found themselves out in the clean air once more.

Rosalyne stopped and nudged him with her elbow. "There is the archbishop to our right."

Edward glanced in that direction and saw Courtenay speaking with another man, obviously noble by his dress. They appeared to be deep in conversation.

"Who is with him?"

"Lord Botulf. He has been placed in charge of the wall's construction by King Richard, though all of Canterbury knows he rarely ventures near the work being done."

Rosalyne echoed what John had told him when he left Sirius with the smithy and his young son, Will. John had accused the nobleman of ignoring the work and had even harsher words for the man Botulf put in charge of the crews. He thought he would seek Rosalyne's opinion on Rawlin, as well.

"If Lord Botulf does not lead the work, who does?"

Her teeth caught her bottom lip in thought, causing a jolt of lust to rush through Edward. If she only knew what a simple gesture like that did to him, she would think twice.

"Henry Yevele, the master builder I mentioned before, has planned out the work on the wall. But there is another man who actually heads up the construction. I am trying to remember his name."

Edward decided to help her out. "Was it Rawlin? I think I heard in passing at the market that he was the one directing the teams of men."

"That's it. Perceval Rawlin. Now mind you, I don't know this firsthand but talk is that Rawlin is deceitful and greedy. He can also be vengeful. I hear he has become wealthy as work has gone on, as has Lord Botulf." She looked at him with concern. "I wonder if you should even seek to be hired at the wall, Edward. Canterbury has other work to be had."

"My heart is set to work on the wall," he told her.

Moving away from the front of the cathedral, Edward heard someone call her name. He looked over his shoulder and saw the archbishop motioning to her.

Rosalyne broke away from him and hurried over, with Edward

following a few paces behind her.

"Lady Rosalyne, 'tis a pleasure to see you today," Courtenay said. He indicated the man to his left. "Have you met Lord Botulf? The king has charged him with making our city safe again."

She kissed the archbishop's ring and then swept a curtsey to the nobleman. Edward did not like the gleam in the man's eyes as Botulf eyed Rosalyne hungrily.

"'Tis a pleasure to meet you, my lord."

"Lady Rosalyne's uncle is an artist of some note," the archbishop explained. "Not only does he paint portraits of noblemen in our surrounding area but he is also preparing a new triptych to be placed in Trinity Chapel." He gave her a pointed look. "And how does your uncle fare with this endeavor, my lady?"

"Very well, your grace. The wood has gone through a long preparation process in order for the paint to adhere and today Uncle Temp is sketching onto it what he will paint. Once the colors have been mixed, the painting will commence. He feels this will be his greatest creation."

"Lady Rosalyne aids her uncle in his work," the archbishop told Lord Botulf.

"Is that so?" The nobleman's eyebrow arched. "I have heard of your uncle and his portraits. Mayhap it is time that I commissioned to have mine done. Do you help him in that, as well, my lady?"

"I do, my lord. I am sure Uncle Temp would be happy to paint you."

"Why don't you accompany me home now, Lady Rosalyne? We could discuss it further." The glint in the nobleman's eyes had grown lascivious.

Before Rosalyne could reply, Edward stepped forward. "My lady, are you ready to return to your uncle's house? Remember that he wanted you to hold his sketches as he drew on the poplar."

"Who are you?" Botulf demanded gruffly.

Edward held both his temper and his true name in check. "I am Edward Munn, my lord, recently come to Canterbury. In fact, I traveled here in order to work on the reconstruction of the wall. Lady Rosalyne just informed me that the king placed you over this project. I am honored to make your acquaintance and hope to work for you."

He saw loathing in the nobleman's eyes, for both a man of a lower class and that he had interrupted Botulf's conversation with Rosalyne.

Edward turned to her and saw gratitude in her eyes. "Thank you for reminding me that it is time to return home, Edward." She looked back to the two men. "Edward rents a bedchamber in Uncle's cottage. He was kind enough to escort me to the market today and was eager to see our city's cathedral."

"Aye," he interjected. "I am most impressed with the work Master Yevele is doing. We also spent time in Trinity Chapel." He bowed his head in a show of respect but he seethed within. Edward knew exactly what Botulf had in mind when he asked Rosalyne to accompany him to his home.

She gave another curtsey. "I will tell Uncle Temp that you are interested in having your portrait painted, my lord," she said sweetly. "He can send word once he has completed the panel for the archbishop. We would love to meet with you and discuss what you have in mind."

"Tell Master Parry that I look forward to what he will produce," the archbishop said.

"Good day to you, your grace. My lord," Rosalyne said.

Edward did not take her hand as they walked away, not wanting to draw Botulf's ire for a peasant placing his hands on a lady. They melded into the crowd and moved down the street.

Once they were out of sight from the pair, Rosalyne gripped his arm tightly.

"I do not like Lord Botulf," she said, her voice shaking.

"Neither do I," Edward replied.

CHAPTER 13

Edward left Temp's cottage and headed toward the wall, where he'd spent the last week laboring. He'd learned quite a bit about the work going on since he'd been hired. Yevele, the master builder overseeing the nave's expansion, had designated the new walls be built on the foundation of the old Roman ones which surrounded the city and had originally included eight gates, erected over a thousand years ago. Time had eroded the structure, which was why the king had called for this massive undertaking a few years ago. Only stone was being used, due to its sturdy nature. When completed, the awe-inspiring wall surrounding Canterbury would be capable of enduring a significant pounding from an enemy and last even longer than the one the Romans built.

Fine stone masonry was used for public works, such as this wall, and Edward found out this was a costly process because of the expense of the materials and the journeyman tradesmen involved, not to mention the expertise of engineering required. Stone had to be hauled into Canterbury on horse-drawn wagons from nearby quarries, where it had been pounded and broken. On site, stone masons chiseled the raw stone into large blocks before craftsmen used man-powered cranes to lift the completed rocks to the scaffolding along the wall. Masons used long ropes with knots placed every meter to measure the space accurately, as well as utilizing wooden triangles with a line and plumb bob suspended from one angle as a level when they placed the stones.

A separate group of workers on the ground took lime, soil, and water and mixed it together to form the mortar that held the blocks together. It, too, had to be transported skyward as the wall grew in height. Edward had grown to enjoy the smell of the mortar.

He had been employed strictly for physical labor since he did not possess the papers marking him as a guild member with a special skill. All but one day he had transported stones from the arriving wagons to the masons near the wall, while once being tasked to mix mortar when another worker fell ill. Edward asked questions of every man he labored beside, playing on his role as a curious country peasant who was eager to know the ways of the city.

Edward had learned that a total of twenty-four towers would be constructed around the circuit and that many of the existing gatehouses were being rebuilt in stone and brick. The towers being assembled atop segments of the wall extended outward slightly, so that the men eventually stationed in them would be able to observe the exterior of the walls on either side.

Every man he observed put in an honest day's labor. No one shirked his duties. Most of the laborers worked in silence but were friendly when he asked them a question. He counted the wagons that arrived throughout the day and the number remained consistent over the week. Each day he watched the progress of stones being placed, both by height and length. It, too, proved steady. The king would be pleased that the men took their work seriously and the wall advanced at a good pace.

Perceval Rawlin had yet to put in an appearance. When Edward brought up the man's name, he caught the disgruntled looks on a few faces. James, a laborer he'd grown close with, even spat in the dirt next to him when Rawlin's name had been mentioned but no one voiced an opinion about the supervisor. Edward wondered how Rawlin was making a profit. Mayhap he overcharged the royal treasury for the stone and other materials used and that was where he gained his wealth.

"You mentioned Rawlin before, Edward. Well, there he is," James said, his voice low.

Edward saw a man coming in their direction, dressed much like a profitable merchant. He had a receding hairline and his brown hair had begun to turn gray. Rawlin's prominent, heavy jowls dominated his face. He walked bowlegged, most likely from the extra weight he carried around his middle. One thing was certain—Perceval Rawlin had not missed any meals.

Rawlin called over a man who supervised the section of the wall Edward had worked on this week. The man never looked Rawlin in the eye, only nodded at what Rawlin said and then moved away. Edward saw contempt in the man's eyes as he trudged back, while Rawlin scanned the area with interest. Edward lowered his eyes and lifted a stone a mason had finished carving and took it to the wall, placing it in the crane and signaling for it to be lifted.

By the time he finished that task, Rawlin had already moved away.

Since it was Saturday, work ceased an hour past midday. Edward lined up with the rest of the men to receive his wages for the week but James told him he would not collect anything yet.

"You have to work on the wall a month before you secure any payment, my friend."

He frowned. "That does not seem fair. I should be paid for the work I have done."

James laughed. "'Tis not the only thing that isn't fair."

Edward joined his friend in line, hoping to learn more about the payment system to the laborers and anything else James might confide to him. Leaning in, he asked quietly, "What do you mean?"

James shrugged. "Stand to the side. Over there. You'll see if you pay close attention."

He did as told, moving near the table where a man sat with a quill in hand. As each worker reached the front, the man spoke to him and marked something on the parchment before him. The worker then moved to his left, where a second man counted out his pence and shillings. Edward noted that the skilled craftsmen, such as the masons and carpenters, received more than the laborers did. That seemed right, for a guild member should earn more than a common laborer, thanks to his years of apprenticeship in a skilled trade.

But what should the unskilled men such as himself be paid?

Edward knew how much he had been told that his wage would be. James, who had worked on the wall three months, probably earned close to what Edward would. He watched carefully as James approached the table and saw the coins counted out. They were far less than what Edward had been told he would earn.

It made no sense.

Why would James make less than Edward when he had worked on the wall for a longer amount of time?

James caught his eye and motioned for Edward to follow him. They moved away from the line of men. Neither spoke till they entered inside the city's walls.

"Did you see how much I was paid?" James asked.

"Aye, and it surprised me. I was told I would earn nearly double that amount."

James gave him a pointed look. "What you are told you will earn and what you are paid are two very different things, Edward Munn."

He stopped. "Explain it to me."

"You are hired for a job and expect to see the money promised you," James began. "Only when it comes time to receive it, you will find much less than expected." His lips twitched. "If you question them, they will explain that you are paying certain taxes and fees for the privilege of participating on the construction of the wall."

"When in truth, those coins go to line Perceval Rawlin's—and Lord Botulf's—pockets, I assume?" Edward finished.

James laughed heartily. "You catch on quickly for a man fresh from the country."

Edward chuckled but inside he seethed. For Rawlin to take from the very men who poured blood and sweat into constructing the wall while never lifting a finger went against everything Edward stood for. If Rawlin did that on such a grand scale, week after week, year after year, the man also must obtain a portion from the cost of the materials, as well. The king would put a stop to this once he received the report Edward planned to give him. Though he well knew that some skimming of funds must go on in construction projects, the scale of Rawlin's cheating went well beyond what King Richard would find acceptable.

Though he didn't know the details, Edward supposed he could return to London and let Richard know what he had learned. But he yearned to stay in Canterbury in order to remain close to Rosalyne. Mayhap, he could continue on a bit longer and see what else he could discover about the corruption and even confront Rawlin, if not Lord Botulf himself. Wouldn't that nobleman be surprised to learn Edward's true identity?

Edward bid James farewell and began journeying north toward Temp's cottage. He stopped at a well for a long drink and decided to cool off by dumping a bucket over his head. Now that June had arrived and he worked outdoors in the heat all day, the cold water refreshed him. He raked his fingers through his hair, smoothing it away from his face, as he continued through the busy streets.

The hot sun dried his clothes by the time he arrived at the Parry cottage. He ducked inside and relished the coolness within. Quiet surrounded him a moment before he heard the snores of Temp, who napped with his chamber door wide open. Edward had never heard a man snore the way the artist did and thought it was probably best that Temp had never become a soldier, for the man's snoring would have given away his position to the enemy time and again. He closed the bedchamber's door, thankful that the snoring was now muffled.

Thinking Rosalyne might be in the workshop, he ventured to it and was taken aback as he stepped inside.

The triptych stood completed.

Mesmerized, Edward slowly walked toward it, taking in the rich, vibrant colors. Stars painted with real gold had been used in the night sky on one portion of the panel, while the bright blue of lapis lazuli formed both the Madonna's simple, homespun clothing and a blanket that enveloped the babe nestled in her arms. In another panel, the Christ's ochre robe resonated with varying shades of red, from a deep hue in the folds to a lighter shade throughout. He was astonished at

Rosalyne's use of shadow and light, from the greens of the grass on a hill to the sunshine that cascaded down on the last picture within the panel.

"Do you like it?"

He turned and saw her standing in the doorway, a hopeful look on her face.

"You are the first to see it completed," she told him. "Be truthful."

Edward went to her and caught her elbows in his hands. "I feel I am in the presence of one with a most rare talent," he said. "You have brought the drawings to life in a way I have never seen before and I have been in churches great and small. I am in awe, Rosalyne."

Her smile spread, moving from her lips to her cheeks and crinkling her eyes in merriment. "I find myself more than pleased with it," she admitted. "I felt the Virgin guiding my hand. I believe our archbishop will be appreciative."

Selfishly, he wished the holy man could know Rosalyne was the artist behind the work but he understood why she would allow her uncle to receive credit instead and discourage Temp from sharing the truth.

"Teach me," he said. "I would love to try to paint something."

"I did promise you a lesson in painting," she mused.

Rosalyne went to the far side of the workshop, where a few bits of wood rested against the wall. She chose one and brought it back. Edward noted it was already coated with enough layers of gesso to make it gleam.

"This is a small piece. Why don't you try something on it?"

"But what would I paint?"

"People are difficult to capture but objects are much easier. Wait here."

She left the room and returned moments later with an apple in her hand. Setting it on the table, she gestured for him to take a seat on the bench. Retrieving parchment and a piece of charcoal, she placed the parchment flat on the table and handed him the charcoal before sitting on the bench next to him. He could smell the faint scent of roses wafting from her.

"First, you need to practice by drawing the fruit on the page."

Immediately, he put the charcoal against the page and heard her click her tongue.

"Is something wrong?"

"You must study the apple first, Edward. Never be in a rush. That is the first secret of art—patience."

He rested the charcoal on the table and gazed upon the apple before he picked it up and eyed it from different angles. He sensed her nodding in approval as he concentrated on the fruit. Finally, he returned it to the table and took up the charcoal.

"When you draw, commit to each line. Think about it first, then capture what you see on the parchment. Remember, there is no rush with a sketch."

Edward focused on the object before him and then drew its likeness on the page.

When he finished, he said, "I know it's not perfect but at least I can tell what it is."

"You have gotten the likeness down," she agreed. Then she told him ways to shade it to bring depth to the flat image.

He tried and only succeeded a little bit. "I think it takes a true artist to do as you ask."

"Still, you grasped the idea," Rosalyne said encouragingly. "Now use the sketch to draw on the wood."

It didn't take him long to do so and he was pleased with his effort when finished since it looked even more like the apple than his sketch did.

"'Tis time to mix the paints. I will tell you what to do but I want you to do the actual work."

She walked him through each step in the process, from cracking the egg and separating the egg's yolk from its white to mixing in the pigments, blending slowly until he had several shades of red to use along with a bit of green for the sprig at the top.

"The egg tempera dries very quickly," she reminded him. "Once you start, keep that in mind." She laid out several brushes to his right to use with the various hues.

Edward dipped a sable brush she handed him into the first egg tempera and outlined the apple's shape on the wood. Rosalyne spoke softly, encouraging him as he dipped into the different shades and swept them against the gesso. He had trouble again with the shadowing, though.

"Here, I can remedy that," she said.

"Don't do it for me," he chided. "I want this to be my own piece."

"All right."

She rose and stood behind him, leaning into him to retrieve a brush. Dipping it into the paint, she handed the brush to him. Once he took it, she wrapped her own hand around his and guided it to the wood. Awareness of her warmth against his back filled Edward's mind. Her breasts pressed into him, her left hand gripping his shoulder for support as she steered his hand along the wood.

He relaxed and let her take over, using him as her instrument. Though Edward held the brush, Rosalyne was the true artist in their combined effort. He watched as the apple came alive before him, looking every bit as good—if not better—than the real one on the table.

"A last stroke or two. There," she said, lifting his hand and the brush away from the surface. "See, you did it. For a first effort, it is quite remarkable."

He turned to look up at her. "I had help."

Her face was so close to his. She turned toward him and his tongue darted out, teasing the corner of her mouth. Her left hand tightened on his shoulder, while the right squeezed the one that helped him hold the brush. Edward brought their joined hand down and forced her to ease up so he could release the sable brush.

Twisting more toward her, his left hand slid against the small of her back and brought her forward. She landed in his lap, her eyes going wide a moment before his mouth crashed down on hers.

It had been over a week since he had kissed her. It seemed like an eternity. Edward didn't know how he had lived so long without sampling her sweetness. He shifted till she was firmly in his lap and he had both arms around her. Her arms looped about his neck. Rosalyne leaned in and opened her mouth to him.

He plundered it ruthlessly, roughly, demandingly. She responded in kind, taking as much as she gave, matching him kiss for kiss. Edward moved to the sweetness of her cheek and down along her jawline. His lips trailed to her throat, nipping playfully, enjoying the sighs and moans that escaped from her.

One hand against the small of her back held her steady as the other came around to the front and cupped her breast, kneading it. He dragged a fingernail across the nipple, feeling it come to attention through the cloth of her gown. Slowly, he circled it again and again and raked his nail across it, feeling her shiver in his lap. His lips moved lower as his hand tugged on the cotehardie and smock she wore, easing them downward, freeing her breast.

His mouth encompassed the round globe, his tongue encircling her nipple, teasing her unmercifully. Rosalyne squirmed in his lap, causing his manhood to begin to swell. He lathed the peak, taunting her until her nails dug into his shoulders and she gasped for breath. Gradually, he slowed his tongue and moved his mouth upward till it met hers again, sinking his teeth softly into her full, bottom lip as he pulled her clothing back into place.

Rosalyne pushed against his chest, forcing him away. Edward thought he had done something wrong until he saw the hunger in her eyes.

"More," she demanded. "I want more. I *need* more."

CHAPTER 14

Rosalyne saw the heat in Edward's eyes cool, turning to bewilderment. She wondered if any woman had ever said those words to him before.

Clutching his gypon, she yanked him close until their lips almost touched. "Your kisses build a fire within me, Edward. Instead of putting it out, I wish to feed the flame." She paused and swallowed. "I cannot even put into words *what* I wish for since no man has kissed me and caused these feelings inside to rage out of control."

Brushing her lips against his, the contact between them caused the butterflies inside her belly to flap their wings again, bringing about a giddiness and joy that made her want to soar as high as the sun. Rosalyne desired more of this feeling, something that overwhelmed her and excited her and left her breathless.

Her fingers opened and rubbed against the hard wall of his chest. She pushed her tongue inside his mouth, teasing the roof, tickling it. Edward's arms wrapped her in a tight embrace as their kiss caused her blood to sing. She wanted to crawl inside his gypon and taste him as he had her. Rosalyne slid her hands slowly down his chest to the edge of his gypon, teasing him as he had her. She pulled the cloth away and pushed her fingers up under it, skimming his bare skin.

He felt heavenly. So different from her. Edward was all firm flesh and unyielding muscle. As her fingers traveled upward, she noticed the soft fur that seemed matted there. Gliding her palms against it, she heard his sharp intake of breath and smiled against his mouth, pleased that she could affect him as deeply as he had her.

Edward somehow took hold of her wrists and removed her hands from him. He entwined his fingers with hers, his breathing now harsh.

"I refuse to spill your virgin blood, Rosalyne," he managed to get out. "But I can pleasure you all the same."

The intensity in his hazel eyes, now a more vibrant green than brown, caused the pounding in her nether regions to slam against her violently.

"Do you trust me?" he asked.

She nodded.

He released her fingers and shifted her slightly so that now she rested on his massive left thigh, his left arm wrapped firmly around her.

"Close your eyes," he ordered, his voice whisper soft.

Rosalyne did as he asked and soon felt feathery kisses along her brow and on her eyelids, his lips warm and reassuring. One hand dropped to her ankle, massaging it with his strong fingers. Soon, the fingers floated up her calf, stroking it lightly. Anticipation built inside her, coiling within, not knowing what to expect.

Edward's fingers continued their seductive march, reaching her knee, then her thigh, his touch soft and then firm. His lips moved to her mouth, his tongue tracing the outline of her lips, bringing shivers down her spine. Then his hand reached where the throbbing originated. He cupped her, warm and sure, as his kiss became more urgent. Slowly, his fingers parted her, one pushing inside, giving her a jolt.

"Oh!" she managed to say, feeling his smile against her mouth.

He began rubbing, stroking, teasing her. Rosalyne's heart began beating wildly, its pounding matching the place Edward now touched so intimately. Another finger joined the first and she began to move against them, her hands clutching his shoulders for support. His kiss became deeper, longer, more insistent.

Then he touched something deep within her, something that shattered her into a thousand pieces. She moaned deeply into his mouth, pushing against his hand, crying out.

Edward tore his mouth from hers. "Ride it, Rosalyne. Ride it, hard and fast."

She did as he told her, holding on for dear life as she moved against the magical storm he created within her. He cupped the nape of her neck, his mouth swallowing her sounds of pleasure as she writhed against him, reeling in the swirling waves that surrounded her. Gradually, the intense feelings began to subside. She grew still against his hand, feeling as if her body had no bones as she limply collapsed against him.

Edward cradled her, murmuring endearments against her ear, sensitive to the warm breath he expelled as he whispered against it. Finally, he grew silent, simply holding her. Rosalyne had never known such peace.

After some time, his hand slipped from under her clothing and smoothed her cotehardie along her leg.

"What did you do to me?" she asked once rational thought returned.

He gave her a crooked grin. "I hope I satisfied you." He kissed her sweetly, a far cry from the storm of passion his other kisses had held. "'Tis but one thing that occurs between a man and a woman. Among many things," he added. "And I would like to show them—and share them all—with you."

His words stunned her. "What do you mean?" she asked, almost reluctant to hear his reply in case she had misread the situation.

Edward looked deeply into her eyes. "I know you have sensed something between us, Rosalyne."

"Aye."

"I believe it is a bond that will stand the test of time."

His tone was so serious. She had never seen this side of him.

"There are things I must share with you, things about myself that you must know." He smiled at her. "But once I do, I hope you will still want me. Want to be with me. For all time."

"You . . . wish for us to . . . wed?"

"Aye." His smile widened.

She had no idea what he might reveal to her. Had he been married before and his wife passed away? Did he have children that she would need to mother? Had he done something awful and run away to Canterbury to escape his past? Was he in debt? Had he killed a man?

"Tell me," she urged.

He cupped her face, his thumbs caressing her cheeks. "My name is not Edward Munn," he said.

Her heart skipped a beat. "Are you an outlaw? Have you assumed another name to . . . escape punishment?" Rosalyne prayed that wasn't the case. Edward seemed like such a good man. She couldn't imagine him being a criminal.

Edward laughed heartily. "No, my love, I am no thief, much less a murderer." He kissed her swiftly. "My true name is Sir Edward de Montfort. I am a knight of the realm and a member of the royal guard, here in Canterbury on a mission for King Richard."

Rosalyne leapt to her feet. "What?"

He rose and closed the distance between them but did not touch her. "It's true. I want no secrets between us."

"So . . . you are not . . . Edward Munn," she sputtered, her mind reeling at his news.

"Nay, but I have tried to be truthful with you when I could. I did come to Canterbury to work on the wall. The king wanted to see how the construction fared beyond the official reports he receives, so I have become his eyes and ears as I have labored. And I have told you about my parents and my brothers and sisters, so you know all their names."

"But not who they truly are. If you are a knight, then they are also of the nobility."

"Aye. Mother and Alys are healers as I said, though Mother is also the Countess of Kinwick. Alys is married to an earl and lives at Brentwood. She and Kit have three children, twins whom Alys claims might be the devil in disguise and their youngest, who is her angel. Alys is the oldest of the de Montfort children, only a minute or so older than Ancel."

Rosalyne gave him a pointed look. "Then I suppose Ancel is no farmer as you claimed."

"Ancel is the Earl of Mauntell. He and his wife Margery lost their first babe but have a son named Cyrus, and Margery is expecting another child in the fall. Ancel does love the land and everything about farming. If he were here, he would talk your ear off about ways to improve crop production and new methods of binding wheat."

"And how is your brother, Hal, seeking his fortune in London?" she asked boldly.

Edward had the decency to look sheepish. "Hal is in the king's royal guard with me. He is a favorite with the ladies at court, as he is a marvelous dancer and knows just how to pay the right compliment."

Panic flooded Rosalyne. "But if you are serving the king and we wed, then I would have to go to court!" She began wringing her hands. "I cannot do that, Edward. I have nothing in common with those ladies. Though I am of the nobility, I have been raised in humble circumstances. I have not the clothes nor the manners required. I wouldn't know what to say to any of them."

Even though Edward was being truthful now, Rosalyne still reeled from these revelations. He had come into her home under false pretenses. He had blithely lied to her and Uncle Temp about his identity. Why, he had *kissed her!*

Suddenly, Rosalyne wondered if he'd spun other lies—and just how much she could trust this new Edward. By the Virgin, even she knew of the de Montfort name and how Geoffrey de Montfort had been one of England's premier knights in the wars against the French. She found herself shrinking from him.

Edward gripped her shoulders and shook her lightly, forcing her to look at him. "Rosalyne, I have no intention of staying at court. I did not want to go in the first place and had no way of turning down the king's offer of joining the royal guard when it occurred. I long to return to the country—to Kinwick, my home—and live out my life there." His palm touched her face. "With you. And our children."

His words briefly reassured her. Then she thought of what she loved. And how she would miss it.

"But what of my painting, Edward? 'Tis the thing that brings me true happiness."

"Silly goose," he chided. "I would not ask you to give up your art once we wed. In fact, I hope you will teach our children how to draw and paint. Surely, one or two of them will receive that special talent out of the dozen or so we will make."

Rosalyne's cheeks burned at the thought of their children. Of what she and Edward would do together to make those babes.

"You will paint my mother and father, of course. They must be your first portraits. And Alys and Kit will want theirs done, as will Ancel and Margery. Then there are my cousins. Oh, Rosalyne, you have no idea how many cousins I have and the children they've birthed. And then there's Raynor and Beatrice. Uncle Hugh and Aunt Milla." He paused. "Oh, and Lord Hardwin, the earl I fostered with, will certainly want his likeness and Johamma's, his wife. And their two boys. You could spend the rest of your life painting de Montforts and our kin, Rosalyne, and never run out of people."

Edward had thrown so many names at her, she fought the confusion that fogged her brain. He had countless people who loved him, while she only had Uncle Temp. She berated herself for not guessing he was a knight. From his regal bearing and assured manner to his warrior-like build and fine speech, Edward was no commoner. She had turned a blind eye to all of the clues, wanting him to be a simple man.

But he was much more than that. And it frightened her more than anything ever had.

He embraced her, holding her close, trying to reassure her. Lifting her chin with his finger, he said, "I love you, Rosalyne. So very, very much. I thought love might never come to me and if it did, it would be years and years from now." His eyes grew moist, causing her heart to ache. "But there you were, a woman unlike any I have ever known. Intelligent, fascinating, talented, and beautiful. My heart whispered to me that we are meant to be together."

Her throat grew thick with unshed tears. "I must ask you something, Edward."

"Ask anything, my love. I would keep nothing from you now that you know my true identity."

"Why are you not betrothed? 'Tis the way of the nobility. Did your beloved die?"

Edward tenderly touched his lips to her forehead. "My parents are a love match. They journeyed through Heaven—then Hell—and back again to Paradise in order to be together. Their love is not merely strong. It is the core they have built their lives around. Because of that, they wanted their children to have the same chance, so they did not betroth any of us."

"None of you?"

He shook his head. "I have told you that Alys is a great healer, an art she learned from our mother. Alys came across a man on the road who'd been robbed and beaten. Left to die by a vicious band of highwaymen. She brought him home to Kinwick and nursed him back to good health. They discovered love and wed several years ago. Even after three children, Alys wears a look of bliss when Kit enters the room.

"The same happened with Ancel. During the Peasant's Rebellion four years ago, he met Lady Margery." Edward chuckled. "Literally met her—in the midst of battle. Scooped her up on his horse and brought her to safety. Suffice it to say, they also found a deep, abiding love and are incredibly happy together."

Edward's hands encircled her waist. "Mother and Father told all of us—myself, Hal, Nan, and Jessimond—that one day we, too, would find our soul mates, most often when we least expected it. The person we would love and cherish above all others. The one we would lay down our lives to protect. The one that would make each day memorable for us. For me, you *are* that person, Rosalyne. I cannot imagine you missing from my life, even for a single day. I want to know everything about you. Build a life together. Plant my seed in your belly. Laugh with you. Cry with you. Make love to you."

His words moved her more than anything she'd ever been told. Rosalyne relaxed, knowing he was still the same Edward she had met, a good man.

One who loved her.

"From the moment I met you, I knew you were different from all others, Edward. And with that first kiss, I realized I would never be the same." Rosalyne took a deep breath and bared her soul to him. "I believe we are meant to be together, Edward. In your arms, I feel as if I have come home to the place I always dreamt of. With you, anything and everything is possible."

They shared a simple kiss, not of passion or seduction but one that told of the many promises between them.

When he broke the kiss, Rosalyne said, "I do love you, Edward. Every part of me. Before you came into my life, I was missing the biggest piece of myself—and I never knew it until you arrived and completed me."

"I feel the same." He gazed at her with longing, causing something to stir within her. "I will ask your uncle for your hand. We will need to wait and wed after I have reported back to the king. I am hoping that he will be pleased with the news I bring him and honor my request to return home to Kinwick since I have fulfilled my duty." Edward stroked her hair. "Your uncle is most welcome there. Mayhap Mother will know how to ease his suffering."

It touched her that he would bring Uncle Temp with them to Kinwick. Rosalyne didn't know what she had done to deserve such a wonderful man as Edward de Montfort.

"In the meantime, I am toying with an idea," he began. He released her and turned toward the triptych. "Because of this, I think your future holds something remarkable."

"Ah, so you have seen the finished panel, Edward," a voice from the doorway called.

Rosalyne turned and saw her uncle standing there, his hair mussed from his long nap. She thanked the Blessed Virgin he had not awakened earlier and seen her and Edward in their love play.

"Since you have returned, mayhap you would like to help me take it to the cathedral now," Temp said. "The archbishop is eager for it to be on display."

Edward gave her a mischievous wink and then turned to her uncle. "I would be happy to see the triptych delivered to the cathedral, Temp. That way all of Canterbury can view it when they attend mass tomorrow."

CHAPTER 15

EDWARD RETURNED FROM mass and broke his fast with Rosalyne. Temp Parry had not risen yet, so Edward sat next to her, his hand resting on her thigh and their shoulders touching. Just being next to Rosalyne put a smile on his face. Already, he better understood the looks he'd seen passing between his parents over the years. He couldn't wait to make Rosalyne his—in every way.

She glowed today, basking in the warmth of praise that had come her uncle's way once Archbishop Courtenay viewed the triptych two days ago. Though Edward knew she had convinced her uncle that she couldn't take credit for the painted panel, Rosalyne still heard the effusive compliments heaped upon Temp by the archbishop.

They had also attended mass at the cathedral yesterday and made time to go to Trinity Chapel and see the panel in its place of honor. While they stood nearby, many pilgrims and townsmen passed through the chapel and stopped to view the triptych since Courtenay had mentioned it during mass. Some of them genuflected before it, while others marveled at the three scenes and bold use of color. Rosalyne seemed to float through the air beside Edward when they left the cathedral and returned to the cottage.

"Will you continue to work on the wall?" she asked.

"Nay. I have seen all I need to there. Today, I will meet with various men who supply materials to build the wall and see if any corruption exists in their ranks. If so, and I believe it does, then I will confront Perceval Rawlin."

She frowned at him. "But look at you, Edward. Though I trust who you say you are, no one will believe you are a representative of the king from the way you dress. Even Rawlin has seen you at work and thinks you are a common laborer."

His squeezed her leg affectionately. "That is why I will return for my horse and change into my de Montfort clothing. I also carry a missive from the king himself that identifies me as his representative." He grinned at her. "You may not even recognize me the next time you see me."

Edward dipped his head and gave her a long, sweet kiss. He broke it before he could be distracted by his need for her.

"Where is this horse?"

"I left Sirius with a blacksmith who lives not far from the city gates. I will set out now and retrieve him. It will save time riding Sirius from place to place rather than walking."

"Be careful," she entreated him. "Rawlin is a powerful man in Canterbury."

He gave her a steady look. "And I am a knight of England who represents our good King Richard. Rawlin should be wary of me." Edward kissed her once more and left the cottage, his bag containing his clothes to change into in hand.

It took him just over an hour to pass through the city gates and arrive at John's forge. The smithy pounded away, sweat glistening on his face.

"Good day to you, John," he called out.

The blacksmith lowered his hammer and smiled. "And a good one to you, Edward." He stepped from behind the anvil. "I'll venture you have returned for that fine bit of horseflesh." He clucked his tongue. "My boy will be disappointed. Will has grown attached to your horse and the beast seems taken with my boy."

"I know you and Will have cared well for Sirius. I appreciate you looking after him."

"'Twas no bother. I did ride him as you suggested, with Will in front of me. I've never seen a finer horse. But come, I'll take you to him."

Edward followed John around the shed and found Will brushing Sirius, talking away as though they were the best of friends. The boy looked up and smiled when he saw Edward, then his face fell.

"Are you here to visit Sirius? Or do you take him with you?"

"I have need of him," Edward confided, "but I am grateful for how you and your father have watched out for him."

Will stroked the side of the horse with his hand. "'Twas a real treat having him here."

Though he had much to do, Edward said, "Mayhap you would like to ride Sirius once more before we must leave."

The boy's eyes lit up. "Can I?"

Edward looked to John, who nodded his approval. "Would you like to ride with Will?" he asked John.

"Nay, I have work to do. You may take Will out in my place."

After greeting his horse and showering attention on him, Edward saddled Sirius. He lifted Will to the saddle and swung up behind him. They took off, Edward giving Sirius his head and allowing the horse to gallop happily. Squeals of joy erupted from Will as the countryside flew by. Edward let them ride for a quarter of an hour before returning to the blacksmith's forge. He wished he could spend more time with the boy but a full day's work lay ahead.

Wishing the pair a fond farewell and pressing a few more coins into John's hand, Edward returned to Canterbury. His first stop was the public bathhouse, where he scrubbed the grime of the past week's work away before he dressed in his own clothes. Though he now felt more like himself, he would miss being Edward Munn. Mayhap a part of Munn would stay with him. That Edward had been a hard worker but a carefree sort and he was the man Rosalyne had fallen in love with. He only hoped that she would still love the man he now became and would remain.

His first stop of the day was outside Canterbury. He rode to the nearest stone quarry. Though he'd discovered that three different quarries supplied stone for the rebuilding of the wall, this one provided the bulk. If Rawlin cheated here, he would at the others, as well.

Edward rode into the area and saw several workers eyeing the rock before them, some feeling it with their hands and squinting. He knew they were reading the rock face in order to see the lines where the stone would fracture. Others pounded into the corners of holes driven into the rock, causing shock waves to ripple through the stone, breaking it apart. Even more laborers transported the broken boulders to a group of wagons lined up in a row, the drivers waiting to haul them to the masons at the walls.

He dismounted near one of the wagons. "Who is in charge of the quarry?"

"Piers Cassy, my lord," replied the closest man. He pointed over his shoulder. "You can find him over there."

Edward thanked the man and led Sirius in the direction the driver indicated. He waited for Cassy to finish speaking with a worker and then asked, "Are you Piers Cassy?"

"I am." The slender man eyed him cautiously. "And who might you be?"

"Sir Edward de Montfort. King Richard has sent me to speak with you."

Edward pulled out his missive from the monarch, a rolled parchment with the king's seal still intact. He handed it to Cassy, whose eyes went wide when he saw the emblem. Cassy pushed the missive back at Edward.

"The seal alone lets me know you are who you say. Save us both time and simply tell me why you are here, Sir Edward."

Edward appreciated Cassy's forthright manner and chose not to mince words. "The king has reason to believe that Perceval Rawlin is cheating the royal treasury. What deal has he struck with you regarding the stones you provide for the reconstruction of Canterbury's walls?"

Cassy braced himself, drawing in a long breath. Within minutes, he explained exactly how much stone his quarry provided and the cost incurred by the Crown. Edward, who'd always had a good head for figures, took it all in and quickly calculated the profit Rawlin earned on each load.

"Will you speak to Rawlin?" Cassy asked. "I'll tell you now, he will deny the numbers I have given you. All of Canterbury knows how they receive one price for the goods they supply and how Rawlin charges another to the royal treasury." He turned and spat on the ground. "Though no one is privy to the exact arrangement, 'tis common knowledge that Rawlin splits his earnings with Lord Botulf."

"I will talk with Rawlin," Edward promised. "And I venture to say that the king will replace him."

"Good," Cassy said.

He thanked Cassy for his time and left the quarry, riding back into Canterbury. Edward called at several shops which supplied goods and materials to the wall workers, from rope to lime. By early afternoon, he had gathered ample proof of Rawlin's deceitful practices. Instead of riding to confront Rawlin, Edward decided to go straight to Lord Botulf with what he had learned. At this point, Rawlin would be expendable to the nobleman. Edward would do his best to give Botulf a gracious way to explain the irregularities and a chance to recompense the king—and hopefully save the man's head, though Edward already disliked the nobleman because of his interest in Rosalyne.

It took almost half an hour to weave his way through the busy streets of Canterbury before he arrived at Lord Botulf's home, which lay near the cathedral. The nobleman's house easily was the largest in the city, rising three stories high and made from the finest quality of stone. Edward cantered through the gates and was immediately greeted by a servant, who offered to take Sirius and provide the horse water and feed. He thanked the man and thought about how differently Edward Munn would have been treated if he'd approached Lord Botulf's residence on foot in his mean clothing.

Knocking on the door, a woman answered, her face so full that her eyes seemed mere slits.

"I am Sir Edward de Montfort and need to speak with Lord Botulf at once."

She ushered him in and said, "Lord Botulf is with others at present, my lord. May I offer you some refreshment while you wait for him?"

"Do you think he will be occupied much longer?"

The servant shrugged. "I couldn't say, my lord. 'Tis an artist he visits with, an important man in Canterbury who paints portraits. Why, he even painted the most remarkable panel for the chapel in the cathedral. I saw it yesterday after mass. The Holy Mother looked alive, all gentle and with eyes full of love."

Edward tamped down the uneasy feeling that stirred within him. Rosalyne had not told him that she and Temp would be seeing Lord Botulf today, though Edward remembered that she had promised the nobleman once the triptych had been completed that they would discuss his portrait with him.

"You refer to Master Parry and Lady Rosalyne?"

"You know them?"

"Very well," replied Edward. "I am certain Lord Botulf would not mind if I spoke with him in their presence."

She looked uncertain.

"I am on the king's business and have little time to spare," he said with authority.

"Very well."

The woman led him through the hall and up a staircase. They arrived at a door and she indicated for him to enter before scurrying off. Edward did not bother to knock.

As he stepped inside, his eyes swept the room and spied Temp Parry. The artist sat alone, sipping from a pewter cup. Surprise crossed his face.

"Edward? Is that you?" he asked, his features perplexed. "But why are you not working at the wall? And what is this finery you wear?"

"I am not Edward Munn, Temp, but rather Sir Edward de Montfort."

"De Montfort?" He thought a moment. "Is Geoffrey de Montfort your father? I met him many years ago."

"He is."

"A fine man, Lord Geoffrey. But why—"

"I will explain later, Temp. Where is Rosalyne?"

His brows knit together in thought. "They should have returned by now. Lord Botulf was uncertain what he wishes to wear when I paint his portrait. He asked Rosalyne to help him decide."

Trepidation filled Edward, knowing Rosalyne was alone with the man. "Where did they go?"

"Lord Botulf said he would have his servant show her to his wardrobe."

Edward fled the room without explanation, knowing no servant would be involved. Botulf planned to seduce Rosalyne.

He only hoped he wasn't too late.

ROSALYNE FOLLOWED LORD Botulf from the room, leaving her uncle behind. She had selected the clothing to be worn in portraits he painted for several years now since she had a good eye for color and could tell what shades would best suit a subject's coloring. Besides, even though Lord Botulf would never know, she would be the actual painter who captured his image.

Uncle Temp agreed with her on this point. Though his cough had disappeared, the tremor in his painting hand had worsened in the past week and the other hand also did the same. They had discussed it a few days ago, the fact that he would never be able to paint again. For now, he could hide the slight shaking from others. They had planned to carry on the subterfuge as long as possible.

Or would they?

With Edward expressing his desire for them to wed, the need for pretense would come to an end. Rosalyne would finish this commitment to Lord Botulf, which might be the last portrait she painted for coin because, in the future, Edward would provide for her. She longed to meet his large family and become a part of it, bringing Uncle Temp along.

Lord Botulf stopped a servant in the corridor and spoke to her briefly before they continued on their way.

"I asked for Curtis to be sent to my wardrobe. In the meantime, I will show you where it is and you can look at what is available with Curtis. He devotes his time to care for my clothing and dresses me each day."

As Rosalyne trailed after the nobleman, she couldn't fathom what it would be like to have a servant do nothing but attend to someone's clothes and dress them daily. It made no sense.

They arrived at a door and entered the largest bedchamber she'd ever seen. The focal point was a massive bed with curtains of rich burgundy pulled on all sides.

Before she could comment on its splendor, Lord Botulf motioned to her. "This way." He led her to a second door, which he opened.

Rosalyne followed him inside—and couldn't understand what she was seeing. An entire chamber, as large as hers and Uncle Temp's combined, contained shelf after shelf of clothing. Various trunks lined the room and she assumed these also contained more items for Lord Botulf to wear. Pairs of boots, too many to count, sat on the floor. She also saw hats and cloaks in every color of the rainbow.

And all for one man.

She thought this wardrobe might clothe half the citizenry of Canterbury. Even if Lord Botulf donned something new every day, it would take him years to wear each piece a single time. The waste astounded and appalled her.

"I hope you will find something flattering for me to wear in my portrait," he said, oozing false modesty. He gazed at her longer than she thought he should.

"Frankly, I don't know where to begin," she admitted, turning away. "Do you favor a certain color, my lord?"

Before he answered, she thought she heard a noise in the bedchamber. "Is that Curtis?" Rosalyne rushed to the portal and hurried through it. She no longer felt comfortable alone in Lord Botulf's company and wanted the presence of his servant to act as a buffer between them.

But she found no one in the enormous bedchamber.

Nervously, she paced around the room, reluctant to return to the wardrobe until Curtis arrived.

"Ah, I see they brought the wine for us."

Rosalyne turned and saw the nobleman standing beside a table. Two silver cups rested on it. He poured a wine of deep red into both and offered her one.

"Nay, I am not thirsty," she said quickly. "I think I will return to my uncle now that I have seen the array of colors you possess. I will mix various shades that would enhance your appearance and let Uncle choose the one he prefers."

He gave her a crafty look. "Surely, you have time for one glass of wine, my lady. I purchase it from the best vineyards and promise you 'tis the finest wine in all of Canterbury. I would say it even rivals what the king himself drinks at court."

"I am not parched," Rosalyne repeated firmly as she moved toward the door. She reached for the latch and tensed when Lord Botulf placed heavy hands on her shoulders.

Before she could shrug them off, he spun her around and pressed his body against hers, pinning her to the door. She opened her mouth to protest his actions and he forced his tongue inside her mouth. Rosalyne gagged as he attempted to kiss her. Where Edward's kisses seemed heavenly, only revulsion filled her with this man's tongue invading her.

Drawing her hands back, she slammed her palms against his chest, knocking him back a step.

Lord Botulf quickly recovered and, instead of anger, Rosalyne saw a glimmer of interest in his dark eyes.

"So, Lady Rosalyne, you like your love play to be rough? I appreciate a partner who tastes mirror my own." His smile spoke of pure evil.

Rosalyne screamed.

CHAPTER 16

THE SCREAM RIPPED a hole in Edward's soul, knowing Rosalyne was in peril. He raced down the corridor and shoved the door open.

Lord Botulf dragged a struggling Rosalyne across the room, one arm locked around her waist and a hand now covering her mouth to muffle any more attempted cries for help. She caught sight of Edward and ceased moving. Her eyes reflected her faith in him to remedy this situation.

"Release her," he ordered.

Lord Botulf's face reflected confusion at finding a stranger inside his bedchamber. Edward saw the nobleman tried to place where they had met as Botulf dropped his arms. Rosalyne, her head held high, walked with dignity across the room toward him.

When she reached him, she said, "Don't kill him—even though he deserves it."

"Find your uncle and return home," Edward told her quietly. "I will see you there."

He waited until she safely exited to confront Lord Botulf but the nobleman spoke first.

"I know you. You claimed to be a tenant of Templeton Parry. A common laborer working on my wall."

"I am Sir Edward de Montfort, sent to Canterbury by King Richard the Second."

Botulf's eyes grew wary. "What business have you with me, de Montfort?"

Edward narrowed his eyes. "The king wanted to see how construction on the wall progressed. He understands it is a lengthy process and wanted to ensure all went well."

"Does it?" Botulf challenged as he glared at him.

"You know how it fares. The king came to the throne with a depleted treasury, thanks to the lengthy wars in France and constant skirmishes with Scottish rebels. Yet, he still committed to the citizens of Canterbury, wanting to see them and their city safe from invading forces that could land in southeastern England."

"I know all of this," Botulf said dismissively. "The king and I spoke of it at length when construction first began."

"Then you also know how the crown has been cheated, either by your design or Perceval Rawlin's."

Anger sparked in Botulf's eyes. "I had nothing—"

Edward held a hand up. "Save your protests, my lord. After my investigation, I know just how much Rawlin profits—from overcharging for supplies to stealing a portion of the men's wages each time they are paid.

"And I know he divides those gains with you."

The anger in Botulf's eyes died. They flickered now in fear.

"I could take you—and Rawlin—into custody today. But I won't. Instead, I offer you a chance to reimburse the crown."

Botulf grew flustered. "I wouldn't know where to start," he sputtered. "Or how much would be owed."

"Oh, I think you do," Edward said smoothly. "It may or may not save your head. That will be up to the king, of course." He paused. "I will return at this time tomorrow and gauge the progress you have made regarding this matter."

Defeat deflated the nobleman's posture. "Thank you for the respite, Sir Edward. I will send for Rawlin now and clear up this matter." Botulf studied him. "Mayhap I could personally fund all the work on the wall for the next five years. If it would please his majesty."

"Make it ten."

Botulf started to protest and thought better of it. "I will speak with you tomorrow, Sir Edward."

Before he left, Edward had one more item to address. "If I hear of you touching any lady—especially Lady Rosalyne—I will personally have your head with no reprieve. Do I make myself clear?"

The nobleman nodded sullenly.

"Until tomorrow."

Edward left the bedchamber and hurried from the house, eager to see Rosalyne. A groom told him he would fetch his horse. As Edward waited, the courtyard became a flurry of activity, with soldiers scurrying everywhere. Edward assumed a group had been tasked to bring Perceval Rawlin to meet with Lord Botulf.

The groom appeared with Sirius in hand and Edward mounted the horse, riding quickly to the Parry cottage. He secured his mount and entered the abode. Temp Parry sat at the table.

"Where is she?" Edward asked.

"With her chickens," the artist replied.

"I love her," Edward told the man. "I want to wed her. With your permission."

"You have it."

"Thank you."

Edward went to the kitchen and then through the door leading to where the many chickens were kept outdoors. He spied Rosalyne at once, her eyes closed, stroking a hen sitting in her lap. He waited to speak, drinking her in. Sunlight struck her hair, turning it into shades of spun gold.

She must have sensed his presence because she opened her eyes and gave him a brilliant smile. Rising, she released the hen, which scampered toward a strutting rooster.

Opening his arms, Rosalyne stepped into them, her arms wrapping around his waist and her cheek resting against his beating heart. Edward enveloped her and simply held her, reveling in her warmth and scent.

"Thank you," she murmured. "I knew you would come."

He kissed the top of her head and cupped the nape of her neck in his hand.

"You are unharmed?" he asked.

"Aye." She shuddered. "He kissed me, a most unpleasant experience but, other than that, I am all right."

Rage burned through Edward at the thought of the liberties Botulf took with his beloved but he remained calm for her sake.

"What did you discover today?"

"That Perceval Rawlin and Lord Botulf are as corrupt as I expected," he said. "When I confronted him, Botulf's guilt led him to offer to personally fund the wall's reconstruction for the next five years." He paused. "I agreed to ten."

Her eyes widened. "That is a fortune!"

"True," he agreed. "But it goes to show how much Botulf has gotten by ill gain since the king appointed him to supervise the construction process."

"What will happen now?"

"I plan to return tomorrow to speak with him again and then leave for London. Once I have discussed matters with the king, he will send a representative from the treasury to finalize the details Botulf agreed to and put them on paper."

"Then Botulf will be legally responsibility for his promise?"

"Aye."

Rosalyne hugged him tightly. "And what now for us, Edward? Once you report to the king?"

He stroked her hair, enjoying the silky feel of it against his fingertips. "Remember I told you I had an idea?"

She nodded.

"I want to bring you and Temp to court. To paint the queen's portrait."

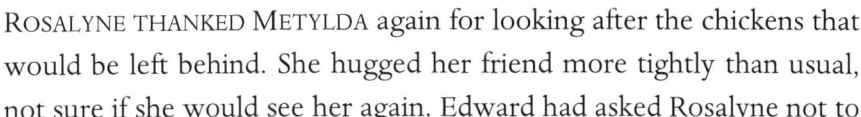

ROSALYNE THANKED METYLDA again for looking after the chickens that would be left behind. She hugged her friend more tightly than usual, not sure if she would see her again. Edward had asked Rosalyne not to speak to anyone about where they were going or their plans to wed. He told her he didn't want any kind of information about them reaching Lord Botulf's ears. From court, Edward knew information was a choice of weapon for some. He did not wish to give any advantage to Botulf.

Edward had met with the nobleman again to solidify their agreement. When Rosalyne asked what would happen to Perceval Rawlin, Edward merely shrugged. Something told her that he kept from her what might befall Rawlin—or what already had occurred. She suspected Rawlin would suffer for his role in scheming to defraud the king.

She watched as Edward helped her uncle into their wagon, which was loaded as usual when they left for a portrait painting session away from home. The back held not only their clothes but all of Uncle Temp's painting supplies, from wood to pigments to brushes. Even a few wooden crates containing some of their best-laying hens accompanied them since they never knew where they went if they would have access to good eggs with fresh yolks to mix their paints.

Edward slipped his hands around her waist. "Do you mind driving the cart?" he asked.

"I have done so in the past," she explained. "The last few times, when Uncle's hands bothered him."

"London is just over twenty leagues," he said. "If you tire, let me know. We will stop and rest whenever you wish."

He hoisted her to the driver's seat and she settled in next to her uncle, taking up the reins. Edward mounted Sirius, his dark brown coat gleaming in the summer sun.

"I'll ride slightly ahead to scout the road but I will always stay in sight," he promised.

They traveled for three days until reaching London's gates. Rosalyne marveled at how large the city was.

Uncle Temp laughed. "I haven't been here in a score. Never thought I'd return."

She glanced at his hands, nestled in his lap. Today was a good day and the tremors seemed held at bay. He had moved more slowly than usual, though, in recent days, and Rosalyne also noticed that he seemed slightly off-balance since they'd left Canterbury. She'd made sure to take his arm each time they'd left the cart, holding him steady when they went into inns to sup or stay the night.

"I thought Canterbury was huge. London seems thrice as large," she said.

"It is an impressive place but the smells are thrice as worse." He chuckled. "Lara enjoyed London, though."

Rosalyne stilled. "You rarely speak of Mother."

Temp shrugged. "I thought it made you sad to hear about her."

"Nay!" she proclaimed. "I would enjoy hearing more about her."

He sighed. "You resemble her a great deal, though your hair is lighter. Hers was a darker blond. But your features are the same, from your eyes to your mouth. Even your height is relatively the same now that you are a grown woman."

"What else?" she asked eagerly.

"Oh, Lara was full of fun. She had a gaiety about her that drew people to her. She was friendly with everyone she met. People loved her." He frowned.

"Is something the matter?"

"Nay," he said brusquely. He looked around. "London is more crowded than the last time I visited."

Rosalyne knew she would get no more from him regarding her mother. She wondered why he stopped speaking about her so abruptly. Why would the mention of everyone loving her bother him?

Edward slowed Sirius until she pulled the cart next to him. He said, "We are going to Sir Harry Pratt's house. I am hoping that you and Temp will be able to stay with him."

"We are not going to the palace?" She hoped she didn't sound too disappointed.

He chuckled. "Nay, my love. I need to convince the king that the queen's portrait must be painted before springing you and Temp on him."

As he rode beside them, she asked, "How do you know Sir Harry?"

"Mother met him at court on one of her many visits there."

"Your mother comes to court?"

Edward nodded. "Father served as an unofficial adviser to King Edward. The old king wished for Father to sit on his royal council but Father's heart never lay in London. He loves Kinwick and the country and did not want to be away from Mother and his children for extended periods of time. Still, he would come frequently to London and, sometimes, Mother accompanied him. King Edward and Queen Philippa were quite fond of her. My sister, Alys, and my cousin, Avelyn, even served in the queen's household."

"Does Sir Harry act as an adviser at court?"

"He did for the old king. When Richard came to the throne, many things changed. Father and Mother rarely come to London now. But years ago, Mother helped Sir Harry's wife, who went through a difficult time carrying her second babe. The child was born early and Mother moved in with Lady Ursula, caring for her and the child day and night. Eventually, the babe began to thrive and Lady Ursula returned to good health, birthing two more healthy sons. Sir Harry was grateful and told my parents if they ever needed anything, they could come to him."

"And you are going to call and ask that we lodge with him?"

"Aye. Lady Ursula has passed on and Sir Harry's sons and daughter are grown. I think he would enjoy the company and be pleased that the favor has finally been claimed."

They arrived at Sir Harry's residence, a grand house on a busy London street.

"Wait here," Edward told them. "I won't be long."

True to his word, Edward returned a few minutes later, grinning from ear to ear. Accompanying him was a short, rotund man with sparkling blue eyes.

"This is Sir Harry Pratt," Edward said. "He insisted upon greeting you himself."

Edward assisted her and then Temp from the wagon.

Sir Harry kissed Rosalyne's hand and welcomed Temp. "Edward

told me you need a place to stay while in London." He glanced around at the wagon. "And your chickens, too, I see."

"We brought them for their eggs," Rosalyne explained. "We use the yolks to mix our egg tempera paints."

"Edward told me you both are painters." Sir Harry rubbed his hands together in glee, much as a small boy might. "I am delighted to have you stay with me. I look upon Lord Geoffrey and Lady Merryn as family." He winked at her. "And Edward tells me that you will soon be family to him, my lady."

Sir Harry took her arm and began leading her to the entrance of the house. "I want to hear all about painting. Did your uncle teach you? Do you paint portraits as he does?" He paused. "Mayhap, I should have mine done. That would be exciting."

Rosalyne looked over her shoulder and saw that Edward had taken Uncle Temp's arm and escorted him.

"We would like to repay you for your generosity in allowing us to stay with you, Sir Harry. Painting your portrait would be a small way of saying thanks."

He beamed with pleasure. "Excellent idea, Lady Rosalyne."

"Harry?" a voice called out from a distance.

She turned and saw a man riding toward them. He leapt from his horse and raced toward them. For a moment, she worried that he might do them harm by the odd look on his face.

The bearded man pulled up just short of them and stared at her, speechless. Rosalyne grew uncomfortable.

"Greetings, Benedict," Sir Harry said. "Meet my guests. This is—"

"Lara," the newcomer said, his gaze boring a hole into her. "Lara," he repeated.

"Nay, my lord," she said, her voice trembling.

"I am sorry," he apologized, shaking his head. "My heart knows you are not Lara. You are Rosalyne. Rosalyne Bowyar."

"How do you know this?" she demanded, afraid to hear his response.

"Because I am your uncle. Benedict Bowyar. And I loved your mother with all my heart."

CHAPTER 17

*T*HIS MAN WAS *her uncle?*

"You . . . you . . . loved my mother?" Rosalyne asked.

Uncle Temp stepped between them. "Get away from her!" he ordered. "You wanted nothing to do with her then, Benedict. Leave her be now."

"You know the truth, Temp."

"I know that you were not man enough to stand up to that witch of a wife." Temp began to sway.

Both Rosalyne and Edward grabbed an elbow to keep him upright as Sir Harry looked on with unabashed interest.

"Shall we take this inside?" their host asked. "I am curious to hear what Benedict has to say regarding this matter."

"Only if Rosalyne agrees," Edward said.

She looked at him and nodded.

"Come, Temp. Lean on me," Edward ordered. "Rosalyne deserves whatever truth this man utters and you can tell her if he speaks right from wrong."

Sir Harry took her arm again. "Let me escort you inside, Lady Rosalyne." The nobleman looked back to his friend. "Benedict, please accompany us."

The group entered the house, with Sir Harry leading them to a large room with ample seating. Edward lowered Temp into a chair and asked that wine be brought as the older man mopped the sweat from his brow.

Rosalyne took a seat next to her uncle—and stared at the other man who claimed to be a different uncle of hers, a relative from her father's side. They sat in silence until a servant brought refreshments for them all. Temp took a sip and sighed.

"Are you certain you are well, Uncle?" she asked. When he nodded, she said, "Then I want to hear what this man has to say."

"Very well," Temp said. "But remember that I warned you. What you hear might not be to your liking, my sweet girl."

Edward came to stand behind her. His hand rested lightly on her shoulder in support.

Rosalyne looked at the nobleman claiming to be her blood relative. "Explain yourself, my lord."

Benedict Bowyar pushed his hands into his hair, frustration obvious on his face. "I never imagined I would see you again," he began. "And I hate that we have started this way." He glared at Temp.

"Look at me," she instructed, her voice firm. "This involves me. Not your dispute with Uncle Temp. Tell me your story," she urged. When he remained silent, she added, "Tell me *my* story."

Bowyar began to weep. He angrily brushed the tears away with a sleeve.

"Temp is right," he finally said. "I was weak." He took a deep breath. "I was supposed to wed Lara, your mother, while my brother, Lawrence, would wed a woman named Amicia." He swallowed. "But Lara and Lawrence only had eyes for one another."

Bowyar stood and began pacing the room as he spoke.

Uncle Temp said, "I see no good coming of this, Benedict. You should leave. Let sleeping dogs lie."

Rosalyne shot him a warning glance and looked to Bowyar. "Please, continue, my lord."

The nobleman sighed. "They came to me. Lawrence first, then Lara. Admitted their feelings for one another. Said they had fought their attraction and lost that battle. No formal betrothal had been made, just a promise between our parents."

He stopped in front of her. "I loved them both enough to step aside. To see them happy." His eyes bore into hers. "To see *her* happy."

Bowyar returned to his chair. "The news bewildered my father but he allowed for the exchange of intended brides. You see, Lawrence was the elder son and had always been his favorite. I tried his entire life to win my father's love—and failed. I thought I could make everyone happy by agreeing to the match."

Rosalyne's heart filled with pity for him. "You must have loved my mother a great deal to give her up."

"I did." He paused. "We Bowyar brothers wed in a double ceremony. Amicia and I went west to live with her parents. My father died not long after and Lawrence became the Baron of Shallowheart."

Temp interrupted the tale. "That's enough, Benedict. Rosalyne doesn't need to hear anymore sordid details. I won't see her hurt by you by dredging up the past."

She grew impatient and sternly said, "Uncle Temp, I have a right to hear about my parents. You never speak of them to me. I don't care if I'm saddened by what I learn. Please, let him speak." Turning back to Bowyar, Rosalyne asked, "Did you grow to love your wife?"

"Never," he spat out. "She was indifferent to me most of the time. Cruel the rest. She resented Lara for stealing Lawrence away from her. Amicia was only interested in power and wealth. As the second son, I had no title. No lands. No money. It made her bitter to have lost Lawrence."

"You became the baron upon my parents' death, though. That should have pleased her."

"Aye. Lawrence and Lara passed close together from a fever raging across England. Amicia and I returned to Shallowheart. You were only a helpless babe but I wanted you, Rosalyne. Wanted you desperately—because you were a part of the two people I loved most." He gave her a wistful smile. "I would have been a good parent to you, I believe.

"But Amicia denied me that."

"That's when I stepped in," Temp said gruffly. "End of story. You can leave now, Benedict. You're not wanted here. Rosalyne and I have gotten on well without you in our lives. We didn't need you then and we certainly don't want you in our lives now."

Rosalyne looked from Bowyar to Uncle Temp. "What do you not want me to hear? You're trying to keep something hidden from me, Uncle Temp."

Bowyar spoke up. "It's the ugliest part of the story, dear. Temp only wishes to protect you. Mayhap, he is right to do so."

"Quit dancing around the truth," she told both men. "I'll have all of it. Now."

"Very well," Bowyar said. "My wife hated you from the moment she laid eyes on you. Amicia insisted that you would never be raised beside her children, much less be treated as their equal. I rue the day I let her dictate what would happen to you." He looked to Temp, who continued the story.

"Benedict sent for me. He begged me to take you before Amicia did you harm."

A shiver passed through Rosalyne. Edward gripped her shoulder.

"Lady Amicia would have . . . she might . . ." Her voice trailed off, the thought too horrible to express in words.

"Without a doubt, she would have carried through with her threats, Rosalyne. Amicia Bowyar was that kind of woman," Uncle Temp said, his eyes burning with rage. "She wished you dead."

"Your uncle did me the kindest of favors by taking you in," Bowyar told her gently. "My wife instructed I was never to see either of you again." He bowed his head. "I foolishly agreed to her demand and told Temp not to let me know where the two of you headed, else I'd be tempted to find you one day." He raised his head, his eyes meeting hers. "I regretted that decision from that moment till this."

Bowyar stood and began pacing again. "Amicia died in childbirth years ago. She birthed one dead babe after another. 'Tis when I knew God cursed me for letting you go."

"So you have no other children?" Rosalyne asked.

"Nay." He came and knelt before her. Taking her hands, he said, "Can you find it in your heart to forgive me, Rosalyne?"

She was torn. On one hand, this man abandoned her, handing her off to Temp and denying any responsibility for her. Yet, in doing so, he may have saved her life.

Rosalyne squeezed his hands. "I do forgive you, Uncle Benedict. I have many questions of you, though, about my parents."

"Thank you for your forgiveness, my child." Bowyar kissed her knuckles, his tears flowing freely now. Releasing her hands, he came to his feet. "I would like to get to know you, Rosalyne. Spend time with you and answer all of your questions. I cannot replace those years we were apart, but never doubt that I have always, always loved you."

"Why don't you give Rosalyne time to ponder things and return tomorrow afternoon?" Edward suggested.

Bowyar nodded and looked to her hopefully. Rosalyne nodded her approval.

"Then I will see myself out. Until this time tomorrow." He fled the room.

She looked at Uncle Temp. "I needed to hear the truth, Uncle."

"I realize that," he said wearily.

"You look exhausted," Sir Harry said. "I can have you shown to your room."

Rosalyne helped her uncle rise. "I will get him settled and return," she said.

"Nay, Rosalyne," Edward said. "You also need some rest—and time to think about all that you heard. In the meantime, I will go to the palace and seek an appointment with the king."

Panic filled her at his coming absence. "You will return tomorrow? When Uncle . . . Benedict will be here?"

Edward took her hand and brought it to his lips, brushing them softly across her knuckles. "I will," he promised. "For now, you will be in good hands with Sir Harry."

His words reassured her. "Till tomorrow," she said.

EDWARD HAD NO intention of making an appointment with the king until he had spoken with Hal. His brother would be able to clue him in as to the happenings at court while Edward had been gone to Canterbury. If Geoffrey de Montfort had taught his sons anything, it was to be prepared going into a situation—especially when dealing with a king. Of all the de Montfort brothers, he had been the one who most took this lesson to heart.

Arriving at the palace, he made his way to the queen's rooms and found that she and her ladies-in-waiting were taking in the air outside. He hurried to the garden that Queen Anne favored and saw her sitting on a bench, eyes closed, her face lifted to the sun. Various ladies clumped together in small groups chatting. Two royal guardsmen stood watch nearby at opposite ends.

One was Hal.

Edward went and stood slightly behind his brother. "Keep your eyes on the queen but fill me in on anything I have missed," he said quietly.

"Good to have you back, little brother," Hal said. "Do you wish to hear about my most recent conquest? Or would you prefer politics to be our topic of conversation?"

He chuckled. "In the time I have been gone, I am sure there have been several conquests, which all ended the same. Politics would be more to my taste."

Hal's head turned slightly as he followed a few of the women strolling by. "The Duke of Lancaster left England yesterday in order to make good on his claim of the title in Castile."

"He wishes to be crowned head of Castile? Is it not enough that he is one of the richest men in all of Europe?"

His brother shrugged. "His wife, Constance, is an heir to the Castilian Kingdom. Lancaster's coat of arms includes those of the Spanish kingdom. For more than a dozen years, he has called himself their king. You know he's gathered about him a variety of refugees from Castile."

"But why now, after so long a time?" Edward asked.

"Since England has decided to ally herself with Portugal and Lancaster's daughter will soon marry the Portuguese monarch, the time is ripe. Our wars with France and Scotland have died down. Lancaster believes he can land his army of five thousand in Spain and seize the throne."

"That worries me," Edward admitted. "Not only that the duke will waste time and coin trying to take a foreign throne by force but what his absence from England could mean. The king's uncle has protected him several times over the years. With Lancaster and those loyal to him gone, Richard will be alone for the first time since he became a boy king."

"Except for that band of young sycophants who gathers about him," Hal noted. "I fear we are in for some uneasy times at court, Brother."

"Father will want us gone from here," he said. "In fact, he never wanted us to come in the first place."

"I actually agree. But how does one gracefully bow out of the honor of being named a royal guardsman?"

"I am going to do my best to find out. I plan to make my report to the king and see if this mission to Canterbury has earned me enough favor to warrant returning home in the near future. With you, of course," Edward said.

"Did you find what you thought you would in Canterbury?"

"Aye. The work is steady but those in charge are corrupt to their very souls and cheating the king blind. They need to be held accountable for their actions."

"He won't like hearing that. Richard has never taken well to bad news."

"I have something else to share with you," Edward revealed.

Hal glanced over his shoulder. "What aren't you telling me? I caught something in your tone." Hal frowned. "You seem different somehow."

"You might as well be the first de Montfort to hear it. We have never kept secrets between us." He paused. "Mother and Father are right. When you meet the one you are meant to be with, you feel it in your very soul."

Hal took a step back so that they stood abreast and gave him a sideways glance. "You . . . found love?"

Edward couldn't hide his smile. "I did, Hal."

"Is she comely?"

"That would be the first thing you asked about. In fact, she is exquisite. But Rosalyne is also caring and talented. Her beauty is both within and without her. I had no reason to expect to find love but I did all the same. She has changed me, Hal, for the better. I look forward to being a married man and spending every day of my life in her company."

"I see. So if the king releases you from duty, will you return to Canterbury for her?"

"Nay. I brought Rosalyne and her uncle with me to London," he admitted.

His brother's mouth fell open. "You what?" he hissed. "I have never witnessed you acting in a spontaneous manner, Edward. Has this woman bewitched you? This is so out of character for you."

"I love her, Hal, plain and simple. I could not stand to be parted from her. And she is an instrumental piece of my plan to seek my release from the king's service."

"How so?"

"Rosalyne is a painter. More talented than anyone I have ever met. I am going to convince the king that both he and Queen Anne need their portraits painted by her."

"By a *woman*? Have you gone mad, Edward? Are you even my brother, or are you someone who only disguises himself as Edward de Montfort?"

"Lady Rosalyne's uncle, Templeton Parry, is a well-known portrait painter. He will be the man supposedly painting our royal duo but, in the end, I wish for Rosalyne to receive credit for the portraits."

Hal gave him a long look. "Now I know it must be love, for you have never acted in such an impossible manner before."

The queen rose and the group of ladies scattered in the garden began rushing toward her.

"I must attend to my duty," Hal said. "Where are you hiding your Rosalyne and her uncle? Hopefully, not here in the palace."

"They are staying with Sir Harry. I will see you later, Hal."

Now that he had a better idea of the political climate, he would be more comfortable meeting with the king. Edward started to leave his brother and stopped in his tracks. Bold actions required bold thoughts.

And his idea was both brash and daring.

Reversing course, Edward marched toward Queen Anne. He had never spoken directly to her since he had come to court.

She watched him coming and stopped, interest flickering in her pale eyes.

Edward bowed and asked, "Might I have a private word with you, your majesty?"

CHAPTER 18

Edward wound his way through the maze of corridors until he reached the hallway leading to the king's rooms. As usual, a bevy of bowmen from Cheshire stood outside, guarding the doors.

He went to the front of the line and said brusquely, "The king is expecting me." A half-truth, at best. The king had told Edward to report to him when he returned from Canterbury but no formal appointment had been arranged.

Without waiting, he pushed the door open and stepped inside. No one questioned him or stopped him, so he proceeded through the rooms until he found the king with one of his favorites, Robert de Vere. Edward paused in the doorway since the two men were deep in conversation.

Some minutes later, the king looked up. "Ah, Sir Edward. You are back from Canterbury. Do come in."

He approached and knelt before the king and was granted permission to rise.

Richard turned to de Vere. "This good knight went to Canterbury to evaluate how the construction on the city walls fares."

De Vere looked disinterested. "I thought you were more concerned with the construction of your new bath house, your highness."

"Canterbury is important, Robert, because of its proximity to London," the king explained. "An invading force from France could enter England and overtake Canterbury. The Romans understood that. 'Tis why they built their wall to surround it. I am merely reinforcing what is there. But go, my friend. I will dine with you later."

De Vere took his leave.

The king turned to Edward. "So tell me what news you have. Did you do as you planned and actually spend time working as a laborer along the wall?"

"I did, sire. Of course, I am not a registered guild member and had not the trade or skill to perform certain tasks."

"Ah, so swinging a sword or mace cannot win you guild membership?" The king roared with laughter at his own joke.

Edward chuckled and nodded in appreciation. "Nay, sire. What I was good for was hauling stones from carts." He grew serious. "I can tell you that those who toil on the wall earn every pence they receive. I found the men employed, be they common laborers or skilled craftsmen, do their best every day. Though it will still involve many years of work to come, you can rest assured that they fulfill their role in the venture."

The king eyed him with interest. "You have more to tell me, Sir Edward. I can tell."

"I do, your highness." He paused. "I spoke to everyone who had any dealings with the wall, from the head of the stone quarry to various merchants around town who provide the supplies used in construction. To a man, I learned that the Crown is being methodically cheated on a regular basis."

Richard frowned. "How so?"

"All workers, skilled and unskilled, contracted for one rate of pay—yet they received less every single time. It is understood by all that they are not to challenge this policy, or they will be ousted. The same is true of materials. Provisions are made to purchase them for one price but each time what is reported to the Crown is a much higher one."

"And the extra coin stolen from me went into whose pockets?" the king demanded, splotches of red darkening his face in anger.

"I determined it came down to two men, sire. Lord Botulf, the nobleman overseeing the construction, and his man, Perceval Rawlin, who handles the daily affairs."

"I will have both of their heads," the king growled, his words seething with hate.

"I have a better plan, your majesty," Edward said, and bravely pushed ahead. "Lord Botulf assured me that Rawlin has already been dealt with. After I confronted Lord Botulf, he understands how his life hangs in the balance. I had him agree to personally fund everything concerning the wall's construction for the next ten years."

"Ten?" the king repeated, turning over the information. "A good move on your part, Sir Edward." He paused. "But I would rather see it ten and two."

"Thank you, your highness. A full dozen years of paying for all construction costs will see the project far along, possibly only a few years from completion. I also took the liberty of meeting with Master Yevele regarding the matter."

"Yevele?" The king brightened. "I had forgotten about Grandfather's master mason. I had him look at the original walls and make suggestions regarding whether to repair what was there or rebuild it. So Yevele is still in Canterbury?"

"Aye, sire. He is in charge of the work on the cathedral's nave. That keeps him busy since the project will run for many more years. I thought since he would be in the city for so long, he might consider supervising the wall work. If you are agreeable, Yevele will visit sites along the wall each week and make recommendations to whomever Lord Botulf next places in charge. That way we would have Yevele's expertise in completing the city's defenses and he could still focus a majority of his time on completing Canterbury Cathedral."

Richard looked at him with new eyes. "For one so young, you drive quite a masterful bargain, Sir Edward."

"All in your name, your majesty. I hated seeing the Crown being taken advantage of. This way, Rawlin has been made to pay. Lord Botulf knows he is being scrutinized and he will provide all the costs for many years to come, relieving the royal treasury of that burden. Besides, the citizens of Canterbury will be the ones who benefit and they will be grateful to you for seeing this project to its completion."

The king rubbed in his chin in thought. "Then I wish for you to meet with my royal treasury officials and explain what legal documents need to be drawn up to guarantee Lord Botulf's participation in the venture. You can accompany them with a group of soldiers so that Lord Botulf can commit to his promise through his signature."

"As you wish, sire."

Edward thought the monarch would now dismiss him and thought his gamble had been in vain. Disappointment filled him, thinking the queen had either let him down or not been able to speak to her husband since their conversation took place several hours ago.

"One more matter, Sir Edward," the king began.

Hope filled him. Mayhap the queen had done as he'd requested.

"While in Canterbury, did you hear tale of an artist who paints portraits?"

"That would be Templeton Parry. I not only heard of him but viewed his work, your majesty. I went to Trinity Chapel to pay my respects to your father, the Black Prince. Parry had recently completed a triptych that rested near the tomb. Not only is Parry talented at painting panels but he also paints portraits and has gained quite a reputation."

Edward was counting on Richard's love of art. The king had cultivated an atmosphere at court where the arts flourished.

"'Tis good to learn you have first-hand knowledge of this artist. The queen has heard mention of him. She would like Parry to come to London to paint her portrait, as a gift to me." His face softened at the mention of his wife.

Everyone at court knew how Richard and Anne had married young and actually fallen in love. Edward used that knowledge when he spoke with the queen.

"I believe Master Parry would capture not only the queen's elegance and beauty but also her sweet disposition," he said.

"Then bring back this Parry when you return to London," the king commanded. "I would have him paint my Anne."

"Master Parry is already in London with his niece who assists him, your majesty. I passed them on the road. They are staying with Sir Harry Pratt."

The king nodded. "Even better. Whatever portrait Parry works on in London can be finished later. I want him to start the queen's portrait at once. Go see him now, Sir Edward. Have him begin first thing tomorrow."

"As you wish, sire."

Richard dismissed him. Edward kept a solemn expression on his face as he left the king's rooms and moved through the royal guard. As he turned the corner, though, he broke out in a wide smile.

He couldn't wait to tell Rosalyne the good news.

"ARE YOU SURE you don't need me present when you meet with Benedict?"

Rosalyne looked at Uncle Temp, who looked worse for the wear. The trip from Canterbury to London had done him in. After they'd arrived yesterday, his balance remained shaky. Nothing had changed with it today.

"Nay. You stay in your bedchamber and rest. Edward is returning for the meeting and I am sure Sir Harry will also be present. I heard the worst of it yesterday. I think our time together today is more for Uncle Benedict and me to get to know each other a little bit."

Temp frowned. "I hate hearing you refer to him that way, like he is family."

"But he is my uncle, as much as you are." Rosalyne hugged him. "You know you are more like a father to me. Nothing will ever change the love between us or my devotion to you." She kissed his cheek. "Edward knows how strong our bond is. Without my prompting him, he offered to have you come to Kinwick with us after we wed. Just think, we will be part of a large family, Uncle Temp."

"You love this man a great deal," Temp observed.

She smiled. "I do. My heart is light and my step happy. Edward de Montfort is the man for me. I have no doubt about that."

"Then I will trust him to look after you." He clasped her hands. "Be wary, Rosalyne. Do not take everything Benedict Bowyar says to be the Gospel truth. I do believe he is troubled by his behavior and how he let Amicia control him all those years ago with her threats of murdering you in your crib. Still, be on guard, my dear."

"I will," she promised. "Get some rest. If Edward works things out, we might soon go to the palace. You need to be ready."

Rosalyne stayed with him till his soft snores began, closing the door behind her.

As she turned, a servant came down the hall. "Lady Rosalyne. You have a visitor."

It was too early for her uncle to arrive. Mayhap, Edward came early and they would be able to spend some time alone together.

She allowed the woman to lead her back downstairs to the room they had met in with her uncle. As Rosalyne entered, a tall man turned and studied her with interest. He looked familiar, though they had never met. Approaching him, she realized exactly who he was.

"You must be Sir Hal de Montfort. I am Lady Rosalyne Parry."

His blue eyes swept across her, assessing her. He stood an inch or so taller than Edward and was as broad through his shoulders as his brother. His hair seemed quite dark.

"Edward said you were talented and beautiful. He neglected to tell me you were intelligent."

She shrugged. "Merely observant, my lord."

"Part of being an artist."

"So he told you that?"

Hal nodded. "He did. And that he loves you a great deal. I had to come and meet you for myself. To see if you are worthy of my little brother."

"Edward is not so little," she retorted. "And he does have a mind of his own." Rosalyne softened her tone, not wanting to alienate this man, whom Edward held dear. "But I know how much he cares for his family and how close he is to you, Sir Hal. He will want your approval, so I must win you over, I suppose." She gave him a warm smile.

"I already like you, my lady. Come, shall we sit? I'd like to learn a little about you. Edward did not have much time to speak with me, so you are a mystery to me."

He led her to a chair and they seated themselves.

"The two of you are very alike," she said. "Your gestures are similar. So are your looks."

"But we are very different in our outlook. Edward is usually a most somber young man. Full of living up to his ideas of duty and loyalty."

"I know he believes those to be of utmost importance but I have found Edward quite lighthearted and cheerful."

Hal laughed. "Then you are most certainly the woman for him, my lady, for you have changed him. Mother says that the love of a good woman will change a man for the better. Edward was already a kindhearted person and one of the most capable knights in England. If you have brought laughter and light into his life, then you will be accepted into the de Montfort family with open arms."

He leaned forward and said, "From this moment on, you are not like my sister. You *are* my sister, Rosalyne. I will afford you with the protection, respect, and love that I give Alys, Nan, and Jessimond."

She was taken aback by his intense declaration and saw how Edward and Hal reflected the same depth of character and honesty.

"Then I will look upon you fondly, Hal, as my new brother. I have no siblings and by wedding Edward, I am pleased that I will find myself with many."

He burst out laughing. "Oh, you will get your fill of family, Rosalyne. The de Montforts. Our cousins. All the children. You will soon find you might never have a private moment to yourself once you come to Kinwick." He waggled his eyebrows at her. "Except for those times you and Edward sneak away and enjoy love play."

"Hal de Montfort!" she exclaimed, feeling her face flame in embarrassment. "Is this what having a brother is like?"

Grinning from ear to ear, he nodded. "Brothers are known for teasing their sisters. I am merely preparing you for what your future holds." He sighed. "But tell me about yourself, Rosalyne. Where did you grow up? How did you begin to paint? Why do you enjoy it?" Hal laughed. "I sound as curious as Alys. She is usually the one who finds out everything from everyone. I cannot wait to lord over her that I met you first and how much I know about you."

Rosalyne couldn't help but laugh. Already, she enjoyed knowing Hal and thinking of him as a brother. She told him of her life in Canterbury with Uncle Temp and how she had always been attracted to the smells and colors of paint. They passed a pleasurable half-hour that way and then Hal told her a few stories of growing up with Edward and fostering with Lord Hardwin at Winterbourne.

Finally, he rose. "I must return to the palace, dear sister." He kissed both of her cheeks. "I am thrilled that you and Edward have found one another. Hopefully, I will be seeing you and Uncle Temp at the palace, your paints in hand."

"So you know of Edward's plan to have me paint the royal portraits?" she asked.

The door opened and Edward entered. Surprise registered on his face.

"I looked all over the palace for you," he playfully chided his brother. "And you were with Rosalyne all along."

Hal smiled. "I wanted to be the first to welcome her into the de Montfort family." He paused. "And I wanted to see the woman who had turned your world upside down, little brother. When you approached the queen yesterday, 'twas more out of character than anything I have ever seen you do. I had to meet the delightful creature who could cause you to act so fearlessly, all in the name of love."

Hal bowed to Rosalyne. "I'm off to the palace but I look forward to seeing you soon—and will keep your secrets, of course." He gripped Edward's shoulder. "An outstanding choice, little brother. If you had not laid claim to Rosalyne first, I might have enjoyed winning her heart."

Edward bid his brother farewell and turned to her. "And Hal is only one of my siblings. You only have four more to meet. Plus, two parents, multiple nieces and nephews, and an assortment of cousins."

"I look forward to it."

He wrapped his arms around her and gave her a lingering kiss. Rosalyne tingled from head to toe by the time he released her.

"And before your uncle arrives, I must share the good news with you. The king is eager for Templeton Parry to paint the queen's portrait. You and Temp are to come to the palace tomorrow morning in order to begin. I have arranged everything with the queen."

Equal bits of excitement and nervousness shot through Rosalyne. "So soon?"

"Aye." He kissed her again. "And the queen knows that you will be the true painter."

"You told her?" Surprise filled her.

Edward grinned. "That—and also that I am in love with you and plan to marry you."

Before Rosalyne could respond, Benedict Bowyar entered the room. He came and kissed her cheek and offered Edward his hand.

"I overheard that the two of you plan to wed," he said.

"We do. Temp has granted me his permission," Edward revealed. "I love Rosalyne very much."

"I hope 'twill be a happy union blessed with many children," Bowyar replied sincerely.

Edward looked to her. "I will leave you with your uncle. I know that you looked forward to his arrival."

Once he left, Bowyar asked, "Where is Temp?"

"Resting in his room."

"Shall we go see him? I think it's important he be included in our first conversation or two."

It surprised her but she agreed, leading this new uncle upstairs to Temp's bedchamber, though she warned him they might find Temp asleep.

"Then we'll sit by his side for our conversation."

They found Temp awake. He told Rosalyne he'd enjoyed a good nap as he warily studied Bowyar.

"Stay in your bed, Temp. We can speak here."

Temp frowned at his brother-in-law. "Say what you want. I can't stop you."

"I didn't expect you would. I'm only here to learn more about Rosalyne and the life she's led and tell her something about her parents."

"I want to her about Mother and Father first," she insisted. "What they looked like. What they enjoyed doing. What their life at Shallowheart was like."

"Lawrence was larger than life. A few inches taller than Father or me and shoulders as wide as a doorway. His laugh was deep and rich and made you want to join in. He was two years older than I was and I worshipped the ground he trod. He got us into more mischief than possible but always had a way of extricating us from too much punishment."

The nobleman told her about several escapades they'd been involved in as children and Rosalyne found herself laughing till her belly ached.

"What about my mother?" she asked.

"Ah, Lara had the tiniest waist and feet of any woman you've seen. Hair a few shades darker than yours. She was petite in height and build and had a smile that lit up any room she entered. People were drawn to Lara, like a moth to a flame. She was irresistible, as full of mischief as Lawrence was. No wonder they made a good pair."

Bowyar told of a picnic they'd gone on and how Lara shed her shoes and hose and hiked her skirts up above her knees so she could wade in the cool water.

"She slipped on a rock and her feet went flying. Lara wound up soaking wet from head to toe. 'Twas shallow so she was never in danger but I can still see the water dripping from her nose." He chuckled, shaking his head.

Rosalyne found out about the horses her parents kept and the cat that always slept on their bed after they wed.

"Lara loved that cat. Brought it with her to Shallowheart. It followed her about everywhere she went." He frowned.

"What happened to it?"

"Amicia banished it to the barn," he said too quickly. "She refused to have a cat in the keep."

"There's more," Rosalyne prodded.

Her uncle raked his hands through his hair. "Aye—but do you really want that truth? I'll tell you. She didn't banish the creature. She killed it. Twisted its neck till the poor thing was paralyzed and then flung it into the fire." He shuddered. "I can still hear the howls coming from it as it burned alive. Amicia said she would get rid of everything Lara loved. She did. From you to the cat to Lara's clothes. Tapestries she'd woven. Tore up her herb garden, only to make the servants replant another. Blinded the horse Lara loved to ride and then sold the beast. She even banned Cook from preparing pear tarts and eel pie because they'd been Lara's favorite foods."

Rosalyne found she couldn't speak. She glanced to Temp and saw new sympathy in his eyes for his brother-in-law.

"You were lucky your uncle was willing to care for you," Bowyar continued. "Not many bachelors would've taken on the responsibility of a babe. I used to fall asleep at night wondering where the two of you were. If Temp still painted. If he'd taught you how. I pictured you with paint covering your face and hands and Temp laughing as he cleaned you up. Every time Amicia found something new to rage on about, I would retreat to a world I'd created, one where Temp and I raised you together."

"Why didn't you stand up to her?" Temp asked softly.

"After I gave Lara her freedom and agreed to wed Amicia, I didn't care if I lived or died," Bowyar explained. "Amicia's father was a tyrant. I found myself so beaten down by him that when Lawrence died and I returned home to Shallowheart, I wasn't much of a man. Being her father's child, Amicia recognized that and continued to intimidate and threaten me. It was easier to give in to her demands just to keep the demons at bay."

He looked to Rosalyne. "Though I would have given anything to raise you, being around Amicia was toxic. Giving you to Temp gave you a chance for a better life." Bowyar smiled. "Look at you now. You're beautiful. Intelligent. Talented. Everything I would have wished for you." He turned to Temp. "You did an excellent job raising our niece, my friend."

Rosalyne saw Temp softening toward his this man. "Though Lara loved Lawrence, you may have made the better husband to her, Benedict. I'm sorry for what you endured during your marriage."

"What's done is done. At least we have Rosalyne—if you don't mind sharing her with me."

"Rosalyne is full of love, Benedict." Temp shrugged. "I'm sure she'll find a place for you in her heart."

Bowyar looked at her earnestly. "I have grieved for years for my cowardice, Rosalyne. Once Amicia passed, I searched for you and Temp for a long time. Too many years had passed, though. I never met with success—until now. I hope you and your uncle can see to forgive me for all of my transgressions."

"There's nothing to forgive, Uncle Benedict," she told him. "You put my welfare above all else. It was a gift to be raised by Uncle Temp. I'm only glad we can all come together now. Hopefully, you'll find some peace."

Rosalyne kissed both men tenderly, happy her own family had grown by one.

"I have news to share with you both," she announced. "Uncle Temp and I are to meet with the queen tomorrow morning. Edward confided in her that I am the one who will paint her portrait."

As the men congratulated her, Rosalyne only hoped she would be up to the task.

CHAPTER 19

Rosalyne placed several pieces of parchment and charcoal inside a bag. She smoothed her rose-colored cotehardie again, hoping to calm her nerves. Meeting the queen today would be difficult enough. Painting a portrait that would please both her and the king became more arduous. But to eventually reveal that she—and not Uncle Temp—was the true artist?

It terrified her.

She had imagined every reaction from the monarch while trying to fall asleep last night. King Richard might laugh off her assertion, not believing a woman could produce such a work. Or he could express his delight in finding a unique artist. Then again, he might attack the wood and destroy it in anger at having been lied to. Or even the unimaginable. He might call for her head—and Uncle Temp's.

And even Edward's, for betraying him.

Nerves danced through Rosalyne at all of these possibilities. She wondered why she had ever agreed to go along with Edward's scheme. But she knew he hoped the king would reward him with his freedom, for both his thorough investigation in Canterbury and for bringing a talented artist that would produce the royal duo's likeness. She only hoped their gamble would pay off.

Rosalyne went downstairs and collected the eggs her hens had laid. She'd brought three of them along. Edward had told her they would have easy access to eggs in London but she knew the size and consistency of those her favorites laid and how to work them into her pigments. Better to stay with what she knew than to experiment with such a burdensome commission before her.

Returning to her bedchamber, she collected her bag and then stopped by Uncle Temp's room to escort him downstairs. She assessed his color and balance and found both better today, the best since they'd left Canterbury. Still, she noticed the slight tremors in his hands and wondered if others would, as well.

Edward awaited them at the foot of the staircase, looking handsome and vibrant. It took everything in her power not to fling herself at him and kiss the very life from him. This man continued to stir strong feelings within her. Seeing him, Rosalyne knew she would do anything he asked of her.

Anything.

She only wished he would ask for more. His every kiss set her skin afire. Though she knew it to be wicked since they were not yet husband and wife, Rosalyne still wanted to lie with him. Explore every inch of his bare skin. Rub against him. Satisfy the burning need inside of her.

"Ready to travel to the Palace of Westminster?" Edward asked, his eyes telling Rosalyne how much he loved her. She hoped hers did the same.

Temp snorted. "I never thought I would see this day. Me, Templeton Parry, meeting the Queen of England."

Edward unfolded the cloth in his hands. "I have brought you a present, Temp. This is a short cloak. I had it cut so that you can hide your hands more easily. And since it's not as long or thick as a usual cloak, you shouldn't overheat wearing it inside the palace."

He wrapped it around her uncle. "Very thoughtful of you, Edward," Temp said.

"We can walk to the palace from Sir Harry's. I think you will enjoy getting to see some of the city that way and it's not far away."

They placed Temp between them in order to keep him steady. Less than ten minutes later, they arrived. Temp drew the light brown cloak about him. She was pleased to see that it did as Edward said. By looking at her uncle, no one would be privy to his secret.

The gatekeeper admitted them and Rosalyne couldn't help but admire the architecture outside and the grandeur within once they stepped inside. She had trouble understanding how many people were inside the palace. Servants scurried down hallways and everywhere else, while nobility teemed in groups large and small. She also heard other languages spoken as they passed by and assumed those men acted as foreign ambassadors to England from various countries.

By the time they reached the queen's rooms, Rosalyne felt overwhelmed. She tried to collect her thoughts and stand tall as they entered and went through a series of rooms before reaching a chamber containing close to a dozen women. Some sat sewing. One woman plucked on a lute as another sang softly. Two royal guards, one of whom was Hal, stood nearby.

But it was the queen who drew Rosalyne's eyes.

Anne of Bohemia had arrived in England four years earlier and married the king when she was ten and six. Richard had been a year younger. Though many disliked her upon her arrival, simply because the marriage brought no advantages to England, this young woman had won over the English people with her kindness. She begged for pardons for many who had participated in the peasants' uprising and Anne even fought to save the life of London's former mayor, John Northampton, two years ago, after his arrest.

Rosalyne studied her from across the room and saw the serenity that blanketed Anne. Small in size, she was attractive without being a great beauty.

The queen's gaze met hers. In it, Rosalyne saw immense kindness. No wonder it was rumored that the king truly loved this woman, despite the fact no heirs had arrived since their marriage.

They made their way toward the queen. Rosalyne curtseyed deeply, as Edward and Uncle Temp bowed.

"Master Parry. Lady Rosalyne. 'Tis good, indeed, to meet you," the queen said, her voice lilting, almost musical in tone.

"Likewise, your majesty," Temp replied gallantly. "I look forward to capturing your likeness." He glanced around at all of the ladies-in-waiting who openly stared at them. "This will never do."

"Too many pretty women would distract you, Master Parry?" the queen teased.

Her uncle grew flustered, so Rosalyne smoothly interjected, "My uncle likes to get to know his subject while he sketches him or her, your majesty. He likes their full attention. Having all of your ladies-in-waiting present would disturb his concentration."

Anne nodded. "Then they must go." She motioned to one woman and instructed her to clear the room. Though the woman looked aghast, the queen said, "I will be perfectly fine. Lady Rosalyne will be here." She glanced around. "And I will have Sir Edward to protect me. And Sir Hal may also remain. Now go."

The woman, who obviously served as the head over the others, removed all of the noblewomen and the unfamiliar knight. She was the last one who exited and left reluctantly, after giving Temp a disapproving look.

Now the room only contained the five of them.

"I assume Sir Hal is aware of the unusual circumstances since you are brothers," the queen began.

"He is, your highness," Edward replied.

She looked to Hal. "Then stand guard at the door, Sir Hal. Admit no one while my portrait session occurs."

"Aye, my queen." Hal retreated to the door, his broad frame blocking the portal.

Anne smiled graciously. "I am eager to begin. Tell me what to do. Am I to sit a certain way? Do you like what I wear, or should I change my gown?"

"You only need to sit and converse, your majesty," Rosalyne shared. "A large part of creating a portrait is simply speaking to a subject. Today, we will only talk. Both Uncle Temp and I will draw various sketches of you while we converse."

"No painting will occur?" the queen asked, her disappointment obvious.

"Nay. And when it does, 'twill occur away from you. Uncle and I always work from our sketches. It is much easier to grind our pigments and prepare our paints and have them close at hand. Light is also very important and your rooms are too dark to be conducive to painting."

Anne relaxed. "Then tell me about this process, Lady Rosalyne. I agree for you to draw me as we speak."

Rosalyne engaged the queen in conversation about what the process involved, explaining to her much as she had Edward about how she prepared the wood and mixed the paints. The queen asked intelligent questions and seemed truly interested. Then Rosalyne began to ask the queen about her life as a young girl in Bohemia before she came to England, wanting to know more of her personality and the qualities she possessed.

"My family is quite large. I have four brothers and a younger sister, Margaret, but I also have five half-siblings from Father's previous marriages. Upon my father's death, my brother, Sigismund, became the Holy Roman Emperor. It was Sigismund who planned my marriage and our alliance with England."

After they talked about the queen's family and her childhood, Rosalyne encouraged her to speak of the king. She noted how Anne's face softened and her eyes went dreamy while she discussed her husband. It touched Rosalyne how this political marriage arranged between heads of state had become a great love match.

Two hours later, she knew she had everything needed. Rosalyne had sketches of the queen from every direction and with a smattering of emotions on her face. She could not wait to paint this animated, cultured woman.

THE PAST WEEK had both sped by and seemed like an eternity. Rosalyne knew some of the hours dragged because of Edward's absence. He had gone to Canterbury with three officials from the royal treasury after the men had drawn up documents for Lord Botulf to sign. Edward had told her how the king thought he was clever in making the arrangement with Botulf but that Richard demanded two more years of payment than Botulf had bargained for. Rosalyne hoped the nobleman would agree to the change and not dispute it so that Edward could return to her sooner.

Having him gone the past seven days was as if she had lost the very hand she painted with. Life would be unbearable if she could not paint. Missing Edward was like missing that hand. She would have no purpose otherwise.

Yet, when she wasn't pining for the man she loved, her art filled the empty hours. Rosalyne had continued to sketch the queen from different angles, trying out different expressions that she had seen flit across Anne's face. Once she decided on her course of action, Rosalyne had prepared not one, but two pieces of poplar. Creating two portraits might be risky but her heart led her to do so and Rosalyne had learned to trust her artistic instincts over the years.

Preparing the wood took a full day. Fortunately, Edward had already cut, shaped, and sanded several pieces for her before they left Canterbury. He told her it would be his small contribution to the royal portraits. It also allowed them to leave behind the saws and planes and not have to explain to anyone why Uncle Temp wasn't shaping the wood that he would use.

After multiple layers of gesso coated the wood until it gleamed to perfection, Rosalyne had begun. Fortunately, Sir Harry had a room at the top of his house that had a large window. She set up her wood and paints there and opened the window every day to bring in as much natural light as possible. Her uncle accompanied her each day to keep up the ruse and everyone from servants to Sir Harry had been banned from entering and disturbing their work. Rosalyne could tell curiosity ate away at Sir Harry but she tried to stave it off as best as possible by telling him that his portrait would be next. He seemed mollified by that and had respected their privacy.

She stepped back and glanced from the portrait on the left to the one on the right and found both pleased her in very different ways.

"Come tell me what you think, Uncle."

Temp rose from his chair in the corner of the room and came to stand next to her. He hadn't seen her work till now. She stared straight ahead, afraid to witness his reaction.

When the silence drew out, Rosalyne finally looked at him. Tears streamed down his cheeks. She threw her arms around him, relief filling her.

He drew her back and smiled. "This is your best work, my dear. Far and above anything you have ever produced." His eyes cut from one portrait to the other. "I cannot say which one I prefer."

"I was hesitant on what I should do but somehow I believed both versions needed to be painted."

"You were right."

A knock at the door sounded. Rosalyne rushed over to answer it. She opened the door and found Sir Harry on the other side.

"I know I am to give Temp his privacy but I was hoping he might be finished for the day. This is usually the time he stops."

"He just completed work," Rosalyne assured the nobleman. "The portrait is done."

Sir Harry's eyes lit up. "May I see it?"

"Nay," Temp called out. "The queen should be the first to do so."

"But I may never see it," Harry complained.

"Then I will make it up to you, my lord."

Rosalyne suppressed a smile. Her uncle and Sir Harry had become thick as thieves since they had been in London.

"You may start now," Harry replied. "My daughter has asked us to dine with her. She is excited to meet the man who is the talk of London."

"I am?" Temp asked, a perplexed look on his face.

The nobleman chuckled. "Everyone is curious about the man who is painting the queen's portrait."

His words caused Rosalyne's stomach to twist.

"You, too, are invited, Lady Rosalyne."

"Thank you, my lord, but I must graciously decline." She waved a hand about. "I have brushes to clean and paints to dispose of. And I find I am tired and would like to get some rest."

Sir Harry inclined his head to her. "As you wish, my lady." He looked to Temp. "Will you accompany me to dinner, my friend?"

"I would be delighted. Let me wash my hands and change my clothes. I wouldn't want to come to your daughter's table with paint staining me." He grinned at her. Having him wear a tunic smeared with paint furthered their story.

"Remember your cloak, Uncle," Rosalyne gently reminded, wanting him to keep his hands out of sight as much as possible.

"Of course."

The two men left. She cleaned the brushes and then went to the open window. Looking at the sun's position, she assumed it to be near six in the evening. As she glanced down at the street below full of people moving, she caught sight of a couple. The man's arm rested snuggly against the woman's waist. It made her long for Edward's return.

She didn't know how much time passed as she stood watching the scene but something changed in the room behind her. The air became charged. Then a familiar scent surrounded her. Before Rosalyne could turn, Edward's strong arms snaked around her, yanking her into his muscled chest. His left arm held her snug against him as his right hand slipped up to caress her breast.

Rosalyne sighed in contentment as the familiar tingling enveloped her. His lips brushed along the nape of her neck.

"Sweet Jesu, I have missed you," he said hoarsely, his thumb now lazily circling her nipple.

"Not a tenth as much as I have longed for your touch. For your kiss."

Suddenly, he spun her about. "You missed my kiss?"

"More than words can say," Rosalyne told him.

"Not a minute passed since we parted that I did not wish to be with you, my love."

Edward sought her mouth but before his lips touched hers, Rosalyne placed two fingers against them.

"I want more than your kiss, Edward," she said huskily.

"More?" he echoed, frowning.

"I want—no, I need—all of you. I want you here, now, inside me," she demanded.

"But sweetheart—"

"Do you love me?" she asked.

"More than life itself," he replied.

"Then show me, Edward. Show me how to love you. What to do. Make me yours, now and forever."

CHAPTER 20

Rosalyne took Edward's hand and led him from the sunny room. They encountered no servants as they descended the staircase to the next floor and went to her bedchamber.

She opened the door and pulled him inside, her heart beating wildly as she closed the door and latched it so no one else could enter. Turning to face him, she took his other hand.

He laced his fingers through hers, wordlessly gazing at her. Rosalyne knew he searched inside her heart and hoped her face told him what he needed to know.

"You are the most beautiful woman who walks this earth, Rosalyne. I feel blessed by the angels above to have earned your trust." He squeezed her hands gently. "What we do now, I do not take lightly. Know that I am committed to you, heart and soul. Today. Tomorrow. For all eternity."

With that, he drew her to him and kissed her deeply.

Time stood still as they drank in one another. One kiss blended into the next until Rosalyne found herself dizzy. Just when she thought her legs would no longer hold her up, Edward swept her off her feet and carried her to the bed. Drawing the curtain aside, he lowered her to the mattress, his mouth still on hers. She entwined her arms around his neck and pulled him closer. He responded by stretching out beside her.

Rosalyne turned to her side so they now faced one another. She stroked his cheek, almost moved to tears by the love she saw shining in his eyes.

"I love you," she said. "I need you."

"I am here, my sweetest Rosalyne, ready to love and be loved by you."

Edward kissed her and then rose from the bed. Before she could protest, he slowly began undressing. Bit by bit, he removed every stitch of clothing till he stood before her in naked magnificence. His shoulders seemed broader. His legs and arms longer.

And she was fascinated by his member, which stood at attention.

He caught her looking at it. "This is for you, sweetheart," he said. "You move me in ways I cannot begin to express."

"I want to touch you," she said. "I want to touch . . . it."

He settled next to her, his bare skin feverish to her touch. Rosalyne ran her hands across his chest, playing with the fine, dark hair, smoothing it down. The more she played with it, the larger his member grew. Finally, she skimmed her hand down his flat belly and reached out for his manhood.

It surprised her how smooth it was, especially the head. She gripped it and began to stroke it. A low moan escaped his lips, causing her to smile.

"You like that?" she asked innocently.

Edward gritted his teeth. "Aye. I like it fine."

Suddenly, Rosalyne knew she needed her skin against his. She began tossing her clothing aside. Edward joined in and quickly helped her shed the layers she wore. Once gone, she snuggled against him, rubbing her breasts against his chest as they nestled together. His hand cupped her buttocks as he lowered his mouth and took her breast into it.

Instant heat filled her. Her hands grasped his shoulders, the nails digging in, as he feasted on her with tongue and teeth. Need undulated inside her. She pushed against him and threw one leg over him, using it to pull him even closer.

His fingers parted her as before. Already, her body knew them and hungered for his intimate touch. As he kissed her mouth, his fingers kissed her insides, the strokes building something deeply within her.

Then an explosion occurred and Rosalyne rode against his hand as wild currents zipped through her, the frenzy reeling out of control as she almost shouted into his mouth. It finally began to subside.

Edward withdrew his fingers and whispered, "You are ready for me."

Before she could reply, he nudged her onto her back and hovered over her as he slipped his manhood against her. With one thrust, he plunged inside.

His mouth covered hers, muffling the shriek that erupted from the sudden pain. Rosalyne lay there confused, wondering why he had hurt her.

But he did not move. She now felt him filling her, stretching her, yet the pain had passed. He kissed her softly a few times and then said, "It will never hurt again, my love. I had to breach your maidenhead. Only pleasure will happen between us from now on. Trust me."

She did—and what happened next was nothing she could have imagined. Rosalyne swore she was flying, Edward by her side, as they came together in a dizzying array of physical pleasure. Both reached a peak of pleasure at the same moment, shuddering in unison, their mouths and bodies melded together as one.

Edward collapsed atop her, driving her into the mattress. Rosalyne welcomed his weight, bringing her legs around him and keeping him tightly against her. Their sweat-slickened bodies now knew one another as intimately as a man and woman could.

Then he rolled, bringing her with him, until she was on top. She finally broke their kiss and smiled at him. This man was hers. Hers alone, for all time.

"You are a gift to me, Rosalyne. I promise to cherish you always."

"Even when my hair turns to gray?" she teased, tracing his brows with her thumbs.

"Aye. For it will have done that from the many sons and daughters you give me. Mother says giving birth is the easy part. It is raising children that she claims puts the gray into a woman's hair."

She ran her fingers through his hair. "Your mother sounds like a very wise woman."

He smiled. "She has to be to manage my father, six children, and all of Kinwick. Most people give Father the credit for how well Kinwick is run but he says Mother is the power behind it all."

Rosalyne kissed him. "Then your father sounds as wise as your mother. I look forward to the day I can meet them."

Edward smoothed a stray curl from her face. "You will need to do so as my wedded wife," he informed her. "I had thought we might wait and marry at Kinwick but now we will need to make our vows in London."

"Why?" she asked. "Your parents will be disappointed if they cannot be with us to celebrate that day."

"But you could be with child, my love. Because of that, I plan to wed you tomorrow."

EDWARD KNEW THAT he had to arrange his marriage to Rosalyne immediately. He did not regret making her his last night. Nothing he had ever experienced could compare to making love to the woman who had become everything to him. To think she would soon spend every night in his bed thrilled him.

But that couldn't occur in the barracks where the king's guard slept.

Mayhap, the queen would be willing to help them. Already, she had been amenable to his suggestion of having Rosalyne paint her portrait. He had confided in her, a woman he'd never spoken with, not only about Rosalyne's talents as a painter but how great his love was for her. Knowing the queen was a romantic at heart, Edward had risked all—and so far, it had paid off.

Rosalyne wanted to bring the two portraits to the palace today. If they pleased Queen Anne, then she might be more willing to help them find a way to wed quickly and allow him to return to Kinwick with his bride.

"Let me drape the cloth," Rosalyne instructed.

She fussed with covering the first portrait and then did the same with the second one. Edward wanted to carry both at the same time but she insisted on him bringing them down to the cart separately. Temp guarded the first picture placed in the wagon's bed and gave Edward a wink as Rosalyne ordered him back upstairs to claim the second one. He could tell how nervous she was and stopped her as she wrung her hands absently in front of her.

"The queen will be pleased with your work." He kissed her, hoping it would bring her some reassurance.

"Do you really think so?"

"How could she not? You have done justice to her, Rosalyne."

Edward foisted the second painting from where it stood and carried it down to the cart before helping Temp and Rosalyne up onto the bench. She took the reins in hand and they set off for the palace.

Since he had sent word ahead, Hal awaited them and helped carry one of the pieces of wood while Edward brought the other. He warned his brother how nervous Rosalyne was and that she shouldn't be teased. Besides, Edward did not want anyone in the palace overhearing that she was the true artist and not Temp.

For once, Hal behaved himself and they arrived at the queen's rooms without incident. The soldiers on guard admitted the four of them and they brought the portraits to where the queen sat embroidering a handkerchief. She smiled as they entered and put her sewing aside. Her ladies-in-waiting tittered behind hands drawn to their faces, whispering about what they would soon see.

The queen addressed her uncle. "I was surprised when Sir Hal told me that he received word that you would come today, Master Parry. You seemed to have worked rather quickly on such an important project."

"You were a delightful subject to paint, your majesty," Temp said graciously. "My hand was inspired by your beauty. The piece almost painted itself."

She frowned. "I see two objects draped. What is the second one?"

Rosalyne spoke up. "My uncle found that you were a true inspiration, your grace. He has chosen to paint not one but two portraits of you, in varying fashions."

Her statement caused the gathered ladies to begin frantically whispering amongst themselves but with one look, the queen silenced them.

"Show me what you have," Anne ordered.

Rosalyne nodded to Hal. He stepped forward with his wood. She stood on her tiptoes and removed the cloth before stepping aside. While all eyes flew to the painting, she watched the queen.

A pleased smile crossed the royal's face as her eyes moved up and down and from side to side as she examined it. Rosalyne made sure the more traditional portrait had been revealed first and it made her happy that the queen seemed to like it.

For a moment, Anne's eyes flicked to hers in recognition before she turned toward Temp.

"Master Parry, you are quite the talented artist. 'Tis hard for me to imagine how you worked such wonders, for I am not nearly as attractive and regal as you have made me seem."

"But this is how I do see you, your majesty," Temp replied. "And others, as well."

"Come, ladies. See what you think."

Since the queen now gave them permission, the women who served her came forward, walking around so they could view the exposed portrait. Rosalyne saw their nods and smiles and, for a moment, she relaxed.

But the queen still had one more painting to view.

"The other now, Sir Edward," Anne commanded.

Once again, Rosalyne removed the draped cloth that protected the portrait. This time, she forced herself to view the queen's reaction instead of cowardly looking away.

"Oh!" the queen exclaimed, her eyes widening. Then a brilliant smile touched her face, lighting it up. "I've never seen anything like it."

Rosalyne had decided to paint Anne in an unconventional setting. Instead of standing or being seated in a chair, she placed the queen outdoors under a summer sky, as if she'd been touring her gardens and taken a moment to rest. Instead of sitting straight and tall, she leaned to one side, a hand flat on the bench supporting her. A large tree trunk stood behind her, with green grass and a sea of flowers scattered at her feet. Where the formal portrait had Anne in royal purple, this one showed her in a cotehardie of softest pink, a flattering hue next to her milky white skin and the roses that bloomed in her cheeks.

The ladies-in-waiting exclaimed over it, finally applauding as everyone turned to her uncle. Hal caught Rosalyne's eye and inclined his head to her in a show of respect.

"I think the king will want to see these right away," Anne exclaimed. "And I would like privacy in which to share them with him."

Her chief lady-in-waiting herded the women into the next room. Hal volunteered to summon the king to the queen's rooms.

That left Rosalyne, Edward, and Temp alone with the queen.

Once the door firmly closed, the queen said, "Lady Rosalyne, this is remarkable work."

"Thank you for the compliment, your highness. I thoroughly enjoyed painting you."

"I will be certain you and your uncle are richly compensated. I am curious, though. Why did you decide to depict two versions?"

"I knew the usual type of portrait would be expected, your majesty, but I saw something wonderful in you. Something that could not be captured without breaking the bonds of convention."

"Your talent is astounding. Sir Edward had wanted me to encourage the king to have his own portrait done by you. I feel he will come up with the idea on his own without my having to suggest it. I wish I could do more."

"You can, your highness," Edward proclaimed. "First, when you reveal to him at the appropriate time that Rosalyne is the true artist."

Anne smiled cordially. "That I can do. What else?"

He swallowed and Rosalyne saw that Edward was nervous. She wondered why.

"I told you that I am in love with Lady Rosalyne," he began. He glanced in her direction for support before turning back to the queen. "I already have her uncle's permission to wed her. I wanted to bring her to my parents' home and marry at our chapel at Kinwick."

"Something tells me that you are too much in love to wait," Anne suggested.

A blush stained Edward's cheeks. "I am. I would wed Lady Rosalyne today if it could be arranged."

"Then let that be my gift to you both," the queen said generously. "Once the king has seen Lady Rosalyne's work, I will see that it is done."

Edward dropped to one knee before her and boldly took her hand. He pressed a fervent kiss to her fingers. "Thank you, your grace. Thank you."

"You are most welcome, Sir Edward."

He rose and returned to Rosalyne's side. His hand sought hers and clasped it for a moment before releasing it.

"I know when you left Canterbury you probably did not expect to marry in London, Lady Rosalyne," the queen said.

"Nay, your majesty."

"I thought so. We are of a similar size, are we not? I think I have something that you might like to wear to your wedding this afternoon. Would that be agreeable to you?"

Rosalyne swayed. Edward caught her about the waist.

"That would be most agreeable, your majesty," she managed to get out before she heard footsteps approaching.

A moment later, the king entered, followed by several courtiers and Hal. He glanced around the room, taking in who was present before he went to his wife and pressed a kiss against her brow.

"I hear you are eager for me to see what Master Parry has accomplished."

Anne waved a hand to where the portraits rested now, propped against the wall.

Richard walked to them and stood silently, his head moving from one and back to the other as he mulled over them. Rosalyne tensed, afraid of his reaction. He turned and went straight to her uncle.

Placing both hands on Temp's shoulders, the king said, "You are a master at what you do. A genius to think to paint my beloved queen in two very different lights. I insist that you paint my portrait, as well, Master Parry. And all of my close friends at court."

Rosalyne let out the breath of air she held, basking in the king's words, though they weren't directed to her.

Much to her surprise, the queen said, "Your friends need to give us some privacy, your majesty. I wish to speak about your portrait with you—and the artist."

Richard gave her a fond smile and turned to the group of men who had accompanied him. "Go find something to do. I need to devote time to my queen."

The courtiers shuffled from the room. Hal closed the door behind them. Rosalyne wondered what Anne wanted to discuss as she rose and went to stand next to her husband.

"You truly like my portraits?" she asked, placing a hand on his forearm.

"They are almost as wonderful as you, dearest," he replied. "Master Parry has captured the essence of your beauty and goodness in a way like none other."

"Then I wish for you to meet the true artist, your majesty." The queen held out her hand. "Lady Rosalyne Parry created both paintings for you."

Rosalyne head grew light as the king's eyes bore into hers, then darkness swallowed her up.

CHAPTER 21

Edward scooped Rosalyne into his arms before she crumpled to the ground.

"Follow me," the queen commanded.

He did as she asked without question. They passed through two more rooms before arriving at the royal bedchamber.

"Place her on my bed, Sir Edward."

He hesitated.

"Now," Anne said firmly.

Edward lay Rosalyne on the bed and sat beside her, gathering her cold hands in his. He heard feet shuffling behind him and assumed the others present had followed.

"You frightened poor Lady Rosalyne," the queen chided her husband.

"I did not," the king said, sounding put out.

"I have seen that cold stare when you have turned it upon others," the queen said. "'Tis most effective when dealing with your troublesome advisers or asserting yourself with a foreign ambassador." She paused. "But I take offense to it when used upon someone who has done me a great service. I am quite fond of Lady Rosalyne and captivated with the portraits she did of me."

Edward bit back a smile as the queen continued to scold her husband. No one in England would dare speak to Richard as his wife did.

"My love, I was merely startled that a woman claimed to paint these works."

"She did not claim to do so. She *did* paint them. She also hoped to paint you but I can see you are too stubborn to allow her to do so."

"I cannot believe—"

"That a woman could possess such talent? Or could produce such art?" the queen asked. She sighed. "Master Parry, you tell him."

"It is as the queen says, your highness," Temp admitted. "I raised Rosalyne from the time she was a babe and I taught her all that I learned in Italy. She has surpassed me in what she creates. Recently, she completed a triptych for Canterbury Cathedral but could not claim it as her own work, for no one—least of all Archbishop Courtenay—would have believed her."

Edward glanced sideways at the royal couple and saw the king listened thoughtfully.

Temp lifted his hands from the folds of his cloak and extended them. "Look, sire. See how they tremble." Silence hung in the air. "Once, I thought myself the best painter in all of England but now some malady has struck and causes my hands to shake. For years, Rosalyne prepared my woods and mixed my tempera paints to allow me to concentrate on my subject and how I would capture him or her. Now? She has assumed my place with her brush in hand and exceeds anything I could dream of creating. Do not punish her, your majesty. If anyone is guilty of lies, 'tis I."

"No one will be punished," the queen assured Temp. "Will they?" She looked pointedly at her husband.

"Nay," he agreed. "I was merely surprised when the queen revealed the true painter's identity to me."

"Rosalyne has only wanted to support us financially," Temp continued. "We both thought it best for others to believe I was still the artist." He looked to Edward. "But now that my niece and Sir Edward plan to wed, this gallant knight has offered to take me in. He wants to return to Kinwick, his family's home, where he believes his mother might be able to ease my suffering."

Edward looked the king squarely in the eye. "I would ask to be relieved of my duties in the king's guard, your highness, in order to bring my wife and her uncle to the country. You know Mother's reputation as a great healer. I hope she will be able to help Temp with his pain and prolong his life."

Richard crossed his arms over his chest. "I would hate to lose such a fine knight from my service but I can understand your request and will grant it." He sighed. "But before you go, I wish for Lady Rosalyne to paint my portrait."

Rosalyne stirred on the bed. Edward watched her eyelids flutter a few times before they opened and she took in her surroundings.

"Oh, my!" She tried to sit up.

"Stay where you are, Lady Rosalyne," the queen urged. "You don't want to faint again."

"I . . . fainted?" Her cheeks flushed with color.

The king stepped closer to the bed. "You did, my lady. In fear of me, I believe."

Her eyes widened. "Your majesty, I—"

He waved a hand. "Nay. I did frighten you and apologize for doing so. The queen's news that you had painted both of her portraits stunned me." Richard smiled broadly. "But I like them very much, all the same."

"You do?" Rosalyne asked.

"Of course. What loving husband wouldn't want to see his wife portrayed that way? But I must caution you that I only want one portrait from you and I need to look regal and commanding in it. As a king must."

"I can do that, your highness. I will need to spend some time speaking with you. As I do so, I will sketch you from several angles. Only then will I return and work on your portrait, away from court."

Richard brightened. "So, I do not have to stay frozen for hours upon hours while you paint me?" He laughed heartily. "I already approve of this, my lady. And of you."

"Mayhap, the king would like to attend your wedding," Anne interjected. Her words got her husband's attention. "I have promised Sir Edward and Lady Rosalyne that I would arrange for them to wed this afternoon. Saint Margaret's Church is next to the palace. I believe they would be happy to accommodate us on short notice."

Richard brushed his lips against his wife's temple. "If you wish, we will go witness this ceremony, my queen."

"Then I have much to do between now and then," Anne said. "Sir Hal? Call for my ladies-in-waiting to return, then you and Sir Edward go to Saint Margaret's and speak to a priest there about performing the ceremony. Mid-afternoon will be convenient. Lady Rosalyne will prepare herself here and see the two of you at the church's door in a few hours."

Temp said, "I will find Benedict Bowyar and bring him and Sir Harry to the church to act as your witnesses."

Edward saw how his words pleased Rosalyne.

"What are you men waiting for?" The queen stamped her foot. "Go. Now."

Edward leaned in to claim a quick kiss from his bride-to-be before exiting the room. "Till we meet again," he said before he released her hands and left with Hal.

As they made their way along the corridors to the outside, Hal said, "Congratulations, little brother. You have gained a bride and your freedom from Richard's guard all in the same day."

He halted in his tracks. "But . . . I forgot. I wanted to obtain your release, too, Hal." It angered him that he had not thought of his brother and that Hal would be left behind.

His brother shrugged. "Mayhap, I am meant to stay in London with the king and queen," he mused.

"Hal, you yourself told me how the political situation grows more complicated. You need to come with us to Kinwick," Edward protested.

"I should be the least of your concerns, Brother. First, let us arrange for your marriage to take place in a few hours. And we must find Lady Rosalyne a ring. Then I believe a trip to the bath house and a shave and trim should be next. Mother would insist that you look your finest for your bride."

"I will wear the last gypon she made for me so she will be there with me in spirit."

Hal slung an arm around him. "You know she and Father will adore Rosalyne. Temp, too."

Edward grinned. "I know."

ROSALYNE ALLOWED HER husband to escort her through the Palace of Westminster, her hand resting on his arm. It gave her a thrill to think of him as her mate for life.

Yesterday's wedding had flown by. Rosalyne actually remembered very little about it other than both her uncles beamed at her as she spoke her vows with the man she loved. She glanced down at the ring resting on her finger which proclaimed to the world that she belonged to Edward de Montfort.

That outward symbol of their love was for the world to see but what had passed between them last night was for them alone. The queen arranged for Edward's things to be taken to Sir Harry's, where they would stay until the king's portrait had been finished. That way, she and Edward could spend private time together. Rosalyne already longed to return to their bedchamber to learn more about the mysteries of love.

It pleased her beyond measure that both the king and queen had looked on as the priest had Edward and her repeat their pledges to one another so that the marriage was consecrated. Their party, which also included Hal, entered a chapel at Saint Margaret's and sat through the nuptial mass. When they left the church, she stepped out not as Rosalyne Parry or Rosalyne Bowyar but Rosalyne de Montfort.

The queen had also arranged a celebratory feast for them inside a small banqueting room in the palace, though she and the king did not attend. Still, their small group enjoyed the delicious food and wines provided for them. Hal told a few tales about Edward and him that had everyone laughing to the point of tears, while Uncle Temp had spoken about his years with Rosalyne and how he looked forward to the children she and Edward would soon produce.

What moved her most, though, was as they started to depart and Uncle Benedict pulled her aside.

"You are a more beautiful, more perfect version of Lara," he told her. "Both she and your father were soul mates. I can see you and your Edward are the same." He kissed her cheek. "I hope one day you might consider traveling to Shallowheart Castle so you can see the place of your birth and where your parents were together and at their happiest."

Rosalyne had promised that she and Edward would visit but she needed to work on the king's portrait and then go to Kinwick first in order to meet Edward's parents.

They arrived at the king's rooms and gained immediate entrance since they were expected. Rosalyne dipped into the lowest curtsey she could manage in front of the monarch. Edward helped her to rise as she listened to the murmurs from those gathered in the room.

Richard gleefully rubbed his hands together. "What do we need to do, Lady Rosalyne?"

She glanced around, disappointed that the room was filled with well over a dozen courtiers and two servants, along with a few royal guardsmen standing at attention along the wall. Edward had already told her how the king was constantly surrounded by others. The queen had taken unusual liberties by dismissing her ladies-in-waiting while Rosalyne sketched her. She would not fare the same in the king's presence.

"We will simply converse, your majesty," Rosalyne said. "I have brought parchment and charcoal and will draw you as we speak."

"The queen told me not to ask to see your sketches," he said.

"That is correct. No one sketch in particular will be used. Instead, I combine parts of several to create the final portrait."

With her words, the men in the chamber began a low rumbling, conversing among themselves. Rosalyne could tell they seemed both offended and perplexed as to why the king would allow a mere woman to paint his portrait.

"Silence!" the king cried.

Immediately, the only sound in the room was that of breathing.

"Come, Lady Rosalyne," the king said in honeyed tones. "We can sit over here."

He led her to two chairs placed near a window wider than any she had ever seen and seated her before he took the one opposite her.

"My queen tells me that light is important to an artist. Open the window," he instructed, and a servant raced to do his bidding.

Edward had followed them and handed over the satchel containing her supplies. Rosalyne removed the pieces of parchment and set them in her lap. She placed several bits of charcoal along the windowsill and kept one to sketch with. Edward moved away from them and went to stand on the other side of the room.

Rosalyne glanced around and found this was as private as possible. All she needed to do now was draw the king out so that he would reveal to her who he truly was.

"What did you like to do as a small boy, your majesty?" she asked.

The king cocked his head and pursed his lips thoughtfully. "I enjoyed hunting. And fishing. I was raised in Aquitaine, you know."

"I was not aware of that," Rosalyne replied as she moved the charcoal across the first page, capturing the emotions flitting across the monarch's face.

"I was born at the archbishop's palace in Bordeaux, during the feast of Epiphany. Three kings—from Castile, Navarre, and Portugal—attended my birth."

Richard spoke for some time about his early years and his great love for his father, the Black Prince. He grew sad when he recounted memories surrounding his father's and older brother's early deaths and how he was brought to England as the heir to the throne. The king laughed as he recounted stories about his grandfather, the old king, and spoke of his great friends, Suffolk and Oxford.

Rosalyne asked him about his marriage and enjoyed capturing the joy and adoration on his face as he spoke about his queen. He told her they eagerly looked forward to the birth of their future children. After discussing hunting and riding for longer than she thought necessary, she put her charcoal aside and decided to wind down their conversation.

"You have been so thoughtful and expressive, your majesty," she complimented. "I will have a difficult time selecting from all the many wonderful drawings I was able to do of you."

"And you are certain I'm not to see any of them?" he asked, his tone conveying that he hoped she reconsidered her stance.

"Nay. They are for my work ahead and not meant to be seen by anyone except myself." Seeing his obvious disappointment, she added, "But if you like, I will make a gift of them to you once your portrait is completed. That way, you will have something different from the queen and can share those sketches with her."

He rewarded her with a wide smile. "I can agree to that, my lady."

Rosalyne slipped the parchment into the satchel and rose. By then, Edward had crossed the room and stood next to her.

"When can I look forward to seeing my portrait?" the king asked.

"Within the week, your highness. These things cannot be rushed."

"Then I will expect you one week from today," the king said. "Come at midday so you and your new husband can join the queen and me as we dine."

Rosalyne curtseyed once more and then allowed Edward to lead her from the room. All eyes watched her as they left. Her heart pounded viciously, knowing that many of these men wanted—even expected—her to fail.

She would prove every last one of them wrong.

CHAPTER 22

ROSALYNE STEPPED BACK and carefully eyed her work. After studying the king's portrait a few moments, she dipped her brush into the tempera paint again and swept a few more strokes onto the wood.

"Perfect," she said aloud, a satisfied smile crossing her lips.

The past week had passed quickly. Edward spent his days finishing up his commitment to the royal guard, returning each night to Sir Harry's—and their bed.

Rosalyne learned several ways in which she could please her husband. He, in turn, had pleasured her beyond her wildest dreams. It still amazed her how much a simple, tender touch could move her. Every day, she fell more deeply in love with her handsome, thoughtful husband.

Now that King Richard's portrait was completed in the time he had requested, they could take it to the palace tomorrow and finally leave London behind. She thought the country air would be better for Uncle Temp and hoped Lady Merryn's array of herbs would be able to help his hands and balance.

Her only regret would be leaving Uncle Benedict behind. They had met daily since her wedding. Rosalyne would paint most of the day and her uncle would arrive to see what she had accomplished. Afterward, they would wander the streets of London for an hour, getting to know one another, before returning to Sir Harry's.

Learning about her parents brought deep satisfaction to her. Uncle Benedict told stories of her grandparents and her father as a boy. The two brothers had fostered together and Rosalyne learned more about that custom.

But most of all, she treasured the stories about her mother. Having grown up without a mother, she had longed for female companionship. Uncle Benedict had loved her mother so much and what he shared with Rosalyne about Lara Parry made her feel as though she understood herself better now, knowing more about the woman who gave birth to her.

A knock sounded at the door and Rosalyne went to answer it.

"Am I too early?" Uncle Benedict asked. "I don't wish to interrupt your time to work."

"Nay, Uncle. Come in. I am pleased to tell you that I have finished."

His eyes lit up. "May I see it?"

"Of course."

Normally, she and Uncle Temp never shared their art with anyone who was not the subject of the portrait. But this man was part of her family. She enjoyed seeing his reactions and asking his opinion.

"Simply outstanding, Rosalyne," declared Uncle Benedict. "I see the king when I am at court, so I am familiar with his looks. You have captured his dignity and strong presence yet at the same time you have given him an approachable air. He is definitely portrayed as a man meant to rule but there is a remarkably human aspect to him."

"He warned me that I must make him appear regal, probably because he is still so young. I hope he will not be upset that I also included vulnerability since I did see some in him when we spoke."

"King Richard will be astounded. So will the queen." He paused. "I am eager for you to work on painting me someday."

Rosalyne had promised to paint her uncle when she and Edward visited him at Shallowheart in the future.

"I also look forward to that—and seeing the place of my birth."

"I hope it will be soon," Benedict said. "From what your husband tells me, Shallowheart is but a day and a half's ride west from Kinwick. You know, I actually met Lord Geoffrey and Lady Merryn here at court, though I have never been a guest at their estate."

"Truly?" Her uncle had not reveled this in any of their previous conversations. "What are they like?"

"Sir Edward is much like his father. He has Lord Geoffrey's height and build. I have noticed his hair appears dark till he stands in the light and it becomes a burnished red. That comes from his mother, who has long, thick, chestnut hair that many women envy. I would say the de Montforts are very kind people. Both are intelligent and well thought of by others. I know the old king favored them and made several visits to Kinwick during his summer progress over the years."

"Aye, Edward told me a bit about that. He said his parents named him in honor of their friendship with the old king."

She brushed a lock of hair from her cheek. "Would you like to go for our late afternoon stroll? I could use some air and would enjoy stretching my legs."

He offered her his arm. "Lead the way, Niece."

They left Sir Harry's house and walked slowly through the streets, reaching a local market where goods and food were peddled. Uncle Benedict had learned of her sweet tooth and bought her a sweetmeat as a treat. She thanked him for it and said she would always think of him when she ate one.

"I saw Sir Harry when I arrived today. He asked me to dine with you tonight. Harry favors pike, so I told him I would purchase some while we were out."

Benedict led her to a stall and said, "The fishmongers' guild was one of the earliest guilds established in London. They have existed in the city for over a hundred years. Thanks to the guild, prices and sales are watched carefully to ensure freshness and quality."

It amazed her how much her uncle seemed to know about many topics.

While Uncle Benedict looked at the fish on display, Rosalyne glanced around and saw a booth that sold spices. She thought she might bring a gift to Lady Merryn and touched her uncle's sleeve.

"I want to look at the spices for sale to take some to Kinwick."

He nodded and she wandered over, seeing the woman had everything available from cloves and pepper to mace and cinnamon. She would need to see if Uncle Benedict would buy some for her and have Edward reimburse him tonight.

Someone brushed against her. Rosalyne glanced to her right and saw a man with a dirty cloth wrapped around his head, dipping low to hide one eye and his cheek. It bothered her that he stood so close and made no effort to take a step away. Since his presence made her uncomfortable, she decided to make her way back to Uncle Benedict.

As she turned to leave, an arm suddenly went about her and something sharp pressed into her waist.

"Walk with me, my lady, else you'll have a hole in your side."

Rosalyne chastised herself for being so careless. Edward had warned her to be wary of cutpurses that stalked the London streets.

"I have no coin on me," she informed him, hoping he would release her.

"Move," he ordered, his voice low so others would not hear. "Do not speak."

"I could give you my wedding ring," she offered, naming the only thing of value that she wore. Though Rosalyne would hate to part with it, she would rather lose the ring than her life.

"I said *move*." The thief's fingers dug into her, while the blade pricked her side. "And don't call out, or you and your uncle will be dead."

The man nudged the blade against her again. Rosalyne knew that if she screamed or brought any attention to herself, he would make good on his threat and shove the dagger into her. She would be dead before she hit the ground.

Reluctantly, she began walking, allowing him to guide her through the crowds. With each step away from Uncle Benedict, fear multiplied within her. She hoped this man would be satisfied to take her ring and set her free without further harm.

The robber led her down a narrow alleyway. Rosalyne heard the sounds of a wailing babe as rats scurried in front of them. She would meekly submit while he held the weapon against her side and wait till he lowered it to make her escape. As they shuffled along, she looked around for anything she could use to grab and strike him.

They arrived at a doorway. He opened the door and roughly shoved her inside the dark abode. Rosalyne fell on her hands and knees. A dreadful stench made her gag as she pushed herself from the floor.

Then pain coupled with a wave of dizziness forced her back onto all fours as the man struck her. The back of her head felt split in two. Vaguely, she was aware of being dragged along the floor and propped against a wall.

She must have passed out, for when she awakened, she couldn't move her hands. Glancing down brought a sharp wave of pain, so she raised her head and leaned it against the wall. The hard wall hurt the tender spot on her scalp but having her head upright again lessened the ache.

Rosalyne pulled on her hands and found her wrists bound tightly together with rope. Her legs, stretched out in front of her, were also shackled at the ankles. Cold sweat broke out along her hairline. She glanced around the shadows falling about the room and saw the stranger lurking, watching her.

"What do you want?" she asked warily.

He lit a candle and came closer to her. She placed his age at a few years shy of two score. His scraggly hair fell into his uncovered eye, which stared at her in hate.

"What do I want?" he growled. "I want my life back, Lady Rosalyne."

So he knew her. This had been no random robbery.

"Are you from Canterbury?" she asked, hoping to discover who this man was and why he had taken her.

"Am I from Canterbury?" He laughed harshly then glared at her. "I used to *own* Canterbury," he roared.

Without being told, Rosalyne guessed who the stranger before her was.

"You are Perceval Rawlin."

Astonishment crossed his face. "You know me?"

"I know of you. That you worked for Lord Botulf on the reconstruction of the wall surrounding the city. That you cheated the Crown, keeping ill-gotten gains for yourself and awarding half to Lord Botulf."

He crossed his arms over his thick chest. "And what if I did? I came from nothing and had to fight for everything I got."

"Whether you earned it or not."

He slapped her.

Rosalyne felt the sting of his hand printed against her face.

"I had to be cunning," he said. "I wanted to keep it all for myself, but Lord Botulf was too wily. When he discovered what I did, he demanded that I keep doing it—only if he could share in the enormous profits."

Rawlin rubbed his chin. "And then I lost everything, thanks to your husband."

Fear knotted in her belly. "Taking me is about revenge?" she asked.

"What do you think?" he asked. Slowly, he unwound the cloth from his head. Dropping the fabric to the floor, he raised his head and stared at her.

She gasped.

As Rosalyne suspected, he was missing one eye. The side of his face was still raw, with angry new scars laced into it.

"Why didn't Sir Edward come to me first?" Rawlin mused. "But he didn't. He and Botulf cut a deal between them, dooming me."

"You make it sound personal. Edward represented the king. He arranged for Lord Botulf to pay for ten years of the wall's construction from his own funds. If the nobleman took out his anger on you, it wasn't at my husband's request."

His face came within inches of hers, his breath hot and fetid. "Lord Botulf tortured me," Rawlin ground out. "By the end, he knew where every pence I had lay. He took my home. My furnishings. My lands.

My gold. I was left with nothing but a ruined reputation."

Rawlin stroked his chin again. "He took my eye. Ripped it from its socket. Shoved a poker into the hole. But that wasn't enough for the rich bastard, to steal from me. While I screamed, he watched his men cut off my very manhood. Then his soldiers dragged me outside the city gates and left me to die."

Rosalyne thought she might be sick. Though this man had done an immense wrong, he should have been imprisoned for his crimes, not cruelly tortured and maimed. And she guessed the money Lord Botulf took would be what paid for all of the construction, keeping his own funds intact.

An evil smile turned the corners of Rawlin's mouth upward. "Before he ordered me from his sight, Botulf assured me none of it would have happened if he hadn't needed everything I owned to pay for the wall. He named Edward de Montfort as the cause, Lady Rosalyne, and told me if I wanted to hurt Sir Edward as I had been hurt, the best way to do it was through you."

CHAPTER 23

EDWARD STEERED SIRIUS through the streets, his heart light as he returned to Sir Harry's home. He would stable the horse tonight at Harry's and take Rosalyne to the Palace of Westminster tomorrow. She had shown him her progress last night, so he knew they would be able to deliver the royal portrait tomorrow as requested.

And then start their new life away from court.

The only regret he had would be leaving Hal behind. His brother had been a constant in Edward's life since his birth. They had spent almost every day together, from playing as children through years of fostering and then fighting.

Now Rosalyne would be his other half, instead of Hal. Edward looked forward to the life they would share. The children they would raise. The many nights of love play. Rosalyne already was the center of his universe. He could not imagine life without her.

As he drew closer to Sir Harry's house, he suspected he would find his parents had arrived. Edward had written them to announce his marriage to Rosalyne and tell them something about her before they met. He also wanted his mother to know Templeton Parry would accompany them to Kinwick and had described Temp's problems as best he could so that his mother might be able to prepare a mixture of herbs that might help give the older man some relief.

A messenger from Kinwick let Edward know that Lord Geoffrey would send a guard to escort them home. Knowing his parents, they would accompany the knights who came to London to see them safely to their destination.

Riding through the gates, he immediately headed for the stables and dismounted. Once inside, he searched for an empty stall to place Sirius in. Many were full, with a few horses he recognized, so Edward knew the Kinwick contingent had already arrived.

As expected, he rounded a corner and caught sight of Sir Hammond, who had served the de Montforts for many years and was a master swordsman.

"Greetings, Hammond."

"Edward!" the knight called out as he closed a stall door and approached him.

Edward dropped his horse's reins and the two men clapped each other on the back, happy to see one another.

"So, you are a married man now. You're a crafty one, marrying on the sly and denying Lady Merryn a wedding to plan. But I guarantee you will have a great feast upon your return. Your mother has already started the preparations."

"Rosalyne will appreciate her efforts. She is excited about coming to live at Kinwick. My wife is truly an amazing woman. So much that I think Mother will grow to like Rosalyne more than me."

Hammond chuckled. "I hear your bride is an artist."

"Aye," Edward said with pride. "She recently completed a triptych for a chapel inside Canterbury Cathedral and has now painted the king and queen's portraits, as well."

"An artist who paints portraits? And you a mere knight?" Hammond laughed. "Lady Merryn will definitely favor your bride over you." He punched Edward playfully in the arm.

"By any chance, did my parents join the escort party?"

Hammond's brows rose. "You even think to ask that? Of course, they came to London. In fact, you need to go see them now." Hammond reached for Sirius' reins. "Here, I'll care for your spoiled horse." He rubbed Sirius between his ears. "'Tis good to see you again, Edward."

"I feel the same, Hammond."

Edward left the stables and entered Sir Harry's house. Hearing voices in the room to his right, he headed toward them. When he entered, his mother rose and held out her arms. Edward went straight to her, embracing first her and then his father.

Merryn de Montfort studied him. "You have matured since we last saw you, my son. I worried about you being at the palace but I believe the time away from Kinwick did you some good."

"Of course, it did," Geoffrey de Montfort declared, "for it led our son to Lady Rosalyne. And love."

"And love," Edward echoed.

"We feel we already know your bride." His mother indicated Sir Harry and Temp. "These two have sung her praises ever since we arrived." She paused. "I hope Rosalyne will allow us to view her work on the king's portrait before you take it to him tomorrow."

"I think she will," Edward replied and frowned. "I thought she would already be back by the time I arrived."

"I explained to your parents how she and Benedict walk together every day," Temp said. "They also know something of Rosalyne's history and why Benedict wishes to know her."

"Bowyar has asked us to visit him at Shallowheart," Edward said.

"I think seeing where Rosalyne came from will be important to her," his mother said.

"Once you are settled in at Kinwick and Rosalyne is comfortable, you should take her to visit her former home," his father interjected. "It's not far from Kinwick, so you wouldn't be on the road for long."

"I will," Edward promised.

A sudden commotion in the hall halted their conversation. A man shouted *"Rosalyne"* several times and then burst into the room.

Edward took in Benedict Bowyar's frantic look and disheveled appearance. He grasped the nobleman by his shoulders and demanded, "Where is Rosalyne?"

Bowyar's eyes clouded with tears. "I lost her. We stopped at the market for me to purchase pike for our dinner tonight. Rosalyne stepped away to a nearby booth to peruse the spices. She wanted to bring some to Lady Merryn as a gift." He looked at Edward with anguished eyes. "One moment, she was there. The next, she had vanished."

Running fingers through his graying hair, Bowyar added, "I have looked for her everywhere but she is nowhere to be found. I fear someone has spirited her away." His shoulders slumped.

"We'll send men out to find her," Edward assured him, fighting his rising panic.

Sir Harry spoke up. "My soldiers know what Lady Rosalyne looks like."

"Then we can pair one of your men with one from Kinwick," Edward suggested. "Send them out in different directions in order to cover more ground."

"I'll see to it," his father said.

"Let me go with you, Lord Geoffrey," Sir Harry offered.

The two men hurried from the room.

Benedict looked to Temp. "Will you search for our niece with me?" he asked, his voice breaking.

Temp nodded and they also removed themselves from the room.

That left Edward alone with his mother. He saw the concern in her eyes but also the core of steel which ran through her. While Geoffrey de Montfort was known as having been one of the best knights of the realm, in truth, it was Merryn de Montfort who was made of even stronger stuff.

"Stay," she told him. "When Rosalyne arrives, she will need you to be here."

Edward noted she said *when* and not *if*.

"I warned her of cutpurses," he began, "but the thought of her being taken off the streets never crossed my mind since she was always with me or Bowyar."

She led him to a chair and sat next to him. "Have you made any enemies at court, Edward?"

The thought hadn't occurred to him. "Why? Do you think someone has deliberately abducted Rosalyne to get back at me?"

Merryn waited a long moment before answering. "It's possible. I have seen it. Been a part of it."

Edward knew something had occurred in the distant past that his parents never spoke of. His cousin Elysande's husband, Michael, hinted at it once long ago. Edward remembered Michael saying something about how he was eager to serve Lord Geoffrey once he heard Geoffrey had returned to Kinwick. The room grew quiet and then conversation had broken out among several small groups. Edward had been young at the time—but old enough to know that something unmentionable was being covered up.

Though he had wondered about it occasionally over the years, he'd never discussed it with anyone. Not even Hal, whom he shared all his thoughts with.

His mother reached for his hand and gripped it tightly. "Long ago, your father did something to anger a powerful earl," she explained. "This nobleman waited until Geoffrey and I married and then had him abducted the day after we spoke our vows."

Shock reverberated through Edward. How had this been kept a secret?

"How long was Father gone?" he asked, afraid to hear the answer.

She closed her eyes. "Almost seven years." The words came out barely above a whisper.

Edward sat, stunned. Then it began to make sense to him. Alys and Ancel were seven years older than Hal. There had only been two years between him and Hal and three between him and his younger sister, Nan. The reason no children came during the large gap of time was because his parents spent all those years separated.

"How? Why?"

She opened her eyes. "It doesn't matter now," she said quickly. "Those years were ones of suffering for both of us. What is important is that we are now together again, our love stronger because of what we went through. But 'twas a wicked man who sought revenge on your father and knew the best way to hurt him was by keeping us apart. When Geoffrey disappeared, I was distraught. I knew not if he was alive or dead until he finally appeared again at Kinwick."

Edward had dozens of questions he wished she would answer but he chose to respect her privacy. Instead, he asked, "And you think something similar occurs now?"

Merryn nodded. "If it were a mere cutpurse, he would have taken any valuable Rosalyne had. He would not have taken *her*."

"I agree." Edward racked his brain. "I have not grown close to anyone at court since I have been here, much less angered anyone. You know me, Mother. I keep to myself and perform my duties as asked. I've caused no problems between anyone in the guard. I rarely speak to any courtiers. I have not been involved with the ladies, as Hal has. But . . ." His voice trailed off.

"What?"

"In Canterbury. I recently returned from there."

She thought a moment. "You found problems there?"

"Aye. The king sent me to observe construction on the wall since it is a long-running project and he and his advisers thought the costs seemed too high. I discovered the Crown losing vast sums of money, being cheated by the nobleman Richard placed in charge. It was carried out by a man named Perceval Rawlin that Lord Botulf hired to oversee the work."

"What was the outcome?" she asked.

"Lord Botulf asked to handle Rawlin himself. I returned to Canterbury after informing the king of the situation, bringing with me several advisers from the royal treasury. Botulf agreed to personally fund every aspect of the wall for the next dozen years and signed the papers affirming his commitment."

Her eyes widened. "That is quite a costly undertaking. 'Twould give him good reason to lash out at you."

"I need to find out if Lord Botulf is in London," Edward said, determined to find the nobleman. "Or go to Canterbury and see if he is there."

And hopefully find Rosalyne, as well.

His father and Sir Harry reentered the room. Edward quickly explained to them the possibility that Lord Botulf might have had something to do with Rosalyne's disappearance. He caught the quick glance between his parents. His gut tightened. He could only pray the punishing years apart they went through would not be repeated between him and Rosalyne.

"Traveling to Canterbury would take precious time," Geoffrey pointed out. "And even if this Lord Botulf is there and you confront him, he could simply deny any involvement in Rosalyne's abduction. Stay in London," his father urged. "You are more valuable here. If you wish, I can send Hammond to Canterbury. He is outside Sir Harry's house, guarding us and keeping a watchful eye as we speak. I know you trust him."

Edward was torn. He had no idea where to look for his wife. He couldn't even say with any certainty that Lord Botulf was behind her disappearance.

"Let go of me!"

He glanced up and saw Hammond entering the room, dragging along a dirty young boy with one hand. In the other, Edward saw a scrap of parchment.

"Quit struggling, lad, or I will squash you like a bug," threatened the knight as he crossed the room to Edward. "The boy tried to leave this note on Sir Harry's doorstep and run away." Hammond handed the parchment to Edward.

"Read it aloud," Merryn encouraged.

Edward cleared his throat and prayed this note would give them a clue as to Rosalyne's whereabouts.

If you value your wyfe, come alone—and unarmed—to Blethin Alley and the door marked with a red X.

Edward knelt and waited until the boy met his eye. "I promise no harm will come to you. What is your name?"

After hesitating a long moment, the boy said, "Timothy."

He glanced to his father. Geoffrey de Montfort nodded. Edward turned back to the too-thin child. "Timothy, do you have parents?" he asked.

A hard look appeared in the boy's eyes, making him suddenly seem years older. "Nay," he said, bitterness laced in the one word.

Edward wondered if the parents had died or worse—if they had abandoned Timothy to live on the streets.

"Would you like to have a home? And a place to work? There would always be plenty to eat and you would make friends."

Timothy eyed him with suspicion. "Where? How?"

"'Tis my childhood home. Kinwick." He pointed. "These are my parents, Lord Geoffrey and Lady Merryn de Montfort. They always need good, strong workers on our estate. Mayhap you would be interested in helping in the stables. Do you like horses?"

The boy nodded reluctantly. Edward saw the glimmer of hope wrestling with doubt in the child's eyes.

"Help me, Timothy. Help us to find my wife. In return, you can come with us to Kinwick."

Timothy's lips trembled. "He gave me a pence to bring the parchment here."

"Who?" Edward asked gently.

Timothy shook his head. "I know not, my lord. He shared half a meat pie with me and then offered me the coin if I would help him."

"Can you describe this man?"

Nodding enthusiastically, Timothy said, "Aye, my lord. He's a fat one. His legs bow out, so he walks funny. And he wraps a cloth about his head. It dips over his eye and hides part of his face."

Edward rose, taming the anger that threatened to explode, so as not to frighten the boy. He would need Timothy's help in finding Blethin Alley.

In finding Rosalyne.

"I know who has taken her," Edward said. "Perceval Rawlin."

CHAPTER 24

ROSALYNE WISHED SHE hadn't screamed for help. All it had done was land her a punch to the face and a filthy cloth tied around her mouth. Now, her eye and cheek ached and the sides of her mouth grew tender from the gag.

But at least Perceval Rawlin was gone.

She had watched him labor over a piece of parchment, assuming he wrote out a ransom demand for her. Rosalyne knew it was common in the wars with France for each side to capture and ransom prisoners. Even King John had been taken by English soldiers after the Battle of Poitiers and held captive in London until the two governments signed the Treaty of Bretigny. France paid a huge ransom and forfeited many territories in exchange for their king's return.

What would Rawlin ask for her?

Obviously, the man no longer had any money or possessions. Would he demand gold for her return? Even if Rawlin did ask for payment from Edward to free her, Rosalyne doubted her husband had enough to buy her release. He might have once served in the king's royal guard but she did not think Richard compensated his knights well, instead offering them the prestige of serving him.

If Edward sent word to his father, would Lord Geoffrey de Montfort be willing to pay a high price to rescue a woman he'd never met? Especially since Edward was not even the heir to Kinwick? The castle and estate would go to his older brother, Ancel, upon Geoffrey's death.

A chill rippled through her.

What if Rawlin did not want money?

Rosalyne recalled how he mentioned hurting Edward. If not wounding Edward financially, did Rawlin mean to do him physical harm? Would he kill her in front of her husband? Or murder them both in his plot for revenge?

Shuddering, Rosalyne knew she must act. She didn't know how long Rawlin would be gone. They had walked a good distance from the market to reach here and Sir Harry's place was even farther away. If Rawlin meant to deliver his missive to Edward at Sir Harry's, then she had some time.

To do what?

Glancing around the small dwelling, the putrid smell continued to assault her nose. She scooted away from the wall, wanting to move to the center of the room to see what was there. Inching her way would take forever with her wrists and ankles bound, so Rosalyne dropped to her side and rolled several rotations until she bumped against something. Wiggling, she sat up and saw she'd reached a broken table. Shards of pottery lay scattered about. A few bones sat on the ground, probably leftovers from a meal.

And then she saw where the smell came from.

A rotting corpse lay curled in the midst of the chaos. The foul smell came from the man who had died here. She wondered if he had been eating when Rawlin overcame him. The man must have fought hard since so much surrounding him had been destroyed. Did Rawlin sneak inside and catch the man while he ate his last meal? Or had Rawlin befriended this poor soul and then killed him?

She guessed her captor had done so in order to have a place to stay in London. Without coin, he would be walking the streets and would have had no place to hold her prisoner. Rosalyne fought the bile that threatened to rush up, afraid she would drown in her own vomit behind the gag. She closed her eyes and swallowed hard, taking deep breaths to try and calm herself.

Gradually, she gained control. The place still reeked of what she now knew was the smell of death but she had a better grasp on her emotions and sense of purpose. Her eyes roamed through the destruction, looking for a way to free herself. The broken shards seemed the best possibility. As she reached for one with her bound hands and lifted it up, her eyes widened.

The man's eating knife lay under it.

Tears sprang to her eyes. Mayhap she could escape before Rawlin ever returned by using this knife to cut through the rope. Just in case, she would return to the spot he left her and work on slicing through her bonds from there. Dropping the fragment of pottery, she picked up the knife carefully with her fingers and flattened them against it before she slowly rolled back to the wall. Once she pushed herself into a sitting position again and leaned against the wall, she ignored the throbbing from the back of her head where Rawlin had struck her and thought how best to use the knife.

Rosalyne slid her feet toward her, raising her knees. She then placed the hilt between her knees so that the blade pointed toward her. Squeezing her knees together in order to hold the knife in place, she placed the rope atop the blade and began pushing her arms back and forth in a sawing motion. She decided she would rather have her hands freed first, in order to strike Rawlin if he came close to her again. She could always lash out and shove her bound feet into him and knock him off balance if she didn't have time to free her legs before he returned.

The work proved tedious because of the rope's thickness. Rosalyne's arms grew tired but she continued to push back and forth, determined not to be used as a pawn in the wicked game Perceval Rawlin wished to play with Edward. She deliberately forced all thoughts of her husband from her mind and concentrated on the task at hand.

Finally, she could tell the rope weakened as she sawed through the various strands. Her excitement grew as she sensed it loosening.

Then she heard movement outside the door. Panic sailed through her, knowing how close she was to freeing herself. Rosalyne grabbed the knife and twisted it, hilt toward her, till it lay against the underside of her forearm. She tilted her hands up and the blade slid up her sleeve.

The door opened and Rawlin called out, "My cousin is improving, thank you. By the Blessed Christ, I will nurse him back to good health." He hurried inside the hovel and shut the door.

Rosalyne's heart drummed loudly. She wondered if she should try and force her wrists apart, hoping the rope was ready to break apart, or if she should wait.

Rawlin made the choice for her, walking over to her in his odd gait. She remained utterly still, trying to slow her breathing after the exertion of working to free herself.

"Your husband is almost here," Rawlin told her. He latched on to her elbow and yanked her to her feet.

Instead of allowing her hands to drop in front of her and the knife possibly falling to the ground, Rosalyne bent her arms at the elbow and raised her restrained hands to her waist, the eating knife now parallel to the ground.

Rawlin snaked an arm about her waist and held her against him as the door crashed open. He raised a blade to her throat and Rosalyne felt the cold steel tip against her bare skin.

Edward entered the dwelling, fury blazing in his eyes. Rosalyne saw he held no weapon and knew Rawlin had instructed that Edward bring none when they met.

"Close the door," barked her captor. "I have a poniard next to your pretty, little wife's throat. Do it!"

Edward shut the door and faced them. He seemed almost within reach to her yet, at the same time, the gulf between them appeared vast.

"Do not harm her, Rawlin," ordered Edward calmly. "Rosalyne is blameless in all of this. It's me you want. Not her. Release her so she can leave. Then we can speak, man to man."

Rawlin snorted. "And have you tear me from limb to limb for even daring to touch her? I think not, my lord. Lady Rosalyne will stay right here, next to me, my knife against her throat."

"For how long then?" Edward demanded. "What do you want?

Gold? Land? More—"

"I want my life back!" shouted Rawlin. "Something that is not in your power to give me."

Rosalyne smelled the fear and desperation on him.

Edward moved toward them and Rawlin growled, "Stay where you are."

Her husband took a step back and dropped to one knee. "I came alone, as you requested." He held his arms wide. "I brought no weapon. I beg of you, man. Let her go."

As Edward spoke, Rawlin moved the blade directly under her earlobe and nudged it into her. She felt the stinging prick, followed by the warm trickle of blood that drizzled down from the tiny wound.

In that moment, Rosalyne decided she would rather die trying to escape this madman's grasp than allow him to torment her husband by causing her pain. She dropped her hands, allowing the eating knife to slide from her sleeve into her palm. Jerking against the rope binding her wrists with all her strength, it came apart. Rosalyne leaned forward slightly and arced her arm holding the knife out, twisting around and slamming her weapon into Rawlin's throat.

The moment the blade pierced his skin, something whizzed by her. Suddenly, a baselard protruded from his one good eye. Both she and Rawlin screamed at the same time.

Strong arms seized her and dragged her away as her abductor swayed and then collapsed to the ground in a heap. Rosalyne closed her eyes and latched on to Edward's waist, burying her face against his chest.

Edward unknotted the gag and pulled the cloth from her mouth. She gazed up at him, his image blurring thanks to the tears filling her eyes. Then his mouth crashed down on hers.

He tasted like freedom. Like love and honor and everything good in life. His kiss promised Rosalyne everything that words never could. It gave her hope. It brought her salvation.

Finally, he broke the kiss and studied her.

"I thought I had lost you," he admitted. "I don't think I could have gone on without you, my love."

"But you didn't," she reassured him. "You came for me. You saved me." She paused, a smile breaking out as she drank him in. "And we will never be parted again."

"Let me free you," he said. Edward released her and walked to Rawlin's still body. He snatched the baselard from the man's eye and strode back to her.

"Hold still," he said. "Unlike you did before." He cut through the rope binding her ankles together and tossed it aside.

"Like before?"

He stroked her hair. "I dropped to one knee to retrieve my blade, which I'd hidden in my boot. I thought if I pleaded with him for your life, I would sound weak and put him off-guard. As I grabbed the baselard and launched the weapon at him, you made your own move against him." He kissed her again, hard and swift. "I thought for a moment that I might have killed you instead. Thank the Blessed Virgin that you are alive."

Edward cupped her cheeks, his thumbs wiping away her tears. "You are quite brave, Rosalyne de Montfort. The bravest woman I know."

She glowed at his compliment. "And I am the luckiest woman in England, for I have you as my husband, Edward de Montfort."

He kissed her tenderly and then said, "I have a few people who would like to meet you."

"Here? Now? Who?"

Edward grinned. "I did not come alone as I said. I had an entire party of people trailing me at a distance. My parents. Sir Hammond, one of their knights. And Timothy also accompanied us. He is the one who led me to you."

She frowned. "Who on earth is Timothy?"

He laughed. "Apparently, the newest stable lad at Kinwick." Smoothing her hair with his large hands, he said, "Mother and Father insisted they accompany me to Blethin Alley. They promised not to enter and endanger your life but I can't keep them waiting any longer."

"And we shouldn't," Rosalyne replied.

Edward wiped the blood from his baselard and slipped it back into his boot before entwining his fingers with hers. He led her to the door and opened it. They stepped outside and found everyone waiting across from the cottage.

Rosalyne found herself being embraced by Lord Geoffrey and Lady Merryn. Then she met Sir Hammond and a dirty child who beamed at her, which she assumed was the mysterious Timothy.

"Thank the Blessed Virgin that you are safe, Rosalyne. We need to get you back to Sir Harry's and let me look at your face," Lady Merryn said. "I have something that will help the swelling. Oh, I cannot believe what you have gone through, my dear." The noblewoman looked upon her with warmth and kindness. "And I cannot wait to have you back at Kinwick. Just think, Geoffrey, we now have another daughter—and our Edward at Kinwick once again."

"Life has been good to us, Merryn." He placed an arm about his wife and looked to his knight. "Hammond, will you take care of things here? Mayhap young Timothy could help you."

"Aye, my lord." The knight frowned down at the boy. "Come along, lad. You can start earning your keep by doing what I say."

"Sir Hammond?" Rosalyne touched his sleeve and the knight halted. "Besides Perceval Rawlin, there is another man inside. I fear Rawlin killed him in order to have a place to hold me hostage. Would it be possible to arrange for his burial?"

"Of course, my lady. I can do that and still be ready for us to leave tomorrow, once you and Sir Edward have delivered the king's portrait to the palace."

"The king!" Rosalyne cried. Sheepishly, she said, "I had forgotten all about him."

CHAPTER 25

ROSALYNE STOOD STILL, her eyes closed, while Merryn gently touched her face.

"I don't believe the king will see anything," her mother-in-law assured her.

"I have you and your poultice to thank for that," she said. "I cannot believe between applying that and drinking the herbs steeped in boiled water, those things could cause the swelling to recede." She paused. "I hope you will be able to work such wonders with Uncle Temp."

"I wish I could. I have observed him since we arrived and we spoke about what ailed him. I know I will be able to help the pain subside in his hands but I will not be able to stop their shaking. Or correct his balance," she added. "Still, I will do for him what I can, I promise you that."

"Thank you," Rosalyne said. "For everything. For allowing Uncle Temp to come live with us at Kinwick. For raising such a remarkable son as Edward."

Merryn smiled. "I am happy you see Edward in such a favorable light. He was always the son I have worried about most."

Her curiosity grew. "How so?"

"Ancel always had a mind of his own and due to circumstances, he grew up quickly and was my little man from a young age, wanting to protect me. Hal, you have met, so you know how charming and gallant he is, and he has never met a stranger.

"But Edward? He is my sweetest boy, always solemn and earnest.

Hard on himself and yet generous to those around him. Of all my children, the girls included, he is the most sensitive. Oh, I don't mean he is weak or delicate. Far from it. Edward is a tremendous warrior and won his knighthood on the battlefield for the bravery that he displayed. But I have always worried that he is more easily affected by things. I knew it would take a unique woman to see how special he is."

"I am confused, my lady. Hal told me much the same, how serious Edward is. I understand he is dedicated to being a knight and knows the importance of his duties. But with me, Edward is jovial and lighthearted. We laugh a great deal when we're together. 'Tis one of but many things that I love about him."

The noblewoman gave her a brilliant smile. "You don't know how pleased I am to hear that, Rosalyne. If Edward laughs with you, then you are most certainly the wife for him. Knowing you have brought out this side of him is almost as important as me hearing that you love my boy."

"I do love him, Lady Merryn. I cannot imagine ever loving any man as I love Edward."

"Please, call me Merryn, for we are family and shouldn't be so formal with one another."

Rosalyne's throat grew thick and she blinked back unshed tears. "We are family now, aren't we," she said softly. "If so, I wish . . . I would so like to . . ." She couldn't go on and turned away.

But Merryn de Montfort was not a woman to be put off. She turned Rosalyne toward her and clasped her hands. "You are my daughter now, Rosalyne. As much as the two I gave birth to and the one I adopted." Merryn looked deeply into Rosalyne's eyes. "I would be most pleased if you choose to call me Mother."

"Could I?"

"Of course."

Rosalyne hugged her tightly. "I always wanted a mother of my own. Uncle Temp did the best he could and I do look upon him as a father but I longed for a mother for so many years."

"And now you have one," Merryn assured her, smoothing

Rosalyne's hair. "It is almost time to go. Let me dress your hair for you."

Rosalyne put herself into her new mother's capable hands and let her brush and twist and plait.

"Would you like to call Geoffrey *Father*?"

She shrugged. "Lord Geoffrey has been most kind to me but . . . well, he is . . ."

"Intimidating?" Merryn suggested.

"Aye."

"That is one of Geoffrey's talents. To be loving and generous and kind to a fault, yet he can slay with a simple glance." She patted Rosalyne's arm. "Then call him Geoffrey for now. That will please him. You can always change your mind later."

"All right."

The two women went downstairs, where Edward already had King Richard's portrait in hand.

"I sent word to the king that Mother and Father and both your uncles will join us in presenting the portrait today."

Rosalyne did not know so many people would be going with them and hoped the king would not be upset. Nerves already shot through her, wondering how he would react when he saw the finished piece. She had confidence in her talent and the work she had done but presenting her art to the king of all of England seemed daunting.

They arrived at the royal palace and headed toward the king's rooms. As they journeyed there, Hal and another knight joined them from a connecting hallway. Rosalyne knew the queen would not be far behind.

Their party slowed and acknowledged her presence when Anne appeared. She greeted them warmly, especially the older de Montfort pair.

"I have not had the pleasure of your company in quite some time, Lord Geoffrey, Lady Merryn. 'Tis very good to see you again. I have enjoyed feeling safe in your son's presence. Sir Hal is certainly a favorite among my ladies-in-waiting."

Lord Geoffrey started to reply but Rosalyne saw his wife's elbow nudge him to remain silent.

"We are delighted that all of our sons have served in the royal guard at one point," Merryn said sweetly. "And I must thank you, your grace, for arranging for Edward and Rosalyne's marriage. It was so thoughtful of you."

"I wanted to do what I could to help their love along," the queen confided. "Being in love with my husband has made me sympathetic to the plight of others."

"I feel the same."

They continued on till they reached the king's rooms, where her uncle, Benedict, joined them.

He kissed her cheek and said, "You look none the worse for your terrible ordeal."

The group shuffled into the king's rooms and was led to a chamber off to the left. The queen entered first and took a seat, while the rest of them stood and awaited her husband's arrival.

Richard swept into the room and went to kiss his wife's cheek. Everyone bowed and curtseyed to him and then waited for him to speak.

His eyes searched the room and stopped when he spied the de Montforts. "I am happy to see you at court, Lord Geoffrey. Lady Merryn. My grandfather was fond of you both and you know the affection I carry for your son, Ancel. He helped me grow from a boy into a man and I will forever remain in Sir Ancel's debt."

"We are delighted to be in your presence, your majesty," Lord Geoffrey said.

Richard's gaze then landed upon Edward. "I see my portrait awaits its unveiling." He glanced to her. "Lady Rosalyne, will you do the honors?"

"Of course, your highness."

Rosalyne threw back her shoulders and walked confidently to where her husband stood. Edward lowered the wood so that she could easily remove the cloth covering it. He winked at her and she refrained from allowing a nervous giggle to escape. Lifting the material away, she stepped aside and bravely turned toward the king to measure his reaction.

His face remained blank as his eyes skimmed the painting, then a slow, satisfied smile lit his face. Rosalyne relaxed upon seeing it.

King Richard crossed to her. "My lady, you have surpassed my expectations. You have painted me as I am—and as I wish to be. I see authority in my bearing but also humanity. There is truth in your art, Lady Rosalyne."

The king took her hand and pressed a kiss upon her knuckles, stunning her. Looking her squarely in the eye, he said, "I do not know how to justly compensate you for your work on my and the queen's portraits." He paused. "Because of your husband's great service to me and now yours, as well, I say that you might ask me for anything, my lady, and I will give it to you."

Rosalyne tore her eyes from his and looked to Edward. He shook his head and shrugged.

"If the happy couple does not know what to ask for, then I do, sire," Benedict said.

The king focused on the man who interrupted. "Bowyar, isn't it?"

"Aye, your majesty. Lord Benedict Bowyar."

"And what is your stake in this, Lord Benedict?" the king asked, interest evident in his eyes.

"Sire, I am Lady Rosalyne's uncle. Her other uncle, the non-painting one."

Everyone chuckled at his remark and he continued.

"My older brother, Lawrence, inherited my father's title and lands. Unfortunately, his life was cut short, as was that of his wife, Lara. They were Lady Rosalyne's parents."

"I see," the king said.

"My wife and I were not blessed with children, your majesty. That makes Lady Rosalyne my closest blood relative. Instead of Shallowheart reverting back to the Crown upon my death, I would ask that it go to Lady Rosalyne and her husband, Sir Edward de Montfort, and that you would make Sir Edward the next Baron of Shallowheart."

His words stunned Rosalyne. She glanced to Edward and saw shock on his face, as well.

"I won't need time to mull over your offer, my lord," the king said. "I reward good men who are friends to the Crown. Sir Edward de Montfort is certainly one of those men. Though I wish you a long and prosperous life, Lord Benedict, I would be happy to see your estate in the hands of Sir Edward. The title, too."

"You are most generous, your highness," Edward said. "As is Lord Benedict. Lady Rosalyne and I are honored to serve you in any capacity."

"That may include another painting or two," Richard quipped. "For when the queen and I have children. We spoke about it and when they come of age, it would greatly please us for Lady Rosalyne to return to court and paint their portraits."

"I would like nothing better than to paint your sons and daughters," Rosalyne assured the monarch.

"Now that we have settled that matter, we would be happy for all of you to join us in a celebratory meal," the queen said.

They filed into an adjoining room and spent the next several hours dining and telling stories. The king remained in high spirits throughout the meal.

As others spoke around them, Edward took Rosalyne's hand. "Your portrait has been deemed a success, Wife." He smiled at her with unabashed affection.

"And you will make an outstanding baron someday, Husband," she said in return.

Edward raised her hand to his lips and pressed a fervent kiss against it. "May all our dreams come true, my love."

Rosalyne smiled at the man who held her heart. "They already have."

EPILOGUE

Canterbury—September, 1405

EDWARD STROLLED THROUGH the bustling main thoroughfare of Canterbury, Rosalyne on his arm. They had not been back to the city since they had left it many years ago. Now, Rosalyne was two score and he would reach that age in another six months.

He glanced down at the woman who had held his heart for so long. Though her blond locks still caught the sun, he spied a few gray hairs mingled within. Tiny laugh lines had been etched around the corners of her eyes but her figure was still trim—even after birthing four sons and two daughters.

"It seems so odd to be back," she remarked. "Everything seems vaguely familiar and yet it's almost as if I have never been here before."

"Cities change," Edward said. "People change. *We* have changed."

Rosalyne gave him a warm smile. "I don't mind change. As long as I am with you." She squeezed his arm affectionately.

"I feel the same."

They stopped where they had once purchased a meat pie and decided to share one. The owner looked the same, as if no time had passed at all, but Edward realized it was the man's son who served them because he caught sight of the father helping someone else.

They returned to the street after they'd eaten. The cathedral loomed in the distance.

"I am glad you wanted to return," Rosalyne said.

"I promised myself years ago that once Master Yevele completed the nave, I had to view his finished work. It was already impressive enough when half-completed."

"At least England has calmed enough for us to travel," she remarked.

The current state of affairs saddened him. Richard no longer held the throne. He had lost it shortly after Edward and Rosalyne left court, when the Lords Appellant took control. Though the king claimed his throne again a year later, he waited years before taking revenge on the aristocrats who had ousted him, exiling some and executing others.

Then Richard's first cousin and childhood playmate, son of the Duke of Lancaster, deposed the king and claimed the crown as King Henry the Fourth. The former king died in captivity soon after. Edward had heard the rumors that Henry starved Richard to death but, knowing the former king, Richard just as well might have starved himself since he no longer held any power.

"Henry has had a rough go of being king," Edward said, "what with Owain Glyndwr and the Percys in a constant state of rebellion against him."

"It would not surprise me if a new king asserts himself not too long from now."

Edward thought his wife might be right.

They walked in silence after that until they reached the great cathedral. Pausing before it, Edward drank in the building's grandeur.

"Shall we enter?" he asked and led Rosalyne inside.

Henry Yevele's new nave had taken a score and five years to complete but it was well worth the wait. Both the nave and transepts had been rebuilt. The perpendicular nave ran from the entrance all the way down the central aisle to the altar far ahead, with the transept crossing it, forming a true cross inside the cathedral. The old aisle walls had been torn down. Tall, slender pillars now supported the structure, with exceptionally high arches in their place.

They walked the length of the cathedral and back, admiring the new stained glass windows that had been placed inside the church. A new choir screen stood at the east end of the nave.

"The details are incredible," Edward said, in awe of the structure.

"It took a true master to create this vision and see it to fruition. As an artist, I can appreciate what it took to bring this to life."

"Shall we visit Trinity Chapel—and your triptych?" he suggested.

They went to the chapel, still full of pilgrims who came to see where Thomas Becket had been martyred. Edward steered Rosalyne toward her panel, which remained near the shrine to the Black Prince. It saddened him that Richard, being so young, had never really known his father as the rest of England had. And poor Richard had never had any children of his own. His beloved Queen Anne had died childless. The king mourned her death and only married again for political reasons. His child bride, only seven years of age, became a widow soon after, ending the line the Black Prince came from.

Edward allowed Rosalyne to study her work at length. He knew she viewed it with a critical eye yet he couldn't help but remember the days in which she had created it. How he had helped her prepare the wood and sand it down and coat it with the sparkling gesso. Those were his earliest memories of their time together. They would go with him to his grave.

"Are you ready to depart?" his wife finally asked.

"Only if you are," he replied.

She nodded and he escorted her from the cathedral. As they took to the streets again, the September sun beat down upon them, heating his clothes to the point where they were hot to the touch.

Much like the many nights of heat and passion that he had spent caressing the woman beside him.

"You know you mean the world to me," he murmured into her ear, sensing her shiver at his touch.

"You *are* the world to me, Edward de Montfort," Rosalyne told him. "You always have been and always will be. My love for you has grown stronger, day by day, as each year has passed."

Despite being in the midst of hundreds of people, Edward stopped and took Rosalyne into his arms and kissed her with all the passion and fire that had never died in the years of their marriage.

Breaking the kiss, he smiled and told her, "I need your bare skin against mine, my sweet baroness. I plan to take you back to the inn and make love to you until we leave for Shallowheart tomorrow."

Rosalyne's palm touched his cheek. "I am forever yours, Edward. Lead the way."

The End

About the Author

As a child, Alexa Aston gathered her neighborhood friends together and made up stories for them to act out, her first venture into creating memorable characters. Following her passion for history and love of learning, she became a teacher who began writing on the side to maintain her sanity in a sea of teenage hormones.

Alexa's historical romances use history as a backdrop to place her characters in extraordinary circumstances, where their intense desire for one another grows into the treasured gift of love.

She is the author of *The Knights of Honor*, a medieval romance series that takes place in 14th century England during the reign of Edward III and centers on the de Montfort family. Each romance focuses on the code of chivalry that bound knights of this era.

A native Texan, Alexa lives with her husband in a Dallas suburb, where she eats her fair share of dark chocolate and plots out stories while she walks every morning. She enjoys reading, watching movies and sports, and can't get enough of *Fixer Upper* or *Game of Thrones*. Alexa also writes romantic suspense, western historicals, and standalone medieval novels as Lauren Linwood.

Alexa loves to hear from her readers. You can connect with her through FB, Twitter, and her website: alexaaston.com.

Facebook:
facebook.com/authoralexaaston

Twitter:
twitter.com/AlexaAston

Newsletter sign-up:
madmimi.com/signups/422152/join

Amazon Page:
amazon.com/author/alexaaston